ALSO BY EDITH SCHEFFER

The Janie Chronicles

Saving Janie

Janie a Broad

Janie on Board

Janie vs. The Big Apple

* * *

Fallen Gracefully

* * *

Winged

THE JANIE CHRONICLES

Janie on Board

EDITH SCHEFFER

JANIE ON BOARD
The Janie Chronicles, Book 3
ISBN 978-1-954174-05-4

Edited by Louise Zanotto

1

JANIE ON BOARD

"So then what are you going to do to me?" I asked, biting my lower lip.

"I'm goin' to kiss ya…starting at yer beautiful lips…moving down to yer sexy neck…"

I let out a little moan of approval.

"…all the way down to yer toes," Cecil said.

My face crinkled up, "Could we avoid the feet?" I asked.

"Why, what's wrong with yer feet?" he asked.

"Nothing! I just walk barefoot a lot," I answered. "I know where they've been."

"So what if I had a foot fetish?" Cecil inquired.

I rolled this thought around in my head and was happy he couldn't see my face through the phone. Finally I asked, "Do you?" trying not to sound judgy.

Cecil laughed, "No. It was just my way of sayin' *every inch of ya.*"

I smiled from ear to ear and got comfortable, "Well, okay then…go on…"

I had been home from Ireland for two weeks and still had not adjusted to the changes around me. Between my mother and my *Southern Belle* landlady, Betty, my house had gone through some transformations of its own.

I had been told that my house was to be painted and had expected this. I had not expected the flower boxes on my windows, the used brick pathway that led to my new front porch and wrought iron screen door.

When my cab pulled up out front, I did a double take. Then I stepped inside…all new wood flooring that led to my completely redone kitchen; new stainless steel appliances, new cupboards and sink and a huge wrought iron cart that held my top of the line espresso maker that Fitz had finagled for me when a 'Home Store' employee attacked me in aisle two. I had no idea where my coffee cups were, and more importantly, where my wine corkscrew was. (I could drink wine out of the bottle if I could open the damned thing) My whole kitchen was like a great adult scavenger hunt. I had been adjusting and had to admit, it was beautiful, so thank you Betty and mom.

The biggest adjustment I had to make wasn't the new house, or mom and Betty's newfound friendship (which was the epitome of opposites attract), it was missing Cecil. During our time in Ireland, Fitz, short for Sarra Fitzpartick (my best friend since naptime was still *a thing* in class), had been working for and staying with the Callaghan's. Callaghan's turned out to be a manor. Well, more of a castle. In fact it was a 300 year old castle. And the family business you ask? Whiskey! The family not only owned the castle, but the Callaghan distillery.

Fitz had been dating the eldest Callaghan son, Scotty, when his brother Cecil and his dad, Martin, made their way to the US to handle distribution deals that would bring their whiskey to the States.

I had met Cecil on that fateful trip and was immediately attracted to him. Okay, parts of me were. He had a reputation as a bad boy and possible man-whore, and *that* was never my thing. Their father Martin had seen my work, and hired me to do two paintings for him; one of the Castle and the other of the Distillery.

Fitz, with her flaming red hair, green eyes and skin that looked like fresh milk, was the perfect Irish lass to be the new spokesmodel for the Callaghan product. So off to Ireland we went. Our stay was one of great mishaps and misunderstandings, but what I did find out was Cecil wasn't really a bad boy and I really cared for him. We also found out that Cecil would be taking over his dad's company in Ireland, and Scotty would be handling the newly found Callaghan distribution in America. This was great for Fitz, who had become engaged to Scotty on that trip. It was not as good for me as Cecil and I had admitted we had feelings for each other right before I headed home. And home is where I'm at… missing him, all day, every day.

We have been calling and texting as much as possible, but with the time difference, we were always on a different page. My day was just beginning as his was ending, and vice versa.

Truth was, I hadn't left the house much during the last two weeks. I had made every excuse in the book not to go to Fitzpatrick's Pub or even Sunday night dinner at my parent's house. If I didn't know better (and I'm not sure I did, having never felt this way before), I'd think I had let a little depression creep in. But tonight, I'd have no choice. Tonight was Fitz's engagement party and the maid of honor/best friend's attendance was not only expected, it was required.

I unglued my ass from my couch and hit the shower. While I soaped up, I heard my phone ringing. I took off like a bolt, grabbing a towel as I ran. I slid across my new wood floors and came to a halt right in front of my phone. But it was too late. One missed call from Cecil was flashing on my cell. I called right back, but it went straight to voicemail.

I never knew what to say to voicemail. It always seemed like a third party was listening, or the recorded message was somehow judging mine. I went for the standard, "Sorry I missed your call. I was in the shower. I miss you." All the way back to the shower, I questioned why I said I was in the shower, like he needed that piece of knowledge.

After my shower, I reached for my 501's and then worried that maybe I should dress up a bit. I mean, it was my BFF's engagement party. Should I really show up the frumpy mess I was on the couch, only washed? I put on a sundress and pretended to do my hair, which actually meant throwing the long blonde mess into a bun. Mascara was applied and some lip gloss was how I finished my attempt at make-up.

I grabbed my purse and sandals and headed south for the eight blocks that separated me from Fitzpatrick's Pub.

I had asked ahead of time if there was anything I could do, seeing as how I would be the maid-of-honor. Fitz's reply was, "Just get your ass here by 7pm." At 6:50pm, I entered the pub. I wasn't surprised to see that we had a fill-in bartender. After all, the Fitzpatrick family, who usually manned the bar, would be sharing in tonight's festivities.

Fitz saw me enter and made a B-line my way. She was clad in a cream colored, body hugging satin dress that went to the floor and boasted a plunging neckline with diamond collar. Her long red hair was swept up and clipped with a diamond barrette. Long ringlets fell around her perfectly painted face. As always, she was stunning.

"I have to talk to ya," Fitz said, grabbing my arm and leading me to the closed restaurant on the other side on the building.

"What's up," I asked when she closed the door behind us.

"Somethin' horrible has happened," she started.

Panic entered, was it mom, dad, Cecil, "What? What's wrong?"

"My best friend has been M.I.A. for nearly two weeks. I'm scared she's gone fer good," she gave me a hurt look.

"I know, I've been kind of...wonky," I said.

"I get it. I do. But this is to be the best night of my life so far, and I need ya HERE."

I nodded, "I know and I get it. I'm so sorry. I will be HERE," I said. "I'm really happy for you, Fitzy," I hugged her.

"I know. It just needed to be said," she hugged me back.

"You look amazing, by the way," I added.

"Good start on that best friend comeback," Fitz laughed. "Now let's go find some cocktails."

Back at the bar, I ordered a Black & Tan and a shot of Bushmills. People were everywhere. Our high school friends were woven in with family. I said *"hello"* to the two Fitzpatrick boys I could see, Danny, Andy and their wives. Coming through the crowd to join us was Pauly and his wife Mona. I had to quickly paint on a smile. Mona had a deep resentment for me that she didn't bother to hide. I wasn't sure what I had done to warrant such open disdain from her.

"Oh Janie," Mona began, "I wasn't sure if that was you, or if one of Fitz's old school chums took up cross-dressing."

"Yep, I'm a tall one," I shook my head at her ridiculousness.

"Oh, that's not what I was referring to," her smile getting sticky. "I was just referring to your..." she looked me up and down, "less than feminine ways."

I took a deep breath and was planning my exit route when Pauly piped up, "Stop it Mona," he told his wife through a tightened jaw.

"What?" she asked innocently. "I was just saying..."

Pauly cut her off, "Yes I know what yer sayin'. I'm tired of ya attackin' Janie. Sick of your pettiness," he put his hands up. "Yes, I had a crush on her when we were young. Yes, I know now how wrong it was to tell ya. But that was a hundred years, a marriage and two kids ago. Fer God sakes, let it go, woman!" his Irish accent thick with anger.

I stood there uncomfortable and dumbfounded while the other wives laughed behind their hands. I never had any idea that Pauly had a crush on me. And finding out this way was more embarrassing than flattering.

Mona stormed off, barreling through the crowd. Pauly apologized before he took off after her.

"Well," Danny raised his glass, "guess we finally know why she's such a bitch to ya, huh?"

Andy laughed, "It wasn't a big deal. We were playin' a stupid game, and it was like five years ago. It was Pauly, Mona, my wife and me. Pauly had to admit to a crush he had, but had never revealed. He said you," he pointed to me. "And he also said it was when we were kids and it lasted fer like two minutes, but Mona just couldn't let it go," he shook his head.

I nodded, at least now I had some understanding of her dislike of me, even if it was ridiculous.

Fitz saw the scene from across the bar and came to find out what was going on. As Danny filled her in, she nodded, "Well there ya go, that's why she's such a bitch to ya, and why she hit on Cecil."

The brothers both raised their eyebrows, "She hit on Cecil?" Andy asked.

I tried to play it down, but Fitz kept the ball rolling, "She sure did! She was sittin' in his lap, and said she was *keepin' him warm* for Janie!"

"Tis true?" Danny asked me.

"Well, um, it wasn't really…" I started, but Fitz cut me off.

"She sure did! Heard it with my own ears, saw it with my own eyes!" she nodded.

The brother's raised their brows to each other again and nodded.

"What? What's happenin'," her eyes darted between her brothers. You two are havin' one of those *mental conversations* that's meant to keep me out!" Fitz gave one eyebrow a raise. She was learning how to do the Mom look. Or in her family, the Mum look. I had to admit, she was getting pretty good at it.

It took a moment, but Andy finally nodded to Danny, "They've been on the rocks fer quite some time now. Pauly has even mentioned the '*D word*'."

I was busy guessing that their '*D word*', wasn't the same as mine.

"No," Fitz brought her hand to her mouth, "Divorce?"

See, not the same, I thought to myself.

The brothers nodded in unison.

"So, is she blaming Janie fer this?" Fitz asked.

"What?" I finally piped up. "How? We never dated, or even kissed. How the hell could I be blamed for this?"

"Well think about it? If she's batshit enough to torture ya for a crush ya didn't even know about, I'm guessin' she's crazy nuts. Crazy nuts people need to blame someone," Fitz added like it made perfect sense.

My fear was that in Mona's mind, it did make sense.

"Don't ya worry luv," Danny patted my arm. I'm sure it'll be fine. Once she's sober," he added.

"And if not," Andy interjected, "my money is on you," he smiled.

I faked a smile and looked at Fitz, "BAR!"

2

DRAMA, DRAMA, DRAMA

Cocktails were needed for this kind of drama, I thought as I ordered two Bushmills and another beer. When the Bushmills came, Fitz grabbed one and we shot them down.

"Wow, it's so strange to finally find out why she's been so awful to ya, all these years." Fitz said.

"It's just crazy though. It was when we were kids. I mean, who cares about a child's crush?"

Fitz made a face at me. It was old information for me, but newly acquired by Fitz, that I had had a secret crush on the youngest of the Fitzpatrick boys, Barry, since we were kids. That lifelong crush had slowly faded away when he met the woman of his dreams in Ireland and announced their engagement. Then, I met Cecil. My feelings for him, as new as they were in comparison, made any crush on anyone else *null* and *void*. I was deeply in…*like* with Cecil, I assessed. But I had to admit, once upon a time the feelings I had for Barry were very real to me. Maybe Mona's *crazy* was just as real to her.

"Speak of the devil," Fitz grinned as her brother Barry approached.

"There ya are Fitzy," Barry said pulling her off her stool via bear hug. He swung her around, "I'm so happy for ya, sis," he kissed her cheek before putting her right on her feet. He turned to me and nodded, "Janie."

"That's all I get?" I laughed. "Usually I get a hug, too. You don't have to spin me though."

Awkwardly, he hugged me; one where he wasn't sure where to put his hands or how long to hold on. As he pulled away, Fitz gave him a crooked grin, "Are ya blushin'?"

"No," he answered quickly. "I'm fine. Can I get a Black & Tan?" he asked the barmaid as she passed by. "So I saw Mona and Pauly havin' it out in the parkin' lot. What's goin' on?"

"Oh that," Fitz began. "Apparently Pauly called Mona on her treatment of Janie, told her to knock it off."

Barry nodded, "Yeah, I've never understood her problem with ya," he nodded to me.

"Well I think it's been made crystal clear now. Turns out, Pauly had a crush on Janie and Mona knew about it," Fitz explained.

Barry looked from me to his sister, to me again, "He has a crush on ya?"

"No, no," I shook my head, "he HAD a crush on me when we were kids, that's all."

"And he just blurted this out?" Barry asked. "Just, *I have a crush on ya, Janie*?"

I stammered, " Um no, it was more like, *'I said I had a two minute crush on you when we were kids and Mona can't let it go*, type of thing," I explained.

Just then, Fitz's mom (Mum as we called her), and her crazy Aunt Marble came up and took me into an embrace.

"Oh dear girl, we just heard through the grapevine, that Pauly is in love with ya," Aunt Marble said. I looked around frantically, who was the misinformed *grape-viner*?

Mum chimed in as my head began to shake 'NO' furiously, "I

feel like a bad person, especially since that woman has given birth to two of my grandbabies, but oh, how I wish it had been you!"

"Oh me too," Aunt Marble nodded to Mum. "Can ya imagine what a great mother Janie would have been?"

"You have the wrong idea," I practically plead.

"Ya don't like Pauly," Mum asked, with visible heartbreak.

"I do, I love him…but as a brother, Mum. He's like a brother to me. Nothing more," I added.

I was trying not to hyperventilate, what the hell was happening? Barry looked upset as he stood and walked toward the front door.

"Mum," I had to say to pull her attention out of her own thoughts, "Pauly's not in love with me. Not at all," my head shook. "He just had a small, fleeting crush on me as a kid, that's it," I put my hands up.

Mum and Aunt Marble rolled this around in their heads then looked to Fitz for validation. She nodded, letting them know that the *grapevine* had been mistaken.

Mum looked back at me, "But then…why are they gettin' divorced?"

I don't know that they are," I stammered. "I really don't KNOW anything."

"Oh," Mum said, looking very confused.

"We really don't know what's happenin', Mum," Fitz added.

"Well okay then, dear," Mum said to me and kissed my cheek. "My mistake," she and Aunt Marble left in search of the *grapeviner* to clear-up the misinformation.

I turned to Fitz, "That was weird," I said.

Fitz's attention was elsewhere though "Barry just took off. It's my engagement party, and he just left?"

"Maybe he went to find Pauly and check on him. After all, Mona is kind of relentless," I added.

Fitz nodded, but looked upset. Barry wasn't just my favorite of the brothers. Fitz and Barry were the closest in age. She loved them all well, but had a soft spot for Barry.

The party raged on and at stroke of midnight, Fitz's finance, Scotty, took the microphone and addressed all gathered for their engagement celebration.

"I'd like to thank everyone…not only fer bein' here for this amazing night, but makin' me feel so welcome." His Irish accent, I noted, had been well pickled. He raised his glass to his new in-laws, "Ya raised a fine woman and I am so proud to call her mine. And Fitzy," he took her hand, "I'll move Heaven and Earth if need be, to make ya the happiest woman in the world."

Fitz replied, "I'll never need the world, my love. You will always be more than enough for me!" they kissed.

People hooted and hollered, while a few women dabbed tears from the corner of their eyes. It was beautiful. Just then two women in baker's uniforms carried out a three tiered platter of silver and gold topped cupcakes and presented them to the couple.

Fitz said into the mic, "These are to be the colors for our weddin', silver and gold. To twenty-five years, then twenty-five more," she raised a champagne glass to her husband.

Taking a silver iced cupcake from the top tier, she fed it to Scotty. Again the crowd roared their approval.

I was so overjoyed for her but somewhere inside, I was missing Cecil and couldn't help but wish he was here with me. Just then, over the microphone I heard, "There you are, you bitch!"

Heads turned and everyone's eyes searched the crowd. Mona was standing in the middle of the pub looking a bit drunk, and a lot pissed. People moved as she made her way through the party. Fitz's brow furrowed, trying to assess just to whom Mona was referring. I, on the other hand, had no doubt as her eyes burned into mine.

"Look at you," Mona slurred, "just standing there without a

care in the world. No thought at all given to the home you've wrecked. YOU HOME WRECKING WHORE!" she screamed.

I had to admit, I was somewhat used to being called a bitch, but whore wasn't a word usually thrown my way. I started shaking my head as Mona drew near.

Fitz lunged but was restrained by her brother Danny, "Yer not fightin' at yer engagement party," he informed her. What he said next, made me wince, "Janie can handle this."

Fitz was still struggling against Danny when he said, "Fer God's sakes woman, think of the dress!" Fitz looked down at her beautiful handmade and perfectly tailored gown, and nodded to her brother.

Out in the crowd family and friends began whispering to each other behind their hands. Great, I was going to be the talk of the town.

"That's right, Red. Back off!" Mona slurred to Fitz. "This has been coming for some time and it's between Janie and me," she said turning her attention my way.

I put up my hands in a submissive pose, "Look, Mona, I'm a little confused about whatever's happening here. Maybe you and I should talk. Ya know, clear the air."

"Clear this, bitch," Mona said, as she grabbed her crotch.

I wasn't 100% certain, but I think she just told me to suck her 'D'. I couldn't help making the face of confusion wrapped with revulsion.

"Look," I said, "I really don't know what you're thinking, here. I mean, if it's about that ridiculous crush thing, from childhood," I added, "it's no big deal. It means nothing!"

"No," Mona breathed, "It means nothing to you!" she hissed, jutting out her chin as she drew nearer. "That's the problem, little Janie, it means nothing to you," she shook her head. "My heartbreak: nothing! My discomfort of having to see you at every holiday, every birthday, every fucking occasion: Nothing to you!

Because apparently, this family, treats you like you ARE family," she teetered on.

"Thicker than blood," Fitz said, needing to be restrained again.

"Oh, that's right, Fitzy. Always there to fight her battles! Just once, I'd like to see this mess of femininity, stand her own ground," Mona said.

"Crap," I whispered under my breath. This was not the night I had planned for. Mona kept walking. She was within charging distance now, as the crowd spread like the *parting of the Red Sea.*

"Mona, I didn't even know...about anything...until this evening," I explained. "You're the one who's been hating me, torturing me, for something I didn't even know about. If just once, you had talked to me, we could have put this to rest a long time ago."

"Oh that's right," she stumbled closer, her eyes filled with hate and voice filled with cheap wine. "My Pauly isn't good enough for you, is he? No, not little Janie. No one's good enough for her!" she screamed.

Now I was really confused. Mona had spent years telling me how worthless I was. How I couldn't keep a man. How I was too tall, and awkward. And now she thinks that I think...I'm too good for someone? Where the hell was she going with this? That's what was going through my mind when she put her head down and charged me.

Running at me, all of her five-foot-nothing frame coming fast, I just had time to try and brace myself. Sneering like an animal in attack mode, her arm was coming up from her side and I was sure it was going to be a right hook. But then just before she got to me, I saw it. A gold blur caught my eye. I cocked my head at the sight as if paralyzed by its shimmer. It was coming directly at my face. It connected with my nose and made a smooshing sound. Gold cupcake blurred my sight as I stood in shock trying to understand what had just happened.

Mona backed away from me, eyes still glittering with hate, "Now you know what it feels like to look stupid in front of the people you love. Just like your very existence has done to me for the last five years."

Fitz, who had been struggling against her captor during Mona's run at me, dropped her jaw in stunned silence. The whole bar went deathly quiet. Women covered their mouths with their hands, eyes rounded as they waited for my retaliation to spring into action.

Wiping cupcake and gold frosting from my eyes, I began to laugh. My hair sparkled with golden highlights, as I licked the frosting from my fingers. That's it? After five years of so called torture that I unknowingly put her through, no less, this is what it had boiled down to? I got cup-caked? I guess I figured that this made us even somehow.

"So is this over now?" I asked, more than willing to take one for Pauly and put an end the nonsense Mona had let brew in her head.

"Over?" she asked, eyes wild and more batshit than I remember, "It'll never be over. Every time you turn around, I'll be there. Every bad thing that happens to you, my hand will be involved. Every little bit of bad luck that touches you, it will have been sent by me," she made a strange sign with her hands, (one I didn't know) then turned her back and marched out.

Danny released Fitz as the door closed behind Mona. She ran to my side and started cleaning my face with a napkin, "Damn Janie, ya shoulda clocked her!"

I was still staring at the closed door Mona had just stomped out of, "She really thinks that I want Pauly, or he wants me? This is so…ridiculous."

People started to form groups and soon enough conversations went to other things.

"Well, I'd be careful if I was you. She's a snakey bitch, that one" Fitz warned.

"I just can't see how any of this makes any sense to her," I shook my head.

"I'm not sure in her mind, it has to. Obviously she's a little off her rocker to threaten ya that way."

"Threaten me?" I asked. I guess I had heard what she said, but didn't really think I had anything to worry about.

Mum and Aunt Marble came to my side and were visibly concerned.

"I still can't believe she cursed ya, and all. And in a room full of people, no less," Aunt Marble gave a head nod.

"Cursed?" I asked, wondering if this was more lore I didn't understand.

"Definitely," Mum nodded to me. "Did ya see what she did with her hands?"

I had, and was under the impression it was vaginal symbol. "I did. I have no idea what it means, though," I confessed. I didn't want to throw my *vagina symbol* suspicions out there.

"Oh my dear," Mum continued, "It was the symbol of the *Watchful Eye*." Mum made the symbol with her own hands. "Tis huge in the craft! There's one for protection, and..."

Aunt Marble finished Mum's thought, "And one for the destruction of yer enemies."

I stood there, blank faced for a moment or two. It still looked like a vagina to me. I was under the impression she was calling me a pussy, and a quite large one, at that. "Are you saying...Mona is a dark...," I couldn't find the word or even embrace the notion, "something?" I concluded.

"I've always had my suspicions of that one," Aunt Marble nodded to Mum.

"Aye," Mum nodded in agreement.

I was trying not to laugh, but Fitz was mulling something over.

As most of the frosting was removed, it left a golden glow on my face that put me in mind of C3PO, but I was no worse for the wear. Back to drinking and mingling, I went.

It was just about 1:00am, when a happily plastered Benny took the microphone and called out to bring our attention his way. It was the first time I had seen him in long pants, but I knew that underneath them were the knobby knees with black calf high socks he usually wore with his white Velcro shoes.

"I'm sure as most of ya know," Benny began in his New York accent, "I have been dating Marble for a few months now," he raised his glass to her. "She and her wonderful family have made me feel so welcome." The crowd cheered and raised their glasses to the Fitzpatrick brood. "That's why, Marble," he said, "we're not getting any younger, my dear." Crouching down on one knobby knee, he said, "Say you'll be my bride and we can spend the rest of our lives together."

Mum looked happily shocked, I smiled from ear to ear, Aunt Marble's overly magnified eyes rounded behind her coke bottle glasses as she covered her mouth and nodded 'YES' furiously. The crown cheered, but Fitz's eyes narrowed into slits.

Benny and Marble embraced. Still searching for his balance on one knobby knee, he put a huge diamond on her finger. Everyone was applauding and cheering, cheering again. Everyone but Fitz, that is.

"What's wrong with you?" I asked her. "Don't you like Benny?"

"Course I do! He's a wonderful man," she added, but the look on her face didn't change.

"Okay. So what's the problem?" I asked.

"They're gonna steal our thunder!"

I shook my head, "Whose thunder?"

"Mine. Mine and Scotty's! They're gonna steal our weddin' thunder!"

"I don't think that's gonna happen Fitz. I mean, I can't imagine that they're planning the kind of lavish wedding you and Scotty have in mind," I said.

"He's already proposed to her, at MY engagement party. That's piggy-backin'!" Fitz exclaimed.

"Like I said, I wouldn't worry about it. I mean, he was probably just overcome by all the family and the..." (I was reluctant to say 'moved by the moment', as the engagement party had already seen some not-so-festive action) "...how beautiful you look." I finished, hoping this would make her happy.

Fitz smiled and said, "Maybe yer right. We should go congratulate them." She grabbed my hand and pulled me through the crowd. As we approached though, Aunt Marble's words stopped Fitzy dead in her tracks.

"I love the idea of silver and gold as well. Those should be out colors, too," she said to Benny.

"Anything ya want. Sky's the limit, baby!" Benny told her and kissed her hard on the mouth.

Fitz spun wild eyes my way, "Ya see! I told ya! And there's no way they're makin' it to their 50th!"

I leaned in closer so no one else would hear, "Oh come on! You know Aunt Marble! She's probably gonna put him in a silver shorty-pants tuxedo and wear a gold muumuu.

Fitz rolled the image around in her brain and grinned, "Yer right," she said. "I'm being ridiculous."

"Little bit," I offered. "Now let's congratulate them."

As we turned to Aunt Marble, she said, "Oh Fitzy, maybe we should have a double weddin'?"

Fitz's horror filled eyes turned to me again.

I nodded, showing her that I did see the crazy, then pushed her into an embrace with her batshit crazy Aunt.

3

HOME, HOME, HOME!

I was more than ready to see my lit front porch. And even more ready to see my big comfy couch. As I started to walk the eight blocks home it was all I could think of.

Fitz had offered me a ride in the limo they had rented, but she and Scotty were a little too *into* each other for me to be comfortable on the eight block ride. I was pretty sure the limo driver was about to get a free, live, soft-core porn show.

Around block number four I heard footsteps behind me. I was reluctant to turn around. Since childhood, I had held on to the belief that the boogie-man still existed. Every horror movie I had ever seen had a scene just like this one. Honestly, it was Fitz's older brothers and their means of torture, to give me boogie-man nightmares. One thing I was sure of was, if the boogie-man knew that I knew he was there, he would pick up his pace. So instead, I picked up my own, trying not to show any sign of panic. After all, that's when he gets you, right?

My ears seemed to zero in on his footfall, which increased as well. Now I was speed walking down the lonely street filled with storefronts darkened by the late hour. Nothing was open. No place to escape, no one to hear me scream. Now panic breathing was setting in. I began to wonder if I should just turn around and face whatever was on my heels. If I was going to be forced to fight, I should be facing the boogie-man, not let him get me from behind.

I was now on block number six and the footfalls following me hadn't turned down another street or slowed. Finally, taking a deep breath, I spun on my heels facing my demon. A dark hoodie was covering his face from my view. I balled my fist and got ready to take him on. I was just about to swing, when he looked up and jumped backward.

"Janie, Janie! No, it's me!" he said pulling the hood back on his sweatshirt.

I put my hands to my chest in an attempt to slow my rapid heartbeat. "Pauly, what are you doing?" I asked.

"Are ya okay?" he asked.

"Yeah! You scared the hell out of me. What are you doing out here?" I asked.

"She kicked me out," he said and took a swig off of the half full pint of whiskey he was holding.

"I'm so sorry," I said, reaching for the pint and taking a much needed nerve calming swig. "So what are you gonna do?"

"Well, normally, I'd go to Mum's, but she'll just want to talk about it and I'm not in the mood."

I nodded. I could definitely see Mum forcing a conversation on him.

"I can't go to Fitzy's."

"Yeah probably not," I agreed, trying not to get an unwanted mental image.

"Aunt Marble and Benny are stayin' in grandpa's room."

That was a room above the bar, usually used by way-too-drunk family members. I had stayed there a time or two and couldn't believe anyone would want to stay there on their engagement eve, but to each their own.

"Andy and Danny are at their homes, asleep. I don't want to disturb them."

I nodded again, starting to worry where this was going. "What about Barry's?" I offered.

"Nah, he's pissed at me right now," he shook his head.

"What for?" I asked.

"It's a long story, Janie. Look, I'd never ask ya, but she wouldn't even let me in to get my wallet or I'd go to a hotel. I swear I just need a place to sleep. Could I use yer couch for what's left of the evenin'?"

I made a visible wince; this seemed like a bad idea from every angle. I thought about paying for him to get a hotel, but it was almost 3am. By the time a cab came to pick him up he'd be passed out cold. I sighed, he was like a brother to me and already half drunk to boot. Against my better judgment, I said, "You can have my bed."

"No, I don't want to put ya out," he said.

"Well, if you insisted on my couch, you would be," I smiled. "That's where I sleep every night."

At the house I showed him to the bedroom and brought him a glass of water and Ibuprofen. Grabbing a pillow and my jammies, I headed to my couch. Before I even lay down, Pauly was sawing logs.

Morning came too soon as the garbage truck made its way down my street. The hydraulic sound was burrowing through my dreams. I tried to fall back asleep, but it was no use, I was awake.

I started the coffee and hit the shower. I was grateful for not being hung over. But given all the drama of the night before, drunk hadn't been on my to-do list. I stepped out of the shower, mentally envisioning a hot cup of coffee, when the door opened. I took a quick breath in and tried to cover my stuff, while Pauly covered his eyes and tried to blindly find the doorknob while yelling, " I'm sorry Janie, I'm sorry!"

I tried to help him by slamming the door with my foot, since my hands were full. It swung, and hit him clean in the nose, knocking him out of my view. I wrapped a towel around me and opened the door. There he stood, his hands being used as a makeshift cup to catch the blood oozing out.

"Oh my God," I yelled ushering him to the bathroom sink. "Here, put your head back."

"I'm so sorry, Janie," he said again with his eyes still closed. "I thought ya were under that lump of covers on the couch."

"It's okay," I said, grabbing tissue and putting it under his nose. "You can open your eyes, I'm covered." Somewhere in my mind, all I could think of was that this was the second Fitzpatrick brother to accidentally see my naked upper body in the last few months. Just then, the doorbell rang. "Damn," I said. "You got this?" I asked.

"Yeah sure, I'm fine," Pauly said, taking the tissue from me.

I tightened up my grasp on my towel and ran for the door. As I opened it just a crack, there stood Barry.

"Are ya descent?" he asked.

"Well, kinda," I admitted, opening the door.

Barry stood still, eyeing my towel.

"Well come on. I don't want to stand here in my towel," I urged, just as Mr. and Mrs. Mendlebaum passed by on their morning walk. Great, I thought. My nosey pervert of a neighbor was seeing me in a towel inviting a man in my home at 7am.

Barry stepped inside and I closed the door behind him, "I didn't mean to… catch ya at a bad time," Barry started, averting his eyes.

"Would ya happen to have any ice?" Pauly bellowed from the bathroom.

"Is that Pauly?" Barry asked, his brow furrowing.

"Yeah, I think I broke his nose," I winced.

"Ya what?" Barry's eyes rounded.

"I was in the shower and I hit him with the door," I explained.

"You were in the shower...with Pauly?"

I heard the way it sounded, "No, no, I was getting out of the shower and slammed the door on Pauly's nose when he was coming in the bathroom," I corrected.

"Why is Pauly here?" Barry questioned.

Just then the phone rang. It was Cecil. I put up a finger to ask for a moment while I answered the phone, "Hi," I said.

"How's my girl?" Cecil asked.

I loved it when he called me *His Girl*. I had been missing him so much. "I'm good. How are you?" I asked.

"Ice! Please!" Pauly yelled from the bathroom.

I mouthed to Barry, "Could you get Pauly some ice?" Barry threw his hands up then took off for the kitchen with a bewildered look.

"I'm good, also," Cecil said. "I can't wait to show ya."

I laughed, "Yeah? I'm looking forward to that, too. How is everything?"

Barry, armed with a baggie of ice, headed for the bathroom.

"It's all good. The Distillery is doin' well. Dad and Elanor are takin' some time to travel. Babygirl misses ya like crazy (that was his horse). Everything is good, but I do wish ya were here," he admitted.

"I do, too. I miss you so much," is what I was saying when the fight broke out in the bathroom. My jaw dropped as I heard things crashing to the floor. I ran to the hall, just as Barry emerged with a bloody nose.

I watched in complete shock as he passed me, said sorry, and went out the front door.

"What the hell was that?" Cecil asked.

"I'm really not sure," I told him as I moved to the bathroom door.

Pauly was holding one hand in the other. "I think I'm gonna need more ice!"

I got Pauly more ice and explained to Cecil why Pauly was there. But I still had no idea why Barry and Pauly had quarreled.

Cecil said, "Well I would have had a crush on ya then, too. And I do now, so let Pauly know he's lost his chance," he said good-naturedly. "Be careful though, Janie. His wife's a little nutty. It also sounds like ya have yer hands full, luv. Can I call ya later tonight?"

"Yes please," I said. "I miss you."

"And I, you!" Cecil rang off.

I walked back to the bathroom and was happy to see that Pauly's nose had stopped bleeding. It wasn't broken, thank God.

"So, what happened with you and Barry? I knew you said you guys had an argument, but I didn't expect *this*. Whatever *this* is," I added.

"I really don't know. He said that I was *a married man*, and should have more respect for the sanctity of marriage. I tried to explain, but he asked why I was in the bathroom with ya. I said I walked in on ya getting out of the shower and he pushed me. I told him not to do it again. Then he asked if I saw ya naked, and I admitted that I had, so he pushed me again. I gave him one last warnin' and he pushed me a third time. I went to walk out the door…just get away from the situation, ya know? I don't want to fight my little brother. Especially when it was all just a huge mistake, but I guess he was headin' fer the door when I threw it open. I hit him straight in the nose with it."

"So how did you hurt your hand?" I asked.

Barry threw the door open again and my hand was still on the knob…crushed it into the wall," he looked down at his swollen and quickly bruising hand.

I nodded. At least no punches were thrown, I thought.

"Why was Barry even here?" Pauly asked.

I wondered that too, but had no answer.

I made breakfast for Pauly and I, and told him I would drive him to Mum's where he left his car the night before.

When we pulled up out front Mum was watering her plants. As she looked up and saw who was in the car with me. Her eyes rounded and she made a B-line to my open window.

"Get out of the car boy," she said to Pauly. "Get out now!" she repeated with haste.

I was confused…until I saw Mona coming down the stairs toward my car.

"Oh shit!" Pauly said.

"Are you kidding me?" Mona yelled at Pauly, as she moved closer to the car.

"It's not what ya think," Pauly said, getting out of the passenger side. "At least give me a minute to explain?" he pleaded.

"And you, you bitch, I haven't even begun to make your life a living hell. When I get through with you, you're gonna wish you were dead."

I came close to telling her I was already kinda wishing that, but thought that *smart-assed* might not be the way to go right now. Considering where her mind was at before this, I couldn't really blame her for the 'bitch' thing.

"I'm so sorry, Janie," Pauly said as he headed for Mum's.

"Why the hell are you apologizing to her?" Mona yelled at the top of her lungs. "She's the reason for all of this!"

Mum came to my car window, "Ya might want to make yerself scarce for the moment. Tis goin' to be a long afternoon."

I nodded. "Yeah, I bet. Think I'm going to go back home and try to take a nap."

Mum nodded her approval of my plans and gave me a quick kiss on the cheek. She turned away momentarily then turned back to me, "So, nothing happened between you and Pauly?"

I tried not to look offended, but fell short, "No. Nothing!"

Mum nodded, "Well, a mother can dream," she said, making me smile. "We're having a BBQ tomorrow. I know it may be a little awkward, but say you'll come?"

"I'll think about it. Maybe things will cool off by then," I pulled out of the driveway and headed home.

As I pulled up to my house, I saw Baby Fitz's black '59 Caddy, parked out front. Fitz had a key and was free to drop by whenever. She took to this freedom much like my mother did. I could only hope she wasn't trying to use my espresso maker, since last time she almost caused it to rocket through my roof.

"Fitzy," I said coming through the door.

"I'm in here," she yelled from the kitchen. She had a pink bakery box in her hand. "I thought ya might actually want to eat one of these instead of just wearing one."

"Well, that was sweet of you," my grin sardonic as I grabbed a silver cupcake from the box and dug in.

I was making coffee when I gave her the update of new drama.

"Pauly saw ya naked?" she winced.

But I wasn't sure if the wince was for him or me. Deciding not to be offended, I just said, "I'm pretty sure."

"Why did Pauly stay here, again?" she asked.

"Because, you were…busy." That was my polite way of saying *rockin the headboard.* "Mum would want to talk to him about his failing marriage. You can't blame him for wanting to avoid that conversation." Fitz nodded in agreement. "And the other brothers, who are actually talking to him, went home early with their wives and families."

"He and Barry will work it out soon enough, I hope."

I nodded my head, "I sure hope so." I didn't want to say anything about Barry asking Pauly if he had seen me naked. I wasn't sure what it meant or if it meant anything at all, so I left it alone. "Maybe you should talk to him?" I suggested. "After all, you're the closest person to him. Well, the closest one who won't try to control him."

She nodded, rolling this over in her head. "So, I guess I went a little nutty last night when Benny proposed to Auntie?"

I made the fifty-fifty hand motion.

"I don't know what I was thinkin'? Obviously, Auntie and I have incredibly different taste. I was just a little crazed with all the drama."

"I can't exactly blame you," especially since some of that drama was directed at me. "Plus, I'm the only one who heard you and I'm not saying anything. You can just sweep it under the rug."

"Yeah," she nodded, "that's exactly what I'll do."

"So…have you and Scotty set a date for the big day?"

"Not yet. I'm really enjoyin' bein' engaged. Plus we plan on marryin' in Ireland, probably at the Castle."

Just the mention of the Castle made me smile. Fitz saw and grinned.

"Yer smitten, aren't ya?" she asked me.

I pretended not to know who she was talking about, "With whom?" I asked.

"Well, I hate to tell ya this, but it will be at least a year before we wed. Ya may want to make yer way back to Ireland before that," she raised her brows. "Yer kinda startin' to look like you should be leanin' against the washer durin' the spin cycle of an unbalanced load."

"Ah the stuff dreams are made of!" I laughed.

But she wasn't far off. By my calculations, I was going on roughly nine months without. It's one thing to be dream horny. It's quite another to have a person in mind for the starring role. The night that Cecil and I made-out until dawn was still fuel for my fire. Only now, the longing wasn't present only when sleeping. Now, my mind could trail off to him and linger on that night anytime it chose. And…it did.

"Janie, did ya hear me?" she looked concerned by my *checked out of reality* experience.

"I'm sorry what?"

"The BBQ tomorrow...are ya goin'?" she asked again, I guess.

"I think so. I told Mum I probably would. I just don't want my presence there to cause any more drama."

"Well if yer NOT there, there will be more drama," Fitz said.

I shook my head not understanding.

"Seriously Janie, you've been a part of our family since long before her. And if you stop comin' round because of her, I'll lose my shit...on her. Got it?"

I nodded again, knowing this was a truth that couldn't be denied. "So, what are we doing today?"

Fitz's smile went from ear to ear. "Get dressed!"

4

ROLLIN' WITH MY HOMEGIRL

Showered, I threw on my 501's and *Panic Attack* T-shirt. They were a band out of Norway, but the lead singer, Dave Pickett, grew up in So Cal. I love their sound and listen to them as loud as my speakers would allow.

Southern California was threatening ninety degree weather. As we jumped in Baby, Fitz hit the switch to roll her top down. I was on CD duty. Usually, my first grab is always X, but today we needed a different attitude. I grabbed her old N.W.A. CD and off we went.

It was still early morning when we hit the 405 freeway and headed north. I wasn't informed as to where we were heading, but I was out of the house, had on my favorite jeans and my best friend was next to me singing 'Dopeman'. All was well in my world.

We headed east on the 10 freeway, and I began to panic. I hated the city. It was just too busy for me. In fact, anything off of the 10 between the 405 and 110 freeways, I avoided like the plague. But maybe since Fitz was the driver, it wouldn't be so bad for me. That's what I was thinking when a large truck just kind of merged into our lane, causing me to gasp and Fitz to proudly display her middle finger as we slammed on the brakes. I say "we" because I, too, slammed my foot down on my imaginary break.

Two exits down, my breathing was almost back to normal as we pulled off the freeway into downtown LA. A bunch of turns later, we ended up in a parking lot. I pulled my dark glasses down and read the sign: *Everlasting Love, Bridal Shop*.

I guess I had assumed that when we went shopping for bridal gowns, we would be in a swanky store in Beverly Hills, sipping champagne on fluffy chaise lounges, surrounded by gold statues of cherubs.

"Seriously Fitz? I mean no offense to this place or your taste in bridal shops, but I assumed that you would be buying your dress from some place next to Tiffany's."

"Haven't ya ever heard, 'Don't judge a book by its cover'? You wait, yer gonna be shocked."

As we walked to what I assumed was the front door, (it was hard to tell given the iron barred security gate) she rang the button. I heard what sounded like a zzz-ing sound and looked up at the video camera that was now focused on us.

I looked at Fitz and said under my breath, "We're gonna die in here, aren't we?"

"Shush Janie!" she said and nudged me. "I'm here!" she said into the camera.

A moment passed before I heard what sounded like large bolts being pulled open, and quite a few of them, at that. After about the sixth, *bang-clank-shoook* noise, the door was opened. I still couldn't see who was there, as the steel framed and barred gate blocked out any real view. Finally the gate was pushed open and then…I really didn't know what to think.

Standing in front of me was…well, I was sure it was a man. He was dressed in an orange and gold formless dress that was cut just above the knee. It almost looked like a really fancy sleeveless housecoat. His hair was in a faux-hawk; long on top, but leaning to the side like a rooster's cockscomb. The sprayed stiff hair was at least five different colors and the rest was shaved bald. His face was accented by big square glasses and a shit-ton of multi-colored eye make-up. Eyes were lined with black on the top and bright blue on the bottom. His cheekbones were accentuated by a hot pink line about an inch wide. But by far, the most eye-grabbing part of his ensemble was the hot pink lipstick outlined with midnight blue. I tried not to stare as he took Fitz in an embrace, but he had some other sizable assets that men don't usually have. In fact they were cone shaped and turned upward like they were threatening to take out an eye. It put me in mind of Madonna's famous bra, but it looked a lot different on her.

Fitz turned to me, "This is the amazing Rudolpho," she waved her hand, like Vanna White presenting the completed phrase. I had a phrase or two going through my own head.

"And this is my best friend, Janie," she told him.

As he leaned in to get an embrace, I wasn't sure where to put my own C's, as his seemed to be trying to joust mine. "Oh Zhanie," his Spanish accent thick, "I've heard so much about jew!" he kissed both of my cheeks. "Well come on ladies, let's drink shampagne and gossip a little. And you Fizzy," he turned to Fitz, "jew will tell me all about the handsome man who has tamed you," he roared at her.

Stepping inside, I went into full shock. Outside: it looked like an old business building that not only needed barred windows, but possibly boarded as well. Inside: was a palace. Marble flooring stretched as far as my eyes could see. Great art hung on the walls, chandeliers hung from the ceiling, and overstuffed, gold inlayed red couches formed the amazing space where we were to sit and gossip. As Fitz and I sat, Rudolpho headed off in search of champagne.

"Holy crap," I said to Fitz. "This place is amazing. Who is this…guy?" I finally asked her.

"He's one of the best designers in the Los Angeles. I've worked with him on a few shoots. He's brilliant."

"Why haven't I heard of him?" I asked. "I mean I've heard of most of the designers you've worked with, and for."

"Rudolpho has social anxiety," Fitz whispered. "He had an awful show once…got horrible reviews, and now he almost never leaves his house. He still designs, but under an assumed name, and is VERY choosy about who he creates for."

"Yeah, about this house…" I gave it the once over, twice.

"It's fabulous, right," Fitz cut me off.

"That it is! But, he obviously has money…why is he living in a rundown building on the corner of *drive by* and *chalk outline*?"

"Oh. This building was where his mom worked when they first came here from Mexico…I think he was fifteen-ish. When he came into his own, he bought the building and changed it into this. I guess this was his 'happy place' and where he learned about fashion and design. His mother was a tailor."

I nodded, I got it. "So, where is his mom, now?"

Rudolpho entered with a tray containing three crystal champagne glasses and a bottle of Cristal, "Oh honey, I bought her a house in Bebberly Hills. This was NOT her happy place," he shook his head.

I laughed. Rudolpho threw his hands up in the air and snorted a laugh, making me laugh harder. "Sometimes I forget how funny I am," he said.

The champagne was uncorked with a pop, and we settled back into the fluffy couches.

"So Fizzy, what can Rudolpho do for you?" he asked, crossing his legs, somewhat Sharon Stone style.

I averted my eyes from the attention grabbing red panty shot I had been gifted.

"Well, as I told you on the phone...big news...I'm gettin' married!" Fitz announced.

Rudolpho squealed, then Fitz squealed back at him, and then they both turned their eyes to me. I was late but threw in a squeal of my own. Both of them raised their brows to me. "I'll work on it," I said to their disappointed faces.

"Okay," Rudolpho turned back to Fitz, "jew tell me what jew are trying to accomplish. Jer vision!" he gave her a look I could only describe as smoldering. I kind of lost track as they spoke of designers and models and things like:

"Remember what she wore in '92...on the catwalk in Paris?" Fitz asked.

"Oh jes I do," Rudolpho laughed at a memory I had absolutely no knowledge of.

I sat there wondering just where my fashion gene was. Had it gotten diluted by my height, or was it forced out of my DNA by poly-blended jumpsuits worn by my mother in the 80's? I couldn't be sure, but my 501's had been my go-to for the larger chunk of my life.

As Fitz and I got back into Baby, she explained that she had given Rudolpho full creative leave to create whatever he wanted. I tried not to show my apprehension as I was mentally drawn back to his ensemble.

"So...you have no part in the creative process?"

"Well, I mean, I can make little changes if need be, but for the most part, it's ALL him!" she smiled from ear to ear.

I forced a smile and nodded. I don't know why, but I had an uneasy feeling about this. At the same time, I knew I had no fashion-wiggle-room to question.

Back on the 405, we headed south toward home. The sun was high in the sky, warming Southern California to beach weather.

As we turned onto my street, I couldn't help but notice my mother's gold Cadillac parked out in front of my house.

"Oh good, my mother's here," I said to Fitz with a grin. My mother had pretty much been Fitz's *Mona*, for as long as either of us could remember. Everything I had ever done wrong (or was perceived as wrong by my mother), had always been Fitzy's fault.

Fitz grinned. Truth was Fitz liked being a burr in my mother's side. Kind of a '*You won't* accept *me*, *I'll let my very existence*, *wreck your day*', thing.

Mom also had a key that was overused, so I wasn't surprised that she had let herself in. I was surprised, however, to hear her arguing with someone as I approached the front door.

"I'm telling ya, just leave the damn screen closed and the door open. Get some fresh air in here, before it gets too damn hot!" Betty was saying.

"If we leave the door open, people will know we're home. Better the thieves aren't sure," my mother was reasoning.

I heard Betty laugh, "I dare a dumbass to try and step foot in this house while I'm here. I have a '38 in that pocket," she pointed to her handbag, "a Taser in that pocket and for the less offensive jackass, pepper spray."

It was by far the strangest friendship ever. Betty, my Southern born and raised, 60-ish landlord, was a well endowed, shit kicking, gun-toting, fire cracker of a woman with long bleached hair and hot pink nails.

My mother, Betty's polar opposite, was a housewife who usually wore her graying hair in a tight bun, mascara was dressy make-up, and her clothes were picked and worn to show none of her assets. Where Betty was a free, fun loving spirit, my mom was ever *weary* and *leery* of everything and everyone. But I had noticed a change in my mother after making friends with Betty. Known for her stringent judgment, mom was starting to show real signs of a sense of humor about things that used to only get negative responses from her.

Fitz and I walked in, "Hi ladies," I said.

My mother jumped almost out of her skin.

Betty shook her head, "This is why YOU don't need a gun," she told my mom.

"A gun?" I asked, horrified at the thought of my mother being armed.

"Oh, she's down on my gun. Hear about it all the time," Betty shook her head.

"You know she has one in her purse AND the glove compartment in her car. What if somebody steals it?" My mother fumed.

"I told you before, it's not in the glove compartment. I had a hidden compartment installed. You'd never even be able to find the damn thing if ya looked for it."

"And that's exactly WHY we're driving my car," mom huffed.

"Yeah no better way to be *incognito*, than drivin' around in a Gold Cadillac," Betty's brows lifted.

I laughed then and gave them both a hug.

"So what are you two doing here," I asked.

"We're out for the day, gonna do lunch and some shoppin'," Betty inclined her head toward my mom. "We thought we'd ask if ya wanted to come. Both of ya," Betty put her arm around Fitz.

Mom stood there smiling and nodding at Fitz and me.

I could read Fitzy's thoughts: Spend the afternoon with Mrs. O? (What she had called my mother since 10th grade.)

Finally I nudged Fitz, "Yeah I'd love to," she said quickly. "Are we all to ride in Mrs.O's Cadillac?" Fitz's smile was stretched and forced.

Mom was a horrible driver. She was sure if she went under the speed limit, and stopped at green lights to make a right hand turn, she'd never get into an accident. The fact that she may have been the cause of a few accidents didn't hold water with her.

"Ya know what…" Betty smiled, "I think we should all ride in

Baby. Four beautiful women, a badass Cadillac with the top down," she grinned. "We'll be the talk of the town!"

Fitz and I smiled. Mom, on the other hand, looked like she had just been sentenced to the gallows.

"I'm not comfortable in a convertible," mom said as all of us headed to Fitz's car. "There's nothing to prevent stuff from falling into the car, or rocks hitting us."

"You can sit up front and roll up the side window, if it scares ya. Janie and I will sit in back," Betty said.

Mom turned an apprehensive look towards Fitz as she got in the front passenger seat.

Fitz put on her dark sunglasses and gave my mother her famous *angry-red-headed-fairy grin,* "Buckle up Mrs. O!" she said as she sped away from the curb.

Mom quickly grabbed onto the armrest, panicked, she couldn't find the '*Oh Shit*' handle as her head was pushed back by the force of the V8 engine.

We had picked a Mexican restaurant in Redondo Beach right off of Artesia Blvd. By the time we arrived, mom's bun looked as disheveled as I'm sure she felt. Clawing at the lap belt like a trapped animal, she did all but kiss the ground after she exited the passenger seat.

"Damn do I love ridin' in this car!" Betty fired off a yee-haw. "I need to get me one of these!"

The mental image I got; a white Cadillac with a pair of long horns on the front and Betty behind the wheel, made me grin.

After mom came back from the ladies room where she had fixed her bun, we ordered lunch and margaritas. Mom made a comment about the fact that Fitz wasn't having one. Fitz explained that she didn't drink and drive, I saw my mother's face change a little.

Halfway into one margarita, mom was loosening up a little. She was going to order a second, but Betty reminded her that we had a whole day in front of us, and she didn't want to have to carry her again.

My mom did a little drunken nod and giggled like a school girl.

"I'm sorry, what?" I asked. "I'm afraid I have to hear this story," I said.

Betty grinned, "Well, we were gonna wait till you were thirty, but I think ya can handle it."

I knew that Betty had taken my mom out for drinks when I was in Ireland. This was where their friendship blossomed. What I didn't know, was that mom was almost arrested. As the story was told, Fitz and I were laughing so hard, we almost peed ourselves.

5

THE STORY THAT WON'T BE REPEATED

So Betty begins; "So I took yer mama to that Mexican restaurant on the pier, as soon as it opened. I talked her into a drink and we talked for a while. Then we ordered another and I talked a while longer as she slurred her delayed responses," Betty grinned at mom. "Then there was another round," she looked at me, "that'd be the one you heard on the phone when you called from Ireland."

Nodding, I said, "I remember the call, and mom in the background singing her heart out to Rod Stuart."

"Well, then we had another," Betty continued, "and that's when the officers showed up."

Fitz's brow furrowed, "Why did the police show up?" I asked.

"Well honey," Betty giggled, "they showed up for lunch. But they grew a little concerned since your mama was passed out in one of the booths at lunchtime on a weekday. I had gone to the bathroom, and by the time I came back, your mom was fightin' a cop."

"What?" my eyes rounded at mother.

"She...she doesn't need to hear this," mom slurred a little and shook her head.

Betty smiled and continued, "Apparently, as the officer tried to stand her up, he accidently brushed her boobie. She was out cold, didn't know where she was...hell, I'm not even sure she knew who she was," Betty laughed. "But she knew that whoever had touch her ***girl***, wasn't her husband, and she hauled off and smacked him right across the mouth.

Fitz nodded and stuck her tongue in her cheek. I knew what she was thinking then, too. All those years my mother had judged her, at least she had never assaulted an officer of the law.

My mom did her best embarrassed face before trying to stifle a laugh with her hand.

"So, I had to explain to the officer, and very quickly, what yer mama was all about. Ya know the stick she's been sportin' for the last 25 plus years. He was pretty understandin'," Betty nodded, "until your mama asked if she was supposed to shove a dollar down his pants."

"What?" Fitz and I said in unison with rounded eyes.

"Turns out she was REALLY confused about where we were," Betty explained. "When she saw officer *good-body* as she called him, she thought I had taken her to a male strip club. She wasn't happy about the idea but still wanted to know what the proper protocol was."

Mom was now laughing and hiding her face behind her hands. I had never seen her this way and I had to giggle. Fitz, who had been my mother's excuse for everything *not right* in my life since kindergarten, was a harder nut to crack. But after mom started snort laughing, Fitz couldn't hold back anymore and laughed, too. Leaning over to me, Fitz said, "I like yer mom better drunk."

I nodded in agreement. She definitely was two different people. I couldn't help but think Betty had brought this person out of her. Not the drunk thing, but just listening to her and befriending her. It made me realize that we never get too old to need a friend. I reached out and squeezed Fitz's hand. It was just a small thank you because I never had to know what it felt like to be friendless, and my mom had.

Mom being a little tipsy made the ride to the mall more enjoyable for her. Me? Not so much. I was never a mall person. To me it was like hamsters in cages. And I would be that one hamster who was always trying to figure out how to escape.

We hit a store that seemed way too young according to my mother, but Betty had talked her into at least trying some new styles. "Ya don't have to buy anything, just try it on!" Betty *bottom-lined* her.

As Betty, Fitz and I looked for outfits, mom sat nervously in a dressing room. Handing what we found over the door, I heard her sigh.

"Just try it on!" Betty answered her sigh.

I heard a lot of tugging and sounds of disapproval. Those I knew well. Fitz had wandered off, not waiting for the big reveal.

Mom cracked the dressing room door and peered out.

"Well, come on now, show it to us," Betty said.

"Out there?" mom asked bewildered.

"Well yeah, sugar. How the hell else are we gonna see it?" Betty shot back.

"I thought you would…come in here," mom looked uncomfortable.

"Seriously? We won't all fit in there!" Betty shook her head. "Now pull up yer *big-girl-panties*, and get out here."

I winced assuming that this was where my mom would put her foot down and list the reasons why this was NOT going to happen. But to my clear surprise, she opened the door, set her jaw high, and gave us the view.

She looked incredible. I mean she still had that matronly bun that made her look older than her years, but incredible none the less. For the first time in my life, I realized that I got some of my *assets* from her. She always kept her *girls*, hips and bum, tented.

"See," began Betty, "I went with a floral print dress in pinks, to bring out her great skin…and sunny disposition," she added raising an eyebrow to me.

"I just feel…naked," mom said looking down at herself.

"Honey, yer arms are showin', not yer *girls*," Betty nodded.

"You look beautiful mom," I said, smiling from ear to ear.

"Yeah?" she asked me, looking at herself in the full length mirror.

"Yeah," I smiled. "You really do!"

Just about that time, Fitz walked up with an outfit in her hand. "Wow Mrs. O, hot stuff!" she said. I think it was the first time my mother ever really smiled at Fitz. I wish I had had a camera with me to capture this moment. Fitz handed mom the garment that she had picked for her.

Mom held it up, and couldn't speak. It was the '*little-black-dress'*.

All women hear about it in their teens: *The one* every woman needs and every woman hopes they look fantastic in. *The one* that magically shaves off pounds and smoothes all the curves. *The one* that every great fashion magazine, article or book that has ever been written, has put focus on.

"Ohhh," mom looked at it with a *Do I dare* expression.

"Every woman needs '*the-little-black-dress*'," Fitz grinned.

"And this is comin' from a model," Betty put her arm around Fitz and gave her a squeeze.

Mom's smile changed into one of *I DO* dare and into the dressing room she went. A few moments passed before we heard her say, "I need a zip."

Betty stepped inside the dressing room and said to Fitz and me, "Are you girls ready for this?"

When mom stepped out, Fitz and I both sucked in our breath. But mom didn't look happy.

"What's wrong?" I asked. "It looks amazing on you!"

Mom turned toward the mirror, "I still…just look like…old me in a new dress."

Fitz stepped forward, "That's because ya didn't do it right. Stand still," Fitz said as she took down my mom's hair from the everlasting bun. Down her back, it fell in waves. Fitz ran her finger though it, moving her '*part*' first one way, then the other, before saying, "Ya need bangs. Ya have the perfect face for big rockin' bangs."

Mom looked in the mirror and smiled, as tears gathered in her eyes. She had worn the same look for twenty years and was scared, but ready for a change.

As apprehensive as she was, we found a few more outfits that didn't scream *Mom circa 1940*. Fitz even bought the *LBD* as a gift to her '*coming-out*' as she put it.

Mom said under her breath to Fitz, "I'm not gay, though."

"Yeah, I got that," Fitz grinned and nodded. "I'm talkin' about ya comin' out of yerself. Not comin' out of the closet," Fitz clarified with a nod.

After her outfits were purchased, Fitz told us we all had appointments at the salon. Looking more than confused, I asked, "What? What appointments, what salon?"

While yer mom was trying on her sixth outfit, I called my hairdresser. He's available and owes me a favor…so?" she looked at my mom. "I got you and Betty in for a pedi," she said to me.

Mom was wearing that fearful face again. "I don't know. It's a big change," she shook her head.

Betty piped up, "Again, a model," she used her hands to present Fitz in all her glory.

I wasn't sure if she was reluctant about the change, or fearful that Fitz would be getting her back for years of mental and verbal abuse.

As we hit the salon, I started to fidget again. Well hidden in Hermosa Beach was this amazing salon that didn't take walk-in's and was so exclusive, you had to be 'buzzed' in the door. A man resembling Fabio walked over and kissed Fitz on both cheeks. She introduced Betty and I to Blair by name then presented my mother as the *project*.

Betty and I were handed champagne then led to the pedi stations. Mom pounded a glass of bubbles and headed in the other direction to her hair appointment with Blair. Fitz actually decided to forgo her pedi to stay with mom and to discuss with Blair her vision for mom's hair.

I didn't remember until I lifted my pant leg that it had been a day or so since I shaved my legs. I was hoping it wasn't too bad, when my nail tech made the comment snidely, "Just so you know...we do waxing here, too."

I began to blush. I wasn't anywhere near Yeti status yet. I knew full well that the hair had to be much longer than this, to actually wax, but I just nodded and said sorry instead.

Betty had heard the woman's comment and saw my reddening face, "And just so you know what we do," Betty looked at her, "we tip really well when we enjoy our service."

The woman looked abashed and never said another word, sarcastic or otherwise. I couldn't help but smile.

I turned to Betty, "Do you think mom's doing okay? I mean, this is a lot of...changing for her. "

"Puddin," she patted my hand, "I wasn't kiddin' when I said 'yer mom needs to find out who she is...besides just bein' yer mama'. She's a great lady, honey. She's just spent so much time bein' mama, she doesn't know how to be anything else."

I thought about it and nodded, "You know I still need her to be my mom, right?"

"And ya always will, Puddin, no matter how grown ya get." She looked at me sidelong, "I'll bet ya she'd like to hear that, though."

I smiled and nodded some more. Betty never had children, but she had a way about her. Maybe it was empathy? But when she saw a box, she saw it from all sides and this made her an amazing person.

As Betty and I sat with our toenails all pretty, enjoying our massage chairs and another glass of champagne, Fitz was watching long strands of hair hitting the floor and smiling from ear to ear.

When mom was ready to step out of Blair's secluded room, Betty and I held our breath. Fitz announced, "Will the real Mrs.O, please stand up."

The door didn't open though.

Fitz cracked the door, "Did ya hear me?" she asked.

"Yes. I was standing," mom told her.

Fitz let out a held breath, "That means 'step out'!"

"Why didn't you just say 'step out', then?" mom asked.

Betty looked at me, "I'll work on it."

"Okay, one more time," Fitz said. "Please step out!"

My mother stepped out of the door and my eyes began to well, "Oh my God mom!"

"That's right," Betty popped off with a hoot, "that's what yer supposed to look like. That's you!" Betty pointed to mom.

Mom was sporting shoulder length hair with big waves and face framing bangs that swept to one side. She was also sporting one of her new outfits.

"We left all her new clothes in the car," I pointed out, taking her all in.

"Ah," Fitz waved it off, "ya know as well as I do, ya need the full picture to really make a make-over pop!"

I smiled as my mother hugged Fitz and thanked her repeatedly. Fitz grinned and hugged her back. I grinned and thought; it only took 21 years, the LBD, a haircut and some booze.

Back at my house, Fitz convinced my mom that no make-over was complete until make-up was applied. Mom looked both excited and scared.

Fitz pointed out that this was the easy part. "If ya don't like it, it washes away," she said.

Fitz pulled out one of her make-up caddies that she kept at my house. By last count, she had one here, one at home, one at Mum's, and a small travel size in Baby's trunk, just in case Baby ever broke down and wasn't feeling properly Fitz-a-fied.

Into the bathroom Fitz and mom went. I made coffee and showed Betty a new painting I had been working on. What only took half of an hour seemed like forever as we awaited the final transformation.

As mom emerged from the bathroom she was glowing. It could have also had something to do with the shimmering make-up Fitz had used. Regardless, mom was in full bloom. Her eyes began to well as she looked in my full length mirror.

"We'll have none of that," Fitz told her. "It was hard enough to get mascara on ya in the first place. I won't be doing clean-up as well."

Mom was 100% sober by now and I was worried she'd have haircut remorse, but she smiled from ear to ear. I couldn't stop staring. She looked so beautiful. Mom hugged all of us before going to show my dad. "Wish me luck," she said.

Betty soon said she had to get home. She was running late for her own date with Larry. With cheeks kissed and hugs exchanged, I watched the two women load themselves into their separate Cadillacs and head off to their men.

I put my arm around Fitz, "You did a good thing," I told her.

Fitz nodded, "It was surreal at the very least."

"Seem like things will be different between you and mom, now."

Fitz made the pouty face.

"What?" I asked. "You act like it's a bad thing?"

"Well…she has always been my arch-nemesis. Every great super hero has one," Fitz explained.

"Oooo-kay," I said, "so are you saying that her being nice to you, may be your…kryptonite?"

"Well I certainly don't know what life is like without it," Fitz said. "What if it brings bad juju?" she laughed.

Fitz stayed for a while before saying that Scotty would be home soon. Since the engagement, he had moved into her condo and still felt a little weird being there alone with B.J., Fitz's roommate.

"Will ya be comin' to the BBQ at Mum's tomorrow?" she asked, the look having a hint of *you better.*

"I'll be there," I assured her. Yet after she left, I couldn't help but wonder if all this nonsense between Mona and me would blow over by then.

6

SECRETS, LIES AND ALIBIES

After Fitz left, I looked at my phone. 4 pm., and still no call from Cecil? I squished up my face and I debated calling him. I knew he was usually awake late, but didn't know if this changed when he became the CEO of the distillery. Back and forth my thoughts went. What if I wake him? But he may be happy if I did. After five minutes of debating myself, I hit auto dial 4.

It rang three times, and I was just about to hang up, when a woman answered the phone.

"Hello," said a cheery voice.

I pulled the phone away and looked at the read out, thinking I may have hit the wrong auto number. It was Cecil's number. Now I was confused. I hadn't called the home number, but his cell. It was after midnight in Ireland. Who was this woman answering his phone?

"Again she said, "Hello?" this time as a question.

"Uh, hello," I began. "This is Janie…calling for Cecil."

"I'm sorry, he's indisposed at the moment. May I take your number?"

I bit my bottom lip, "Ugh…he has my number."

"And you said Janine?" asked the woman.

I rolled my eyes, seriously? "No, Janie," I said, hoping that she had heard of me or this rang some kind of bell for her.

"Last name?" she asked.

Nope, hadn't heard of me. I stuck my tongue in my cheek, "O'Connelly," I stated, a little more upset than I wanted it to sound.

"Okay, I'll let him know," said the oblivious woman. "Have a good night."

My laugh was flat, "Yeah, you too." I hung up.

As I set the phone down, my mind immediately went to finding excuses why some random woman, who had apparently never heard of me, was answering Cecil's cell phone past midnight. As hard as I tried, I couldn't think of a good reason, at least not one that wasn't a complete stretch. I could however think of a few bad reasons.

I sat and rolled this around in my mind, hoping my phone would ring any moment now and he would dispel all my negative thoughts. As the hour passed by, 1am in Ireland, there was still no call back. Throwing my phone in my bag, I grabbed my keys and headed out the door. Every part of me wanted to call Fitz so she could tell me how ridiculous I was being. But I knew it was her and Scotty's alone time, and I was reluctant to interrupt that with my *crazy*.

I walked with no destination, and wound up where I usually did when I had no destination in mind. As I entered Fitzpatrick's Pub, I realized how early it was here in Southern California. On a Saturday night, this place would be jam packed as the band rattled the rafters. At 5:15 in the afternoon, not exactly a happening place, except for the regulars who had been coming here for 50 plus years. Within the next two hours, the changing of the guard would happen, as the old regulars filed out to go to their homes and families. Then the new regulars, in their twenties and thirties, would appear to ride out the rest of the night.

I was a bit surprised to see Andy behind the bar. This was usually Pauly's night.

"Ello luv," Andy greeted me. "Usual?" he asked already grabbing a pint glass.

"Hi, and yes please," I said taking a stool. "What are you doing here tonight?"

"I'm fillin' in fer Pauly. As ya know, he's had a few hard days," Andy raised his brow to me. His accent was much thicker than Pauly and Barry's.

I let out a heavy sigh, "Yeah, I know," I shook my head.

"So…I heard he stayed the night with ya," Andy baited me as a big brother would.

"Very funny," I gave him my sardonic smile.

Andy let out the good natured laugh I loved, "Really, I don't know what he was thinkin' stayin' at yer house after all the… drama. But…at least he and Barry are workin' things out."

"Oh, well that's good," I said.

"Yeah, they're in the poker room right now, talkin' it out. Glad I'm NOT a fly on that wall," Andy added.

I turned my head toward the poker room, "Why would they choose to do it here?" I wondered out loud.

"Neutral ground," Andy said, as if I didn't understand anything about men. "This is the easy part, I'd imagine. The hard part…is gonna be breakin' it to Mum."

"Mum?" I questioned. My mind went immediately to Pauly. "Is Pauly getting divorced then?"

"No I meant about Barry!" Andy cocked his head.

"What's wrong with Barry?" I asked.

Andy stared at me for a moment, "Ya really don't know, do ya?"

I was quickly starting to feel very left out of all the loops in my life, I shook my head.

"Damn, I shouldn't have said a damn thing!" Andy berated himself. He let out a heavy sigh before saying, "Look, yer as good as family…and yer gonna find out sooner or later…"

I sat there wondering if it would in fact be later than sooner. Finally, I gave Andy the *and* hand roll.

'Ya can't say anything to Mum, ya understand?"

I nodded, "Of course." Only now I wasn't sure if I wanted to know whatever I was agreeing to.

"Barry's not engaged."

My jaw dropped, but no words found their way out. I wasn't sure I had any. My mind seemed to be put on the spin cycle. Finally, I squeaked out the only thing that came to the surface, "What?"

"I guess Mum went a little nuts…settin' Barry up all the time. It was makin' him crazy. And even though he protested, she would just ambush him with girl after girl, after girl. He almost told her he was gay to get her to stop, but then he knew she'd be ambushin' him with men. And since Barry's straight, that would have been a lot worse for all concerned."

I nodded, knowing a little of Mum's ambushs, having almost been one.

"So when he was in Ireland, his best friend came up with the bright idea of a fake fiancé, to at least give him a moment of peace," Andy explained. "What he didn't think of, was how crazy Mum was gonna go, plannin' a weddin'. Every day she had him out and about, tryin' cake, lookin' at kilts and proper dress for the occasion. She's even been on the phone looking for venues in Ireland," he shook his head. "Now Mum wants to fly the lass here, to meet her future daughter-in-law. It's a bloody mess, I tell ya."

"Oh God…wait till Fitz finds out," I said.

"Fitzy?" Andy looked confused. "Fitzy knows."

It took me a moment to register and I still needed verification, "She does?" I asked.

"Yeah…she's known for a few days. I guess that's why I figured ya already knew, you two bein" thicker than blood, and all."

I nodded, "Thicker than blood," I agreed, as he went to wait on another customer.

Fitz had known…for days? I couldn't help but wonder why she hadn't told me. We came to an agreement in Ireland, when she found out that I had had a crush on Barry since I was a child. We promised then, we would never lie to each other again. But is keeping a secret from someone also lying to them? I went over it in my head as I drank my beer. If Aunt Marble looks awful in her muumuu, but never asks if she looks good…if I don't say she looks awful, am I lying to her? I came to the conclusion that this would be omitting…which in essence was lying to keep from hurting someone's feelings. But wasn't there also omitting to cover your own ass, then justifying it by saying *at least I didn't lie*? No matter how I went around it, I came to the same conclusion, omitting was a lie's right hand. Whether to spare feelings, or save your own ass…that was the only moral question here. After all, if you omit something, having done something you knew would hurt someone, weren't you omitting just to cover your own ass? Because you had to know, doing whatever you had done, that you knew you would have to omit…you shouldn't have done in the first place, therefore it's more on the lying side? I needed another beer. Andy set me up and gave me a shot of Bushmills. I didn't ask for it, but wondered if he knew a reason why I would need one…that had been omitted. I shook my head to make my brain stop going in circles.

So far this week had been kind of a shit storm. Not a full-blown kind of storm, but definitely working up to it. Mona was pissed at me for something I didn't know anything about. And, she had also apparently cursed me, according to the *Scary Sisters* (how

I referred to the Mum and Aunt Marble combo). Cecil...had some random woman (who apparently thinks I'm the random woman) answering his cell phone at midnight, after never having called me back, no less. And the cherry on the cake...Fitzy is keeping secrets from me.

Suddenly Pauly emerged from the poker room and headed for the bar. His face showed surprise at my being there.

"What are ya doin here?" he asked.

I thought it was a strange question, "Having a beer," I raised my glass.

"I didn't mean it the way it sounded," he shook his head and took the stool next to me.

Andy walked down the bar with a beer for his brother, "Did the two of ya get it all worked out?" he asked.

Pauly cocked his head toward me: the universal, *Not in front of her*, head cock.

"I already know," I said.

Pauly looked confused, "What do ya mean, ya know?" he asked.

"I know about the fake fiancé," I nodded.

"Ah that," Pauly said quickly.

"Wait...is there something else?" I asked.

"No, no...just that," Pauly took a long pull off of his beer.

I got the feeling I was just pushed out of the loop again, but just asked, "Where's Barry?"

"Ah, he left. When we were done talkin', we hugged and he went on his way. "

I hadn't seen him, so I assumed he went out the back door. "Oh," was all I said.

"So, um, that guy yer datin'..." Pauly started.

"Cecil," I offered.

"Right, the guy that beat the shit out of John at the BBQ..."

I nodded. Cecil had indeed beat-up my ex after he knocked

me unconscious.

"So where's that goin'?" Pauly asked, making his brother Andy raise a questioning eye to him.

"I, um…" was I supposed to say I don't know? How about some woman just answered his cell, so I'm not sure? "I'm not sure," I admitted. "It's still pretty new."

"Right," Pauly nodded. "But ya have feelins for him, right?"

I was starting to get a little uncomfortable. True enough Pauly was like a brother to me. But he was the kind of brother who never asked about my relationships. In fact, this was a first in our last 21 years we'd been around each other.

"Ummm…I do." I finally answered. "Why?"

"Just wanted to know where ya were at…what's goin' on with ya."

Andy shook his head and walked down the bar to help another customer.

"Well like I said, it's still new. But yeah, I like him," I grinned.

"Good…great," Pauly replied quickly. "Well, I best be gettin' home or Mona will come lookin' fer me. And we both know, it's best Mona doesn't find me talkin' to ya," he downed his beer.

I nodded in agreement, but just then, as if her name had been mentioned too many times, here came Mona through the back door.

Pauly saw my face change and looked in the direction of his quickly approaching wife, "Going to talk to Barry, huh? I didn't believe you and now I know why I shouldn't have. Meeting your girlfriend, huh?"

Before I, or Pauly, could offer an explanation, Andy came forward, "He wasn't here to meet Janie. Barry just left. You can call him yerself."

"I didn't ask you anything," she hurled the comment at Andy. "So why are you answering for them?"

Andy's face became grave as he leaned forward, "Because as

long as I'm behind this bar, you'll be respectful…or leave. Everyone else is puttin' up with yer crazy shite, and I won't have it. Are we clear?" he never took his eyes from hers.

For a moment, I thought she would test him. They held each other's stare, before she huffed and left the way she came. Pauly gave his brother a look then followed behind her with his tail between his legs.

I had never seen Andy less than jovial and was taken aback. "I'm sorry if I put you in her crosshairs," I told him.

"Ah, I'm so sick of it. She's been miserable for years, but now she's making everyone else miserable, too. I have to see her be miserable at every family function. I won't have it at my job, too."

I nodded, but didn't offer an opinion. Soon enough I headed home.

When I walked through the door, I noticed that my answering machine light was blinking. Not gonna lie, part of me was afraid to press play. But maybe, just maybe, it was Cecil. And maybe he would fill me in on the mysterious message taker.

I hit play: "Janie, it's mom," I heard. I tried not to be let down. "So I wanted to call you sooner…but this was the first time I could pry your father's hands off me," she giggled.

I crinkled my nose up at the phone.

"He loves the new look and well…I don't think we're going to have Sunday night dinner this week."

My whole face squished up. I had tried to feign a million different ailments and was still required to show for Sunday dinner. Now because mom was getting some, I get excused? Don't look a gift horse in the mouth, I reminded myself.

"Your dad is taking me for a night on the town!"

I smiled. It was pretty sweet, though. Then in the background I heard my father, "What's my little sex-kitten doing?" My face changed to a look of horror, and I hit *skip message* in a panic right after I heard my mom let out a purr.

I sat there staring at my answering machine and shaking my head NO. Okay, Fitz was right. I was a prude. I should be happy for mom…instead I was just trying to block all mental images.

I turned on the TV, put on my jammies and dragged my comforter back to the couch. I still couldn't believe that Barry had never been engaged, never met the woman of his dreams in Ireland. I did understand his reasoning, though. Mum was determined to see him wed, and had done some strange things to try and get him to the altar. Still…Fitz knew…and didn't tell me. As my thoughts shifted from, Barry to Fitz, to Mona, to Pauly, to Cecil, I thought I'd never fall asleep.

I woke with a fright. A vision of my mother dressed like one of the fur clad actors from Cats…my father pouring her a saucer of milk. I shook my head to clear the vision.

Before I had my coffee made I heard my front door open. "Hello," yelled Fitz.

"I'm in the kitchen," I said. "What are you doing here this early on a Sunday morning?"

"Scotty had to go into the office, something to do with payroll. Guess Callaghan's in Ireland is having a computer glitch. No one here got their deposit. He'll be at Mum's later, though."

I stared at her, wondering if I should open the conversation about Barry.

"What?" she asked.

I shook my head, "Nothing."

"Will ya please make me a quad mocha?" she pled with folded hands. "I'll be your best friend!"

"Sure, what are best friends for?" I answered.

"So, what's new?" Fitz asked.

I stuck my tongue in my cheek, "Let's see," I began. I told her about the woman who answered Cecil's phone.

Her eyes narrowed, but she said it could be nothing to worry about.

I told her about mom's message.

She grinned. "Go Mrs. O!"

I told her about having an impromptu beer at the bar with Pauly and Mona showing up.

Fitz shook her head, "Well, that's not good."

I told her about Andy's response to Mona.

"Yeah, that's Andy," she said, "he won't be takin' shit from anyone…even her."

"Oh yeah," I added, "it turns out, Barry was never engaged," I said to her.

She stopped her coffee cup halfway to her mouth and let out a sigh, "Who told ya?"

"I think the better question is…why didn't you tell me?" I asked.

"It was Andy, wasn't it?" she diverted. "So what else did he tell ya?"

"Nothing," I emitted. "What else is there?" I did a palm-up.

"Nothin'," she said.

I wasn't sure I believed her, but said, "Fine. But why didn't you tell me?"

She let out a sigh, "I didn't know…if ya'd want to know. I knew that you had a huge crush on him for so long…"

I nodded, "Yeah?"

"And I know how yer feelin' about Cecil…"

My brows raised, "And…"

"I didn't want to rock yer boat," she looked me dead in the eyes. "I didn't know what kind of affect this would have on ya. At first I thought ya only liked Cecil because ya thought ya had no chance with Barry. But I know better now…know ya really *feel* for Cecil…I didn't want to make those waters murky."

I slowly began to nod. She was always trying to protect me. This wasn't any different. "You know this doesn't change my feelings for Cecil, right?"

"I do. And that's exactly why I didn't think ya needed to know. If I thought for a moment it would change yer heart's desire," she shrugged her shoulders, "I would have rushed to tell ya. I swear it to ya."

I went to go get ready for the BBQ at Mum's. I was a little sad that my phone still hadn't rang. This wasn't the longest Cecil and I had gone without talking to each other. While trying to get our schedules to meet up, we had played tag once for three days. Even though it had only been one now, I was really missing him.

I put on a cute white sundress that went down to my knees and threw my hair into a long pony tail. For all practical purposes, I was ready for the BBQ.

At 10am, we walked into Mum and Da's house. Da was reading the paper but stood to greet each of us with a kiss and a hug. "Mum and Marble are in the kitchen," he informed us.

In the huge kitchen, Mum and Aunt Marble were at the center island finishing another tray of jalapeno poppers that would eventually find their way onto the grill.

"There's my babies," Mum said as we both circled the island to put a kiss on her cheek before kissing Aunt Marble.

"Anything we can do to help?" I asked.

"Not a thing, luv," said Mum, all decked out in a vibrant orange muumuu with a matching scarf holding back her flaming red hair.

Aunt Marble was wearing what looked like an African Ceremonial dress, it was the only way I could describe it. Beautiful, if not a little too long on her very short frame, "We've got everything ready to go. Now we just have to wait for everyone to show up."

"Where's Benny?" Fitz asked.

"Oh, he had an errand to run, but he'll be here by noon. Ya know what ya could do?" she said to Fitz, "Bloody Mary duty."

"Oh that would be great. I have a gallon of mix in the outside fridge. Would ya mind, Fitzy?" Mum asked.

We headed out to the patio bar and pulled out Mum's Bloody Mary mix and cracked open a bottle of Absolut. Fitz came from a long line of bartenders and bartendresses, in some cases. Watching her make a drink, was like watching great art being made: Hands deft, precise, four drinks being made all at the same time, no measuring and exactly the same from the Vodka to the Tabasco down to the olives and limes. I know there are some who scoff at the magic I speak of, but those are people who have never had one of her drinks.

We each carried one drink for us, and one for each of the *Scary Sisters*. Mum made the "AHHH" sound after her first drink. "Where's Scotty?" Mum asked, finally realizing he was M.I.A.

"Problem at work, computer thing, he'll be here soon, I hope," Fitz said.

"Well ladies," said Marble, "shall we?" she headed outside.

Out on chaise lounges, the four of us enjoyed the sun and our drinks until Mum said, "I keep tryin' to get Barry to let me talk to this woman of his on the phone. She's to be my daughter-in-law," Mum pointed out. "I should get to speak to her, don't ya think?"

I bit my bottom lip. I had never tried to lie to Mum before. And to be honest, I wasn't sure I could. Fitz could keep a straight face for Barry's sake, but the way she looked at me, led me to believe that she had serious doubts that I could.

"Soon enough Mum, soon enough," Fitz said.

In Fitz's mind, she wasn't just lying to protect Barry, but to protect her mother, too. What mom wants to hear that your child lied to you because you were an overbearing presence in their life?

As I kept my teeth buried into my bottom lip, the others began to arrive. First was Danny with his wife and boys, then Andy with his family and soon the only ones missing were Pauly, Mona and Barry.

Barry showed up with Pauly's boys, saying that Pauly and

Mona were out front finishing some personal business.

Mum raised her brows to Fitz and me. I think we were all sure what was happening. Most likely, Pauly was trying to convince her not to cause a scene or be a bitch. I wasn't ready to bet money on how today was going to go.

When Pauly and Mona walked in, fake smiles stretched across their faces, I was sure it was just a matter of time before Hurricane Mona was released.

Benny and the brothers helped Da Bar-B-Que. The women folk had nothing to do for the next hour but refill the men's drinks and gossip. Mona sat guard next to the kids playing Marco-Polo in the pool. Once in a while, she'd shoot me a shitty look that I would feel burning into my flesh. But when I turned my eyes her way, she would switch her gaze. Part of me just wanted to go talk to her…work this out. We'd never be friends, I was sure of that. But maybe we could at least get along?

Barry too, kept sending looks our way. But I wasn't sure who he was looking at. Was it his Mum, knowing he'd have to come clean? Was it Fitz, hoping that she would keep his secret instead of trying to mediate? This was by far the most tension I had ever felt at Mum and Da's house. And that's including the time that my ex, John, crashed a family BBQ and knocked me unconscious.

More Bloody Marys were created and served as we women brought out all the side salads for the meal. Mum and Marble had made a green salad, potato salad, macaroni salad, deviled eggs, baked beans, and some kind of layered Jell-o fruit mold with whipped cream. The men had pulled everything off the grill, hot dogs, hamburgers, tri tip, ribs, chicken, poppers and corn on the cob. It was always more of a feast here, than a meal, at the Fitzpatrick's.

As we all sat at the long table Mum and Da had built for their large and still growing family, I had almost forgotten the weirdness of the day. Almost! Mona and Pauly, having no other space available sat directly across from me. It did make it that much easier for her to shoot death rays at me. Fitz and Scotty sat to my left.

I tried not to notice as Mona stared at me while ripping apart her chicken with angry teeth. At the far end of the table, conversations of marriage took center stage. Benny was asking Aunt Marble if she had given any thought to where she would like to get married.

"Well, I hadn't really thought about it," Aunt Marble said. "But someplace next to water, is a must."

Mum nodded, as if this was an absolute necessity. "We were married in the rain," she winked at her husband. "Tis good luck to be married by runnin' water," she added.

"I'm glad to hear ya say that," Benny said. "Just this morning, I picked up tickets for a cruise to Mexico."

Aunt Marble's eyes widened with surprise, "I haven't been to Mexico in years!"

"Well, that's not all," Benny took her hand, "If you're okay with the idea, we can be married on the ship!"

Marble looked like she would burst, "That's amazin'! I'd love to!"

"And," Benny added, "I have tickets for all of you!"

There were a lot of *WOWS* flying around, as Benny started passing out tickets. Rounding the table, he got to me and held out a ticket.

"Me?" I asked surprised, trying not to catch the '*Death To You, Bitch*' look I knew Mona had adopted.

"Well of course, yer family!" Aunt Marble said, turning a threatening look to Mona.

Mona stood and excused herself.

She was the least of my problems now, though. I hated being in the ocean. I hated boats. In my mind, when we were on land, all fish, even the greatest ocean dwelling beasts, were food. We were in the water, same rule applied, but in reverse. Not to mention, whoever WAS in charge of the ocean, God, Poseidon, Mother Nature, whoever, had made it clear I was not welcome there.

Fitz was so excited and was shaking her ticket in her hand, until Scotty said, "This is for next weekend."

"I know it's short notice," Benny started, "but I got a great deal on account all of those people that got injured."

Everyone stopped and stared at him, "What?" Mum finally asked.

Benny shook his head, "Tragic, just tragic." He explained how a group of seniors in a party bus coming from Las Vegas, had been hit by a semi. "Ya had to have seen it on the news," he did a palms-up as we all shook our heads, No.

"Are they okay?" Fitz asked. "I mean…did anyone…ya know…pass?"

"No, no," Benny offered. "Well…that one guy, but he was 98. All the other people were just injured. Thank God for being drunk, am I right?" he nodded.

"So is this a senior's cruise?" Mum asked.

"Well, mostly, but they allow family to come with the seniors," Benny smiled.

Everyone tried not to look as though the blush had been taken off the rose by the news of the injured elderly.

Scotty piped up, "I won't be able to go," he shook his head at Fitz. "I'm so sorry, Benny, Marble, but we're still havin' computer problems at work. And even if we weren't, I have that big meetin' next Friday with some buyers in New York."

Fitzy threw him a pouty face and let out a breath," I understand."

"We understand, too," Benny said. "Since you're the only one here with a nine to five…" he trailed off. "Anyone else that can't make it?" he asked.

Danny would be the other with a 9-5ish job, being a police sergeant, but he said there was no way he was passing up Mexico, much to his wife's grin.

I was busy trying to find my own way out of this. It was much easier when I could use the *my mother won't let me* excuse. I was really missing that right about now. Fitz looked at me and KNEW what was going through my mind but she just patted my hand instead of making my private fears a scene.

Back onto the patio walked Mona, carrying a full tray of Kamikaze shots for everyone. "I thought we should all toast to the happy couple and Mexico." Pauly smiled at his wife's attempt to fit in with the family and be a good sport.

As she made her way to my side of the table, I grabbed the shot closest to me and handed it to Fitz. Mona's eyes widened for a moment then she grinned at me, "Enjoy," she said before moving on. I inspected my shot, nothing on the glass, nothing floating in the glass. I pounded my shot with everyone else once 'Mexico' was toasted.

We all went back to chatter, mostly the women talked about which ones of us needed a new bathing suit for the trip. Mona wasn't talking though. In fact…she just kept staring…at Fitz.

I wasn't sure what was happening, and Fitz seemed to be oblivious to the mischievous grin aimed at her. I joined in the chatter, too, knowing I would like to wear something more *boaty,* if that was even a word.

It was a jovial and carefree moment until "Bllluurrup" could be heard. Fitz covered her stomach with her hand. Scotty looked to his betrothed just as another sound emerged "Bllluurrup" Fitz's tummy yelled again. She turned her eyes to me. They were wild, frightened, *about to pop out of her skull* eyes, as she took off running for the house.

Standing, I caught Mona's grin and shook my head at her.

"What's wrong with Fitzy?" Benny asked as she whizzed past him.

"Nothing, she's fine," I offered. "Or at least she better be," I said looking Mona directly in the eye, as I passed her.

Mum and Da had five bathrooms in their house. Deduction told me that Fitz hadn't made it far. The door to the hall bathroom was closed, "Fitz?" I inquired.

Her response was a moan, but I couldn't tell if it came from her mouth or her stomach. Scotty was right behind me.

"Baby, are ya alright?" Scotty asked.

"Yes," she said with some difficulty. "Go back to the party, dear."

"Can I get ya anything?" he asked.

"I'm fine. Go back outside now, darlin'," Fitz said again.

"I could get ya…" Scotty started.

Fitz cut him off, "Fer the love God, baby, get the hell away from the door!" she howled.

Scotty looked concerned and confused, "I got this," I told him. "It's okay, go back outside. She'll be fine," I nodded to him.

A moment passed before Fitz asked, "Is he gone?"

"Yeah, he's gone. Are you okay?" I winced.

"Mona! Mona that bitch, she did this!" Fitz replied.

I nodded, "I know. I'm so sorry, Fitzy."

"Don't be sorry fer me," Fitz offered, breathless. "Be sorry fer her…because I'm gonna kill her. Really fuckin' slowly!" she added.

I nodded, "I know," was all I could say.

I went in search of ginger ale to see if maybe it would calm her tummy. Sitting on the counter was a jar of powered **Super Concentrated Ultra Turbo Lax**. I read the directions on the bottle: half a spoonful into water or other fluid. It boasted that it was clear with no chalky taste. I shook my head. I stomped out back, ready to not only confront Mona, but I think to kick her ass, when I noticed that Pauly, the kids and Mona had left abruptly.

"Is Fitzy okay?" Mum asked coming to my side.

"She will be," I said showing her the bottle.

Mum's green eyes flashed and she stomped inside. I had assumed she was heading to the room of hell that Fitz was holed up in, but she grabbed her phone instead.

"I'm gonna say this once," Mum began into the receiver, "ya call me as soon as ya get home. This is not a request. Do ya hear me son? OBEY!" she hung up.

The look on Mum's face made me recoil, "That woman...has gone too damn far."

I just nodded with wide frightened eyes. It was rare to see Mum angry, just not her nature. But screw with one of her kids... Hell Hath No Fury, was alive and well in her.

I knocked on the bathroom door and handed a ginger ale through the crack when it opened. "Any better?" I asked.

When Fitz opened the door, she looked like she had either had the worst stomach flu ever or had been in labor, "I'm goin' to make her so sorry!"

I nodded, "I know."

"So fuckin' sorry," Fitz repeated.

"If it makes you feel any better, I'm pretty sure the shot was intended for me, not you."

"No. That doesn't make it any better...it makes it worse," Fitz answered.

I knew what she meant. We had this unspoken rule: If someone messed with us, it could be ignored. But, if someone messed with family...it was going to get ugly.

As we headed back into the living room, Fitz still holding her tummy as if she didn't really trust it anymore, Mum was on the phone with Pauly.

"Oh, so ya don't think she'd do somethin' like that, huh?" she asked her son through a tightened jaw.

There was a pause before Mum's eyes practically popped out of her skull, “My cookin’? Have ya lost yer damn mind boy?”

Fitz and I both winced, whatever hole Mona had jumped into, Pauly was about to join her.

“Have I…EVER…made ANYONE sick with my cookin’?” Mum posed the question. There was another short pause, “Ya tell yer wife, son…now she has more eyes on her than she could have ever imagined. And fer damn sure, more than she wanted.” Mum slammed down the receiver and let out a growl. “That woman, is not gonna get away with this!”

Fitz and I stood like stones as Mum headed back out to the patio.

“Ohhh,” Fitz shook her head, “she’s picked the wrong fight.”

“Yeah, I know. You’re gonna get her for this,” I agreed.

Fitz let out a laugh, “Hell, I’m the least of her problems, now,” Fitz pointed to her Mum.

Back out on the patio, Barry had taken Mum aside and they were having a private conversation. I shot a look to Fitz, who shook her head, “He can’t possibly think this is a good time to do this?” I told her.

As we took sidelong glances so as not to seem nosey, we both saw Mum throw her arms around Barry’s neck and begin sobbing hysterically.

“Ah, for the love of Saint Peter, Barry!” Fitz covered her eyes and shook her head.

I, too, thought this was poor timing, but was more concerned with WHAT he told her. Did he say he invented a girlfriend to escape his mother’s interference in his life? Did he say she was actually a fairy that went back to *Neverland*? I wasn’t going to have to wait long for an answer, as the two of them headed back to the family. By this time, all of us had questioning eyes, especially the ones who knew what was going on.

Mum wiped her eyes and took a deep breath before she announced that Barry’s fiancé had called off the wedding. “She just wasn't ready to be a bride," Mum nodded. "I understand, but I'm so sorry for ya, son." Mum kissed both of his cheeks, "I have a woman I'd like ya to meet."

Barry looked like he was about to lose his mind and possibly his composure when Fitz butted in, "Ya know what Mum, it's too soon. He's gonna need time to heal his heart."

Barry began nodding in agreement. "It's way too soon, Mum," Barry added.

"Of course, what was I thinkin'? Ya take all the time ya need, son," Mum patted his cheek.

Barry let go of a breath he had been holding. It was the first time I saw him look relaxed in weeks.

My phone began to ring and I almost yipped as I saw Cecil's name on the screen. "I have to take this," I said excitedly as I headed to Mum's garden.

"Hello," I said into the receiver.

"Well, there ya are," Cecil said. "I'm sorry I didn't get to call ya yesterday. I'm sure Fitzy told you, we're havin' a lot of computer issues here."

"I heard," I said.

"I worked so late into the night that I fell asleep on the chaise. Thank God I had one of those put in the office."

I tried not to picture him on the chaise lounge with the strange woman who answered his phone. "So…who was it that answered your cell when I called?"

"Ya called me?" Cecil asked.

"Yeah, about midnight, your time," I bit my lip.

"Someone answered my cell?" he truly sounded dumbfounded. "The only other person here was Shelia. She's the new receptionist. I'm sorry, she didn't even tell me."

I nodded, committing her name to memory. "Yeah it was strange to have a woman answer your cell…at midnight.

"Yeah, we worked late, like I said," he answered. "I'll have to make sure she knows to wake me when ya call."

I smiled. "She doesn't have to do that. Just her giving you the message that I called, would be nice."

"I will let her know that yer call is to go on top of any and every message I receive, always. Now tell me how much ya miss me," he added.

I laughed, "I miss you with every part of me…all day…and all night," I grinned from ear to ear.

"And I miss ya, like the moon…" he was cut off by a woman saying he was needed right now on a conference call from New York. "Damn, I have to go. I miss ya so much."

"I miss you," I said, deflating a little as he hung up.

Part of me missed the lounge about Cecil that was all fun and games. I was really proud of him and all the work he was doing to pay tribute to the family name. But I'd be lying if I said I enjoyed every one of our talks being rushed or interrupted.

I walked back to the patio and took a seat.

"Cecil?" Fitz asked.

I nodded.

She rubbed my shoulder, "I know ya miss him. I'm sorry."

Back at home, Fitz asked if I'd like to get a nightcap but I really wasn't feeling it. "No, you two go ahead," I smiled and gave Fitz and Scotty a hug.

It was still early and I felt too on edge to just collapse on the couch. I headed to my painting room and stared at the painting I had been working on. It was supposed to be a scene of a meadow. Somehow, the giant Willow tree: the one on the Callaghan property, the one supposedly haunted by memories and possibly fairies, had made its way onto the canvass. I didn't just miss Cecil. I missed Ireland. I missed Cecil's horse, Babygirl. I missed the castle. For God sakes, I missed Miss Elanor. I never thought that would happen. I pushed PLAY CD on my stereo and picked up a brush. This painting was to me, what automatic writing was to a psychic. I had no real idea in mind as I started. Things began to appear and I would make them more noticeable, accentuate them and bring them to life.

By the time I was tired, I stood back and looked at what I had done. Fairies with see-through iridescent wings fluttered around the giant willow, happily.

The next morning, I woke to my phone ringing. I only knew two people who woke earlier than I did; one was my mom, the other was Fitz's.

My hello was returned by Mum.

"Good morning Mum," I said, trying to disguise the fact that she had woken me.

"Oh good, yer up, I was afraid I would wake ya," she said.

I grinned, "No I'm up. What's happening?" I asked.

"We have a meeting of the *Ladies* of the *Moon*, tonight, luv. Yer presence has been requested," she said matter-of-factly.

I went over my only two meetings with the *Ladies* of the *Moon*; one had me standing in a plastic kiddy-pool as I was re-birthed. The other had me passing out cold during a full moon ritual.

"I ugh," I began, searching for ANY reason why I couldn't make it. I couldn't find one though, "I ugh, I'll be there," I finally said, squishing up my face.

"Good. 7pm at the pub," Mum added.

"I hate to ask, but is there any specific way I should dress? I mean, will they be expecting me to have on good undies?" I posed the question.

"Not this time, dear. Yer frog boxers would be fine," Mum answered.

My eyes slit, did she really think that the frog boxers were a part of my wardrobe? For God sakes, I only wore those because all my other undies had gone to Hawaii without me. Plus I had tossed them after the oil ritual. "Ah, okay," was all I said.

As I hung up, I wondered what I had gotten myself into. It would be nice to see Diane, though. She had been instrumental in getting me to display my paintings, which in turn had changed my whole life for the better. I felt I owed her thanks.

I was on my second double latte when Fitz arrived. I made her a quad mocha and we headed out to my back patio. It was so pretty right now with all the flowers blooming in their urns that Betty had bought me.

Fitz started the conversation, "So, Barry told Mum he had been engaged, but she broke it off."

"That's what I gathered," I nodded.

"I wonder how long that will buy him…before she starts with the *set-up's* again."

"I don't know," I offered.

"Well he better enjoy this time. Things are about to get much worse for him," Fitz said.

"What do you mean?" I shook my head.

"Think about it, her baby's heart was broken, or so she thinks. She'll be goin' full force at findin' him a mate, now. Not just to see him wed, but to mend a broken heart."

I winced, I hadn't thought about it that way. Maybe it was because I wasn't a mother. Maybe it was because I wasn't bat-shit crazy. Either way, the thought hadn't entered my mind.

Just then, Fitz got an E-mail from the great Rudolpho. As she excitedly opened it, her face changed from an ecstatic smile to a 'WTH'.

"What's wrong?" I asked.

"I'm not sure. Oh my God," she covered her mouth with her hand. "I think this is…a Flamenco dancer's dress."

I laughed, "It can't be that bad."

She handed her phone to me so I could take a look.

My face squished up, not only was it a Flamenco dress design, it was made in silver and gold with a plunging v-neck, ruffles starting at the hips and flowing down a long gold train. It seriously looked like **Flamenco's do Las Vegas** should be the working title for the dress. "Damn!" was all I could say.

"Oh my God," Fitz began to freak out, "I gave him full designer's rights."

"Okay, it's…not that bad?" I said as a question.

"How can ya say that? Yer lookin' at the dress! Fer the love of God," she said again.

"Well, maybe you don't wear that dress," I gave a palms-up like this was an easy fix.

"Rudolpho's comin' to the weddin'! He goes to every occasion he designs for. Sometimes he goes in costume, but he goes!" her eyes were wide with fear.

"Well, you may have to…I don't know, tell him that you're not a Flamenco dancer?"

"He's so fragile…so temperamental. My disapproval of his work could crush him," she surmised.

"Well, it's either his feelings, or you're wearing this!" I showed her the picture again.

Fitz turned her eyes away, "Put it down, I can't look at it."

I felt bad for her, but after the way he was dressed when I met him, eccentric being an understatement, I had to wonder why she expected anything less?

"We need to take your mind off of this," I suggested.

"HOW?" she ran her fingers through her wild red mane and gave a tiny tug.

I thought for a moment, "We need to shop for our Mexico trip? How about we do that, okay?"

Fitz slowly began to nod, "Fine."

As we jumped in Baby, Fitz asked, "Where to?"

I smiled from ear to ear.

"Venice Beach it is!" she grinned.

7

HOME SWEET HOME, AGAIN

I loved Venice Beach in the same way that some people love theater, or opera. It was a magic to me. For some reason that even I couldn't explain, all I had to do was hit Venice Boardwalk, and all the stress, over thinking and drama in my life…disappeared.

Even on an early Monday morning, the Boardwalk was in full swing. People were everywhere. Some wore suits and walked quickly with a cell phone in one hand and a hot dog in another. Others in wet suits, grazed on pizza, ice cream and gyros. It was always *come as you are*, without even the slightest hint of pretention.

Men and women sat in their tents selling whatever they had from hand rolled incense to body oils and perfumes to clothing and even Chinese throwing stars and tattoos. You could find everything you wanted or needed on Venice Beach.

We found a great little shop that had lots of flowing Bohemian print sundresses that were not of the muumuu variety. Trying on a few in a small dressing room made by blue tarps and clothespins, I found my boat wardrobe. Now all I needed were accessories and shoes, two more things that Venice could proudly boast.

Fitz stayed mainly with solid colors saying only after I paid for my brightly printed dresses, "I don't want to look like Aunt Marble."

I stared down into my own bag and squished up my face. Although they weren't muumuus, I could definitely see what she was saying.

I found some cute sandals and a pair of deck shoes as Fitz picked out a pair of silver heels.

After hours of shopping, I saw Madame Zorra's tent. I cocked my head. The last reading I had (one that I must admit I blew off completely), she told me that she could see me going overseas with a redhead. At the time, I didn't make any connections, other than Barry (who has a little red in his brown hair) who had gone overseas and not with me. But less than a month later, Fitz and I were headed to Ireland. She had also been correct when she said that my career was about to take a positive turn. I decided that maybe I would drop in…get the down low, so to speak.

I was surprised, as I entered her tent of magic symbols and incense, that she remembered me by name.

"Janie, come sit," she said extending an overly ringed hand toward a red folding chair. Her red hair was unbridled by her usual swami wrap, and fell down her back in spirals. Her purple floor length dress, embroidered with the moon in all of its phases, flowed as she took her seat behind her crystal ball.

"Nice to see you, again, Madame Zorra," I said, sitting.

"What can I do for you?" she asked, taking my hand.

"Well, to be honest, you were so *dead-on* at my last reading, I wondered if you saw anything…new," I smiled.

She smiled from ear to ear, "Let's take a look."

Sitting on a black metal, three pronged dragon stand, was her bowling ball sized crystal ball.

I too, tried to look into the crystal ball, but saw nothing.

As she took some deep breaths, I watched her focus change. Her eyes took on a dreamy quality, almost hazy, almost euphoric.

"Ah, I see you had a great time overseas," she began.

I smiled.

"Ireland, if I'm not mistaking," she looked to my nod for validation.

"Hmmm, you met someone very special…but you met him here…yet I see him in Ireland," she cocked her head.

"He lives there."

"Ah," she nodded.

"Your art plays a big deal in everything surrounding you there…and here."

I nodded again. I knew all of this but wanted more future information.

"Your stone…a tiny stone with a…zig-zag…?" she made the symbol with her finger.

I nodded, "A lightning bolt, my Rune," I confirmed.

"It hasn't felt the need to watch you so closely, now that things are on the right path. But…it wants you to make sure you take it on the boat?" Her eyes took on a look of concern, which in turn, concerned me.

"Is everything gonna be okay?" I asked. Of course I was picturing scenes from Titanic.

She looked into the ball nodding and shaking her head like she was having a private conversation with someone. "There will be… so much drama surrounding this trip. Yours, other people's, it seems positive and volatile at the same time. I see a wedding," her brows arched at the picture she was seeing. I could only imagine what she saw that made her eyebrows do that.

I made a face, was this my way out of the boat trip? Lord knows I would rather get another bikini wax than go on this trip, and I was very anti-waxing after my first, and last hair-ripping.

Although, I wasn't sure a note from Madame Zorra would excuse me.

"Things aren't always what they seem," she said, shaking her red spirals. "The best advice I can give you, is to stay neutral."

"Anything else," I asked, almost afraid of what she would see.

"I see love."

I smiled happily, thinking of Cecil.

"But…not the way you expected. I see love…and then I see diluted…leaving you."

My smile quickly faded.

"It's going to be a painful loss," she looked at me with sympathy, "but you must go through it. There's no way to avoid it," she shook her head.

This was not nearly as good as my first reading, which I deemed BS until it all came true.

She also said my mother was blooming, my work was to take a twist in another direction, and my best friend was going to be more on edge than normal.

Fitz piled her long red hair up with a clip for the ride home. Getting back in Baby, Fitz asked how my reading went.

"I'm not sure," I answered honestly. I ran everything down to her, except the part about her. I didn't want to be the cause of the superstition that would undoubtedly form in the back of her brain. "It was a little more ominous than I hoped for," I answered.

"Ominous? In what way?" Fitz looked like she was already feeling the impending doom.

"She said I needed to stay neutral…and that love was leaving me," I let my face squish up.

"Don't do that!"

"What? Worry?" I asked.

"No don't squish yer face up like that. It'll give ya wrinkles," she shook her head. "Don't read so much into this, Janie. So she was right last time," she did a palms-up, "that doesn't mean she's right all of the time. Right?" she asked.

I nodded, but the truth was, this had me a little freaked given the woman answering Cecil's phone…the fact that he was a whole ocean away…and the fact that before me, he had that whole man-whore thing going on. Cecil was now a man-whore in recovery. What if he relapsed? It's not like I gave him his drug of choice before I left him. I couldn't be *that girl* for one night? I chastised myself for not giving up the goods.

"Holy crap," said Fitz, drawing me out of my internal dialog. "I've been sittin' here for five minutes, watching yer head nod and shake. What the hell are ya lettin' occupy ya so much?"

I let out a sigh.

"If ya really want somethin' to worry about, ya should be thinkin' about…the *Ladies* of the *Moon* gatherin' tonight," she grinned at me.

"Why? Are they gonna do more weird stuff to me?" I was feeling a flutter of panic in my gut.

Fitz painted on her *angry fairy* grin and sped out of the parking lot.

On the 405 South, we listened to *Garbage* and sang at the top of our lungs. This was a good distraction while it lasted.

We decided we needed coffee. I needed to stop by and see Nance. She had been my boss since I was sixteen. Not working at her coffee house anymore, I missed seeing her on the daily like I used to.

Walking into *Spilled the Beans*, I had that feeling of being home. Nance saw us walk in and beamed. You'd never be able to guess this woman's age, I thought to myself. Nance was a slight woman who had moved here from New York years ago. When she bought this old building, she decided to incorporate two of her favorite things: coffee and art. This building had been the first place to feature my paintings and set me on my path.

Clad in a Bohemian print jumper, purple framed glasses and maroon highlights in her short red hair, she always looked like she was on the pulse of modern fashion.

"Oh, my sweet girls," she walked over and embraced us. "How have you been?"

"Good, but I miss you," I told her.

"Oh, honey, I miss you, too. Both of you," she grabbed Fitz's hand. "Do you have time to sit?"

I nodded and followed her to a table. She called out our standing order; triple latte for me and a quad mocha for Fitz.

When Dante (a teenage boy who had the biggest crush on Fitz) heard the order his head popped up from behind the counter.

Bringing out our drinks, Dante looked solemn. Setting the drinks down and staring at Fitz he said they needed to talk.

Nance and I gave each other the eyes.

"Okay," Fitz said and gave him a nod.

"I don't know how to say this, so I'm just gonna come clean," he crouched down in front of her and took her hand.

Fitz looked confused, but let him take her hand.

"You may wonder why I made you just a regular quad mocha."

Dante was always making Fitz wild specialty drinks that even though she didn't want (and sometimes couldn't drink), she had found them to be a sweet gesture.

"Well, Fitz," he took a deep breath, "I've fallen in love with someone else."

He looked over his shoulder at a teenage girl standing behind the counter. She watched the interaction with hopeful eyes.

"I know this must come as a shock for you," he told Fitz. "I didn't expect this to happen," he shook his head.

Fitz sat dead still, and repeated "Okay."

"I hope you understand," Dante looked down at the floor.

Nance and I were having a hard time not laughing. Not at

Dante and his imaginings that he and Fitz had a relationship of sorts, but just the look on her face.

Fitz, understanding that their interactions meant much more to him than her, decided to be let down easy. She nodded, "I understand," she whispered to him.

"We'll always have something special," he gave her hand a squeeze, before walking away.

The three of us watched as Dante made his way to the teenage girl. She hugged and soothed him, like she understood his pain.

Fitz turned rounded eyes toward us, "So apparently, I've just been dumped fer a younger woman," she folded her arms across her chest.

At this, Nance and I had to laugh.

It was nice to catch up with Nance, who was still dating a great man, still traveling and still drinking espresso like it was the fountain of youth.

"I can't wait to meet that Irishman of yours," she told me. "Any plans for him to come back to this side of the pond?"

"Not as of right now," I gave her a little pout. Madame Zorra's words about '*losing love*' rushed back.

After an hour or so, we exchanged hugs and were heading for the door, when the teenage girl approached Fitz. She was a slight little blonde thing with big brown eyes.

"I just wanted to say, I'll take very good care of him," she nodded to Fitz.

Fitz raised her chin and feigned being heartbroken, "I couldn't ask any more of ya. I wish ya the best."

As we pulled up in front of my house, Betty's car was parked curbside.

"I take it yer mom and Betty are here again," Fitz pointed out.

We grabbed our bags and headed inside. I could hear crying before we ever entered the house. Not normal sniffle-sniffle crying, more of a wailing. I knew it was my mother and followed the howls. My bathroom door was shut and Betty was on the outside trying to reason with my mother.

"Honey, just open the damn door. It can't be that bad," Betty said, shaking her head at Fitz and me.

"What's goin' on?" Fitz asked.

"Well Sugar, she tried to re-create the look from the salon and your make-up job. I guess it didn't go so well. I've been tryin' to get her out of there for an hour. She just cries harder."

"Geez," Fitz said. "Is that all, it can't be that bad. "Mrs. O," Fitz knocked on the door. "It can't be that bad," she repeated. "Open the door and let's see what we can do fer ya."

Reluctantly, mom opened the door. Fitz, Betty and I took a giant step back. I'm sure the looks on our faces didn't help as she burst back into sobs.

The *magician of hair* had told mom that a gentle teasing of the hair, would give it more body, more lift. He failed to mention that it took some practice and you probably shouldn't use a round brush to do so.

The brush hung in a snarl of matted, over-sprayed hair. Her head put me in mind of Liberty Spikes. The make-up, well, she wanted her eyes to pick up the green of her new dress, she explained through wails. Unfortunately she went a little more *wicked-witch-green* as she covered her whole eyelid from her lashes into the brow line. Her blush was put exactly where it should be… she just picked a hot pink blush no one had seen since the 80's, and way too much of it. I'm still not sure where she got liquid eyeliner, but this, too, was an art form that not all possessed. I tried to relax my shocked facial muscles.

Fitz raised her hands in a submissive manner and spoke calmly, like she was talking mom off of a ledge. "Okay Mrs. O, it's not as bad as ya think. I can work with this," she edged cautiously towards my mother.

"Am I gonna have to cut this out," she asked pointing to the hanging round brush living in her hair.

"No. I'm a master of the round brush…and whatever ya have done to yer face."

Mom nodded as Fitz went into the doom-room and closed the door behind her.

Betty and I gave each other looks and shook our heads. Betty said under her breath, "I don't envy Fitzy right now."

"Nope!" I agreed.

Back in the kitchen, I made us coffee and we shot the shit. I hadn't really had a chance to find out what was happening in Betty's life now that mom had become her hobby of love.

"So what's happening with you?" I asked her as we sat.

"Well, that depends on how much ya wanna know about yer mama," she said.

My face squished up. I wasn't sure where this conversation was going. To top that off, I wasn't sure I wanted to know now. "Umm…do I want to know?"

"Well, yer mama and yer daddy haven't been exactly…how do I put this?" she asked, "Affectionate…for the last several years."

My stomach did a flip. I really didn't want to know about their lack of a sex life, any more than their having a sex life. "Yeah?" was all I could say.

"But things have been changin' in the last couple months. She's comin' out of her shell."

"This is a good thing, right?" I asked.

"It is," Betty confirmed. "But I told her that it may be a good idea for her to have an open dialog with you about sex."

My face showed clear horror as I remembered my mom's after (or before), call to me the other night. "Why?" I asked.

"Because, I think it may make her loosen up and make you see her as somethin' more than mom."

I guess I understood Betty's thought pattern, but applying it didn't bring me any warm, happy feelings. "We really aren't… sharers when it comes to…ya know…sex."

"Believe me, I know," Betty laughed.

"I think maybe it's just enough that we both know that at some point, we had it. I mean, I'm proof that she did. That's really all the validation I need," I nodded.

"She's still so closed off. And you, you're a young, vibrant, *girls are power*, kind of person. She needs…well, honey, she needs that kind of woman to pull that woman in her, out!"

"But YOU are that kind of woman," I reasoned. "Can't you do the pulling?" I asked. "I mean, did you talk to your mom about sex?" Even as I asked the question, I was scared of what she would say. With my luck her and her mother may have dated twins, or something.

"No Puddin, we didn't," she shook her head.

I was just starting to feel good about my position and did a palms-up.

"She passed when I was ten," Betty gave a weak smile.

"Oh…I'm so sorry," I said, feeling somewhat like an ass.

"It would have been nice to have her there for all the big steps in my life. Hell, I would have loved to have her there for the little ones, too," she nodded. "But she was needed at home, that's what daddy told me."

I never knew how to react to death, especially when it was a child that had to face mortality. "I imagine it was hard to grow into a woman without a mother's…" I wasn't sure how to finish this thought. My own mother had been so hard on me…Fitz, everyone. "Guidance," is what I finally came up with, because for better or worse, my mom had always BEEN there for me, even if her version of love came with some negative feedback at times.

"My daddy did the best he could. He wanted me to be self sufficient. He always told me, 'The only man a woman should ever depend on, is her daddy'," she smiled. "He taught me how to ride a bike, fish and gut the damn thing," she nodded, "how to cook, shoot, ride a horse, box, change my own oil, replace a fuse, and not to give a damn what anybody thought of me. These were all important lessons."

I smiled, "He sounds wonderful."

"He was, Puddin. He was a wonderful father and a damn good man. But the things he couldn't teach me, that's where I had trouble."

I could imagine. If I hadn't had Fitz in my life, I may have ended up…just like my mother; the woman who had walked out of the bathroom not thirty minutes ago looking like the bride of Frankenstein.

Just then, we heard a scream come from my bathroom and headed towards the outcry. With Betty by my side, I knocked on the door.

"Everything okay in there?" I asked, worried that she and Fitz had an issue.

"Fine," Fitz said, opening the door and stepping out. "She's just a little excited," she giggled.

Mom stepped out, and once again, I was floored. She looked amazing. Fitz had not only taken down her matted Liberty Spikes, she curled her hair in big waves that did indeed give her that runway-ready look. Mom's make-up was subtle, but still had some pop, especially her naturally long lashes. Fitz couldn't help but smile as my mom took her into a huge hug for the second time in a week. (Or more correctly, the second time in twenty-one years.)

"You," my mom said looking Fitz dead in the eye, "you are a miracle worker."

Fitz went for modesty and said, "It's what I do."

"No, really, I can't thank you enough. And after I've been so…" mom began to tear.

Fitz nodded, "I know exactly what you've been…" they stared at each other, "and all is forgiven."

Mom began to sob, "I don't know how you can," she shook her head.

I was smiling, but somewhere inside I couldn't help but wonder, W.T.H. is happening to my mother?

All four of us women ended up out on the back patio sipping coffee. We talked about how beautiful the flowers were blooming in their urns. How nice the day was. How I needed misters for when it got really hot. It was all so surreal. And then, it happened.

Betty started a conversation I wasn't ready for.

"So, I guess your husband really likes your new look," she said to my mom. "Couldn't keep his hands off ya, could he?" she grinned.

Mom was beginning to blush like a schoolgirl, "He loves it," was all she said. I let out a grateful sigh that it seemed the conversation would end there. I sighed too soon.

8

WOMEN TALK . . .

"We haven't been this active in years," said mom, as my eyes rounded. This was what my nightmares were going to be made of from now on. Step aside Boogie-man, I thought.

"That's great Mrs. O," Fitz said, grinning, knowing full well that I was having the stomach spins.

In fact everyone was grinning...everyone but me!

"I thought at our age," mom began, "the best years for, ya know, THAT, were, well...behind us."

Oh God looking at Fitz and Betty I was scared to death a '*behind*' joke was imminent, but they both just grinned and nodded.

"I mean," mom continued, "things taper off naturally with time, and even more so if you have children," she winked at me.

I wanted a safe space, wanted to change the subject, but now I was worried about stifling her. Fitz, who wasn't a prude, sat there enjoying my mom opening up.

"You know how it is, you get busy, exhausted and that part of you just gets put on the back burner," mom explained.

I just nodded like an idiot and forced a smile.

"I knew when we hit three times a week, we had real problems," mom admitted.

Fitz, Betty and I furrowed our brows at this comment.

"Three times a week…is what it tapered down to?" Betty asked confused.

Mom let out a sad sigh and nodded.

All three of us sat there exchanging looks.

"We really forgot about ***us***," mom said.

The remaining **us** at the table, were in shock.

Betty asked one of the questions I didn't want to know the answer to, "Um, Sugar, how often did you two, ya know, do **it** before the taper?"

Mom thought, "Well, once a day. Sometimes twice a day… depending on Janie's schedule, of course. We're not animals!" Mom looked around the table at all of our dropped jaws. "What?" she finally asked.

"Sugar," Betty began, "your taper off point is better than most women who are considered highly active for our age."

Mom shook her head and looked around the table for verification. All of us were nodding to her.

"And this is after twenty somethin' years?" Betty cocked her head.

"28," mom nodded.

"Well, I'm done feelin' sorry for ya," Betty shook her head.

"Maybe there was a good reason I called ya Mrs. O," Fitz added.

"For Mrs. O'Connelly, right?" mom questioned.

"Not quite, but it seems the joke may have backfired in my face," Fitz laughed. Betty laughed. I was still silent with big rounded eyes. I couldn't believe what I just heard. My parents… were sex fiends.

"Well, what is a normal amount of sex?" mom posed the question.

"Have ya never read a Cosmo, or anything about women who only get **it** twice a year?" Betty was still flabbergasted.

"Well of course, but those women just don't want anyone to know how active they really are," she gave Fitz a look.

"Excuse me," Fitz feigned offense, "I've only had three lovers before Scotty, I'm proud to say."

At this comment, I snorted with laughter, "Right!"

"What are ya talkin' about? There have been three," Fitz repeated.

"Oh come on, no judgment here…you can be honest," I shook my head.

"There's been three," Fitz looked dead serious.

I cocked my own head, "But…you've told me about…like a million times?"

"Yeah…I've had a lot of sex…not a lot of partners."

"But what about Dan, and Danny and Daniel…?" I trailed off thinking about the name. "That was all one guy, wasn't it?"

Fitz grinned and nodded. "Ya didn't like any details, remember? So I told ya WHEN I had sex, but no details as per your stringent prude-ism. Truth is, I found lovers who served a purpose. I didn't like the whole datin' thing. So I picked ones that I could get what I needed without the fear of them wantin' a commitment."

"Rob, Robert, Bob and Bobby," I said looking off into space.

Fitz nodded.

"Mike, Michael and Mikey…" I trailed off, still lost in my own thoughts.

Fitz nodded again, "What? Ya thought I was a slut? I'm very discerning about who I let play in my garden," Fitz used her hands to outline said garden.

I shook my head, I was in shock. We had been best friends for over twenty years, how could I not have…known?

"Well, your dad was my one and only," mom said. "But four isn't so bad in this day and age," she squeezed Fitz's hand. "And I commend you on your garden's privacy act."

"Well, I've had more than my share," Betty admitted. "I've had eight...in my garden," she grinned at Fitz.

My mom's eyes rounded as she covered her giggle.

Betty's only had eight…and she's sixty-something? I sat there like a stone, knowing the inevitable was coming.

All three women stared at me, smiling. I could try to lie. I could. But I knew I wouldn't.

Fitz piped up, "Remember…no judgment here," she grinned and folded arms across her chest.

I shot her a shit look, "Five," I announced. "I've had five…in my garden," I continued the metaphor.

Mom began to laugh hysterically and claped her hands, but I wasn't sure at what? "So you're the slutty one!"

My eyes popped out of my head, "What?"

"No, no, sorry honey," she shook her head. "What I mean is… all these years, I was so afraid that Fitz was a bad influence on you…and it turns out, you're the bad one!" she pointed at me.

Personally, I didn't find this even slightly amusing, but Fitz and Betty were rolling with laughter.

"But…I've only had monogamous relationships," I pled my case to no one in particular.

"Well, that's kind of been yer problem," Fitz assessed. "See you've been lookin' fer Mr. Right for a while now, but you've only dated Mr. Wrong. Thus having the relationship fail, thus having more relationships, thus having more partners," Fitz did a palm-up like this was an easy problem to see.

I sat there blank-faced.

"I, on the other hand," Fitz continued, "was never trying to find Mr. Right, or a relationship, so I had less boyfriends and break-ups, and that led to fewer partners."

"You've just single-handedly ruled out the pros of monogamy," I rubbed my temples.

"Not true, I believe in marriage obviously," Fitz showed her engagement ring, "just not tryin' to make every man, the right man. If anything, I've pointed out the cons of persuin' relationships that are destined to fail."

My mother broke out in sobs and covered her eyes, "I did this to you!" she wailed. "If I hadn't worked so hard at seeing you married, you never would have had so many people in your garden!" she was ugly crying.

Betty and Fitz jumped up to soothe my mother's admittance of guilt.

I sat there, dumbfounded as they told her again and again that it wasn't her fault. I shot Fitz a death-ray from my eyes and she said, "Well, it is a little her fault, but it wasn't done maliciously. How could she know she was forcing ya to let people in yer garden?"

At this I threw my hands in the air, "Can we stop already with the damn garden metaphor?"

A moment passed before my mother asked Fitz through her sniffles, "Why DO you call me Mrs. O?"

Fitz, still standing at my mother's side, looked down and said, "I'm gonna get ya the book."

I shook my head. *This*, *it*, whatever *it* was, had been enough for one day.

9

MEANWHILE, BACK AT THE PUB . . .

It was time for the *Ladies of the Moon* to meet. I felt like I had already been through the wringer. What could they do to me?"

As Fitz and I walked in to the poker room where we were to meet the women, they all began singing, *For She's a Jolly Good Fellow*. I assumed it was for Fitz and her engagement, but as I stood there singing my heart out to Fitz, all eyes were turned to me.

"What's going on?" I asked Fitz under my breath.

"Well, they didn't get to celebrate yer birthday with ya," she stated.

I shook my head, "That was a while ago."

"And…" Fitz continued, "the ladies have decided to make us members!" she said excitedly and clapped along with the other women.

I was trying to mask my *oh shit* face with a smile, "Ohhh," was all I could say. I began rolling this around in my mind. I was never a joiner. I didn't play team sports or an instrument basically because I didn't want to be a member of anything. For God sake's, I didn't even have a gym membership. As they took turns hugging us, all I wanted to do was find a way out of this. I wasn't even sure what duties being a member held. I looked around for the kiddie-pool they had once put me in for ritual, but thankfully, I didn't see it anywhere. At least I could breathe a little easier knowing I wasn't going to be anointed with oil. I actually liked this bra and didn't want it ruined.

All the women were dressed in what looked like togas with flower wreaths on their heads.

Finally Diane walked up and took me in an embrace. In my ear she said, "I know it's overwhelming." She pulled back to look me dead in the eyes, "You can say 'no' anytime you want," she nodded to me.

I looked past her to where Mum and Aunt Marble stood beaming like proud parents. I smiled at them and thought to myself, no, I really can't.

I had no idea what they planned on doing to us, but at least this time I wouldn't be alone. I forced a smile at Fitz when we were handed our togas and wreaths then instructed to go change.

Fitz headed for the bar door and I stopped her, "I'm not walking back through the bar in a toga."

"Why do you care?" Fitz asked then let out a sigh. "Fine… we'll change in the kitchen."

Standing in the closed kitchen, we began our clothing change. Fitz was slipping out of her bra.

"What are you doing?" I asked.

"Taking off my skivvies," she gave a palms-up.

"Is that required?" my brow lifted.

"Didn't ya notice? None of the women were wearing bras."

"Well, they didn't tell me to take it off, so I'm not going to," I concluded.

"Fine…be a prude," Fitz shook her head.

"I just don't get the point?" my turn to do a palms-up.

"Do what ya want. If it's wrong, I'm sure they'll tell ya," she gave me the angry fairy smile.

Back in the poker room we went, two large overstuffed beanbag pillows sat in the middle of the room on the floor.

Mum pointed to the pillows, "Please ladies, sit!" she instructed.

The room was aglow in candlelight as I dropped my butt down on the giant purple beanbag. Fitz sat with her back against mine on the hot pink pillow.

"They have chosen," said Rosemary to the others standing around us.

"So it shall be," said Mum. "These colors will represent ya. You, Janie will be purple! And you, my little Fitzy, will be hot pink!"

I couldn't see Fitz, but I was sure this made her smile. She loved hot pink.

Two of the women, Vervain and Hops (no, that couldn't be right, I chastised myself for how horrible I was with names, especially nicknames), each grabbed a glass bowl and moving clockwise starting at the north and south points, made a ring of salt around us. Then they made an even bigger ring of salt outside of ours. All of the women stood inside the big ring and joined hands.

Aunt Marble was directly in front of me, Diane was to her right. I could hear Mum, somewhere behind me, begin speaking.

"Mother Moon, Goddess, bringer of light and life," Mum started. The women I could see had raised their joined hands and chins to the ceiling. "Daughter...of my own womb...wishes to honor the goddess within her. I ask that you are alive and well...in her thoughts...in her actions...in her heart...in her soul! Let her find strength and pride in the divine feminine within her. Let her see generations of life and rebirth, from the womb to the tomb.

Let her acknowledge herself as a small part in the wheel of life that has spun since before time existed."

There was silence and I wondered if it was over. Was that it?

All of the sudden Aunt Marble began speaking.

"Mother Moon, Goddess, bringer of light and life," she began well enough. "Although my womb is barren…no seed to grow… no fertile ground inside me…" I furrowed my brow. "I AM the divine feminine!"

All the women I could see, nodded. From somewhere behind me I heard two separate "Amen's".

"I ask that Janie finds the light and wisdom within her. I ask that she KNOW the strength she carries inside…I ask that she never fear her own heart…her own mind…her own path."

I had to smile, this was so sweet.

Aunt Marble continued, "I hope she finds beauty in all… especially the body…which she's kind of freaked out about."

My face squished up a bit.

"Let her get more, ya know, comfortable with nudity and sexuality…don't let her remain a prude," Marble shook her head at the ceiling.

My eyes slit when I heard another "Amen" emitted from behind me…from Fitz, to be exact.

"Let her understand that genitalia should be worshiped...openly and with love," Marble nodded.

W.T.F. was the only thing going through my head now, as I dropped my jaw.

"Let her see her vagina as a flower…bloomin'…" Aunt Marble was stuck in a thought that I didn't want to think about.

At this point, Diane cocked her head at Aunt Marble.

Aunt Marble carried her thought, "Let her learn to love the smell of the rose as it blooms."

I heard Fitz let out a snort. Obviously she was trying hard not to laugh out loud.

"Although her vagina has had suitors," Aunt Marble went on as my eyes almost popped out of my skull, "I ask that she find the right bee for her flower."

As I began to rub my temples, Diane broke in and cutoff Aunt Marble from furthering my humiliation.

"That was beautiful, Marble. Really lovely," Diane had ended the dialog that was sure to haunt me all of my days.

Mum started again, "As my daughter," she said to Fitz, "so you are *Daughter of the Moon*."

All of the women let go of each other's hands and applauded.

Aunt Marble looked at me with her huge magnified eyes and said, "As my honorary daughter, you are now *Daughter of the Moon*!"

Again the clapping erupted as I sat baffled. Did I understand this correctly? Have I just been spiritually adopted…by Aunt Marble?

I was still in shock as Aunt Marble grabbed the tiny sword and cut the air around me, as she had called it during my first ritual. I was now 3 and 0 on the humiliating ritual score sheet.

Aunt Marble, and I assumed Mum behind me, crossed the salt line. Marble made the symbol of the moon on my brow and then put a kiss there before helping me stand.

As Fitz and I stood, we were presented with goblets of wine, and tiny gifts from each woman. I received a book, bell, chimes, crystals, a tiny rock, with a vagina crudely carved into it (I could guess who that came from), chocolates, candles, and a bottle of tonic made by Diane. As I was sure this was the fire herbed whiskey she had made before, I was elated. Stuff had one hell of a euphoric kick.

"So, are we *Ladies of the Moon*?" Fitz asked her Mum.

"Yer second generation," she patted Fitz's cheek. "You, and Janie, are *Daughter's of the Moon*, now."

Fitz looked a little disappointed, "So when do we become *Ladies of the Moon?*"

"When you have a daughter of yer own to initiate," Mum smiled.

"Or, when we die," Aunt Marble said to me. "You'll take our place."

Both thoughts were equally horrifying to me, but one of those things was horrifyingly inevitable.

Wine was poured and folding chairs were set in a circle so we could sit and chat.

I wasn't surprised when Mum brought up Barry's heartbreak of being dumped. All the women agreed that it was better done now than later.

Marble showed off her ring and announced to the women that she would be married on the cruise we were taking to Mexico.

Rosemary was thinking about going back to school to be a dental hygienist.

The Latin woman, whose name and nickname both escaped me, said that her mother was well. I nodded and listened to all the women's updates.

Soon enough, I was caught in their stares. Eager eyes stared at me from all directions, waiting for me to share.

"Um, well you all know about Ireland…" all the women nodded. "Uh, well…my mother and my landlord have become good friends," I nodded. "My dad is well," I was reaching for something. "Yeah, that's about it," I finished.

All of the women stared, like they had been waiting for something more. "And?" said the woman I was almost sure was called Chamomile. "And…what about you?" Chamomile asked. "What is going on with you?"

I rubbed my tongue on my teeth, unsure of what about me held any interest. "Well," I began, "I'm still painting…not really working at the coffee shop right now. Just…painting," I finished.

Rosemary busted in, "I heard you met that fine boy from Ireland…and while you were there, you started a torrid love affair," she nodded to all the other women that were making wooing noises.

"Well, I did meet a man named Cecil…here actually, at the Pub. He's Fitz's fiancé's brother…and I did a couple of paintings for his dad...in Ireland. There was a lot of drama…but our last night together…we did tell each other that we had feelings for each other." When I said it out loud, I could see why all the women's faces changed from hopeful and excited to *HUH*?

So you were there…with this drop dead gorgeous man…for a month," I nodded, "and nothing happened?" Anise asked (I think it was Anise).

"Well, not nothing," I started to blush.

Rosemary smiled, "See, she's my girl!" she pointed to me. "Okay girl, tell us all about it!"

I started grinning, "Well…we…made out."

"Yep, that's how it starts," Rosemary nodded. "Then what?"

"Um…" I was seriously embarrassed. "That was it," I gave them a shrug of my shoulders.

The women were not doing well at hiding their disappointment. The forced painted smiles said it all.

I guess this is why I felt the need to defend myself, "You see, for most of the trip, I thought he was interested in his ex-girlfriend. Then when I finally found out he wasn't interested in her, but in me…I didn't want to seem…easy…so then, ya know...I know it doesn't sound like much, but I really…like him. I didn't want to screw it up."

I could tell by the looks given by the majority of the women, they thought I already had.

Fitz saw the fear in my eyes. The fear of a misstep, the fear of having made the wrong decision, the fear that would eventually make me crazy. She came to my rescue the only way that Fitz could; the wrong way.

"Take it easy on her ladies, she's just found out she's a slut," Fitz said, rubbing my shoulder.

All the women sent questioning eyes at me.

"I'm not a slut," I demanded. "I've had sixteen relationships and I slept with five of them!"

Two of the women raised their brows to me, the others shook their heads.

Rosemary asked, "You don't suppose since you never slept with the other eleven, that's why they dumped you?"

"Well, yes, but I wasn't ready," I explained. "I think that's a pretty good way to rule them out."

"What's the longest you've dated a guy without sleeping with him?" Violet questioned.

"Um..." I had to think, "six months-ish," I figured.

Now the women were shaking their heads again, "You can't call yourself a slut!" Rosemary put her hands up.

"Well actually, I didn't," I shot a look to Fitz.

"Seriously, I'm with Marble on all that blooming stuff. Hell honey, six months! You died on the vine...then the bee died!" Rosemary offered. "You can't be afraid to get yours," Rosemary nodded her head.

"But if I wasn't ready, and they left me because of it. Doesn't that mean they weren't the right guy in the first place?" I did a palms-up.

"What you need to be asking yourself," Rosemary reasoned, "is why would you date a man for six months who you didn't WANT to sleep with?"

I rolled this around in my head.

"Seriously, you should only date a man whose kiss drives you wild...whose touch...starts a fire in you!" Rosemary was explaining. "The very thought of him, should make bumps rise on your flesh," all the other women *uh-huh'd* and *amen'd.* "You can't date a man who doesn't stoke your flame," she stood and preached it, "You need a man," she balled her fists, "who makes the woman in you come alive…a man who makes your soul SING," she said with great gusto. "You NEED A MAN…WHO WILL RELEASE THE GODDESS IN YOU…LET HER SOAR," I know that's right, I heard another woman chime in. "AND LOVES TO SEE HER FLY! YA NEED A MAN…YA NEED THAT MAN… LORD, BRING HER THAT MAN!" Rosemary shouted to the rafters. She started to calm down, took a few breaths and said, "That's all I'm gonna say," she took her seat.

I wasn't sure if I could hold a candle to her argument. It unfortunately made perfect sense. Why WOULD I date a man I wasn't physically and intimately attracted to? I had one now…kind of had one.

"What about the Irishman?" Diane finally piped up.

In all of this craziness, thinking of him calmed my thoughts. My smile stretched from ear to ear.

"That's what I'm talkin' about!" Rosemary clapped her hands.

"He's…amazing," I said with a goofy grin. "I miss him so much."

"And the kiss?" Diane raised her brows.

I was embarrassed. I didn't usually *share* with anyone but Fitz, and even that was given without any real details. "I lost myself in his kiss…and found myself at the same time."

Diane nodded knowingly to what still baffled me, "To the good stuff," she raised her glass to me. All the women repeated the phrase and raised their glasses as well.

After a little bit, Diane announced "Okay, Vervain and Clary, (which were Mum and Aunt Marble) it's time for you to give your daughter's a name. I know you've given them much thought," she smiled, "please announce your daughter's moon name to the group.

Mum stood and put her hand on Fitz's shoulder, "My baby, I am so proud of ya," she had tears in her eyes. "You are lovely to those who behold ya, and pain to those who would handle ya incorrectly," Mum smiled. "You, my dear, are the Rose."

We all clapped as Mum went over to a small table and picked up a hot pink rose, then presented it to Fitzy.

Aunt Marble looked at me, "You, my daughter, are a healer."

I kind of liked the sound of that, I smiled.

"You heal joint pain…"

Wasn't really the kind of healer I was thinking of but ridding the body of joint pain is good, I guess.

"You heal bone disorders, skin conditions, and fluid retention…" Aunt Marble nodded.

If I was understanding her correctly…I was a diuretic," I bit my bottom lip.

"You heal headaches, varicose veins, gout and…syphilis," she raised her palms.

One brow raised. Did she just say syphilis? Fitz covered her mouth and was trying not to laugh.

"Your name," Aunt Marble placed her hand on my head, "is Clematis!"

No one was cheering like they had for Fitz becoming Rose, and why would they? I was now a cross between a climax and Chlamydia, I thought to myself.

Aunt Marble walked over to the table and brought back a bunch of purple star shaped flowers. At least they were pretty. I brought them to my nose, "don't get those in yer mouth, dear, they're toxic," Aunt Marble informed me.

I sat there nodding, yep that sounded about right.

As the night drew to a close, small groups had broken off chatting about other things. I found Diane clearing the table and asked if I could bother her for a moment.

"You may not," she said grinning, "but you may bless me with your presence."

I smiled, "Really I just wanted to thank you, for everything," I added. "If it weren't for you..."

"You wouldn't have realized how amazing you are?" she cocked her head at me. "I think it's wonderful that you credit me with helping you. I'll take it," she beamed. "But please don't forget, you were the one who became you. You were the one who put forth the effort to become who you really are. All I did," she shook her head, "was hold up a mirror in front of you, so you could see YOU clearly. I'm very proud of you."

I smiled, "Well, I still think you did more than that...and I thank you...for the mirror, kind words..." I trailed off as my eyes began watering.

Diane took me in an embrace and said quietly, "I did try to talk her out of Clematis."

"I appreciate that," I hugged her back.

The next few days were spent playing more rounds of phone tag with Cecil. Every time I started to feel really insecure about us, he would call and be so sweet, I'd forget why I felt insecure in the first place. I had been home for weeks now, and missing him had become just a part of my every waking moment, and some not awake ones, too. The morning I was supposed to board the ship, he called.

"Are ya nervous? I know ya hate boats." His voice was sympathetic. "I wish I was there with ya. I'd find a way to keep ya calm." The innuendo made me grin.

"Is that true?" I stretched out on the couch.

"Yes I would. Who's there with ya right now?" he asked.

I bit my bottom lip, "No one."

"No one, huh?" his voice took on a hint of naughtiness. "Now I really wish I was there."

"Yeah? Why? What would you do, if you were here?" I asked.

"Let's see, first, I would kiss ya…deeply….then I'd strip ya… slowly," he added.

"Mmm," I nodded my head.

"Doesn't that sound nice?" he said almost dreamily.

"Yes it does," I pictured him in my head as my free hand began to roam.

"Then I would lay ya down," he added.

"Mmmhummm," the vision in my head was so good.

"Then…I'd nestle my way…between yer thighs"

"What the hell are ya doin?" Fitz said, stopping dead after barreling through the door.

"Oh my God," I yelled jumping up from the couch. "You scared the crap out of me!"

"Right back at ya, Clematis," she said. "Do ya want me to come back in like five minutes?"

"Oh my God," I repeated. What was supposed to be a Fifty Shades of Gray moment, turned into Fifty Shades of Red.

"Is that Fitz?" Cecil asked.

"Yeah, it is," I told him.

"Oh hey, tell her I said *Hi,*" he added.

"Yeah, I'll do that. Look I'm sorry, but I have to go now. I miss you and I'll try to call you later."

"I miss you, too, my girl. Have a good day. And don't ya be nervous," he rang off.

Fitz stood with her hands on her hips, "If yer gonna do that, you should probably lock the door," she laughed. "Now as much as I hate to make ya procrasti-bate…"

I covered my eyes.

"…are ya packed?" she gave me an evil grin.

"I do kind of hate you right now," I informed her.

As I finished packing, I stared down at the tiny stone with the lightning bolt carved on its face. I had been told by Madame Zorra that the stone no longer felt the need to be with me at all times. Somehow, it made me feel lonely. I knew one thing for sure, though: it was better to not need my protector and have it with me, than to need it and have it sitting on my bedside table. Into my wallet it went. After all, it had apparently earned a vacation, as well.

Scotty had a limo drive us to the Port. As we stepped out, I could see the rest of the family waiting for us by the giant ship. The day was going to be a beautiful one; Sunny with a few scattered clouds that silently drifted like they were in no hurry to get anywhere. Always, I had loved the smell of the ocean, even if the thought of being surrounded by it in bobbing steel, scared the crap out of me.

"Go on ahead," I told Fitz. "I need to do something."

"Yer not gonna finish what ya started on the phone with Cecil, are ya? Cause if ya are, I'm not tippin' the driver," she grinned.

I gave her a mock laugh as she headed for the dock.

A few minutes later, I too, arrived at our meeting point. Everyone turned to look at me.

"What the hell are ya wearin'?" Fitz asked.

"It's just a vest," I said.

"No," Fitz shook her head. "A vest is a clothing accent to keep your core body warm. What yer wearin'…is a life preserver," she raised her brows to me. "A…bright…orange…life preserver!"

Benny gave me a laugh, "You are such a funny girl," he leaned in and pinched my cheek. "This is why I can't wait to make you my family."

What was said as a compliment, made Mona stick her finger down her throat, like the thought was going to make her throw up. Mum threw Mona a glare and she immediately painted on a fake smile.

This was the first time I had seen Mona since the BBQ and she was still dead set on being a bitch. But undercover bitch was more easily accepted than out-and-out bitch. I wasn't sure what happened between her and Mum after the laxative dosing Fitz had received at her hands. Everyone seemed to be on their best behavior, though. But sadly, bitch, was the best I could expect from Mona.

We all checked in our luggage and I began to notice none of the kids were here. "Where are all the boys?" I asked.

Fitz's oldest brother, Danny, smiled so big I thought his face would crack, "We got a sitter," he gave his wife's backside a pinch. "Gonna be a second honeymoon for us."

Andy lifted his brows to his wife, "Us too," he added, winking.

All of us looked at Pauly, who had turned his questioning eyes to his wife, hoping she would show some enthusiasm. Instead Mona folded her arms across her chest and walked away. He gave us a forced smile, "Gonna be a long week for me," he mused.

Finally, Barry arrived right as we were walking the plank, as I referred to it. He was wearing khaki board shorts and a black tee with his converse. He was still drop dead gorgeous. I guess that wouldn't change just because my crush had.

"For Pete sakes, ya almost missed the boat," Fitz said hugging him.

Barry still looked out of sorts. At least he could be reassured Mum wouldn't try to set him up on a senior's cruise, I thought.

I will admit that the ocean liner was beautiful inside... beautiful enough to make me fidget. Chandleries hung from the ceiling that loomed two stories overhead. The plush crimson carpet stretched on as far as my eyes could see. At the desk, we were handed our keys and directions to our rooms. I was amazed for some reason that there was an elevator on the ship. I guess I never thought about it before. Combining so many things that made me uptight; ships, elevators and floating in a huge metal coffin, on the deep, shark filled ocean, was just a slice of hell for me.

Down the elevator we went, two whole floors. Or *50,000 Leagues Under the Sea* as I saw it. Down here, the ship wasn't nearly as luxurious. A compressed hallway, in both height and girth, made me feel like the walls were closing in around me.

Fitz and I were to share a room, so we tried to unpack. The only window in the tiny room was an even tinier porthole, not big enough to squeeze Fitz through. I was having a hard time breathing, but didn't want Fitz to make fun of me again. As we tried to put away our toiletries, we ran into another problem of sorts. It seems that the shower, toilet and sink were all shoved into a space the size of my closet. In fact, you had to move to the far side of the toilet, up against the wall, just to close the door.

"Are ya gonna take off that damned life vest when we go up top?" Fitz asked. "It's a little discomforting to see how much faith ya have in the ship. Yer gonna scare the old people."

I wanted to take it off, I did. I also wanted to be back on solid ground and I didn't see that happening anytime soon, either. "Yeah, I'll take it off," I said somewhat apprehensively.

"Don't worry, Janie. Boats almost never sink anymore. And since the Titanic mishap, they have more than enough life rafts. And besides, ya brought yer own," she pointed to my vest.

I wish she hadn't brought up the Titanic. I also wish I hadn't watched the damned movie two weeks ago.

As I slowly removed my vest, Fitz tried to soothe me, "There are no icebergs in between here and Mexico."

"I know," was what I said. But this comment did start me wondering what else had taken down huge cruise ships; Storms, electrical failures, pirates. I was aware that a life preserver wouldn't do anything to help with the last two, but the first one was also more likely.

I threw the vest on my bed. Fitz and I headed up to an upper deck where we all intended to meet up with Benny and Aunt Marble.

I wasn't really shocked to hear that Barry had been sent with a message; Danny, Andy and their wives would meet up with us later. I grinned, remembering the look on all of their faces; their first vacation in years AND the very first time without the kids? I had no doubt we wouldn't be seeing much of those four.

On deck, we found Aunt Marble, Benny, Mum, and Da already with cocktails in hand. Barry went to get Fitz and me a frothy, colorful beverage with tiny umbrellas. Taking the glass from him, he gave me a devilish grin.

"What?" I asked, looking sidelong at him.

"Nothin'," he kept grinning.

I shook my head at him and took a drink. Very quickly my eyes rounded, "Holy crap," I looked at my glass.

"Yeah, I watched her make it. I wish she had made mine," he grinned.

"Maybe we should switch," I suggested.

Barry grinned, "Nah, how am I

"Nothin'," she shook her head at me.

Under my breath I told her that her *nothin'* was almost as believable as Barry's. But I let it go for the time being.

Aunt Marble wanted to go over the wedding agenda. She and Benny were to wed in just a few days, right here on the deck. They had her and Benny's wedding clothes, back in their cabin. I couldn't help but wonder just what they had chosen. Aunt Marble unzipped a garment bag she had with her and announced that her maid-of-honor, would be wearing this; she pulled out a muumuu with what I thought looked like a brightly colored pattern of tiny piñatas. I narrowed my eyes wondering how, how in God's name, she had come up with this? Another thought started to worm around in my head. Although many muumuus are made for a one-size-fits-all world that doesn't actually exist, this one seemed to be for someone...not mum's size. In fact, there was no way all her sizable assets were going to fit into that thing.

I tried not to show the horror I was feeling when Aunt Marble said, "This Janie, is fer you!"

"Me?" was all that found its way through my windpipe.

Aunt Marble nodded with tears in her eyes as she handed it to me," Yer my daughter now."

I took the dress thing and let Aunt Marble take me into an embrace. "And," she continued, "you are exactly the child I would have chosen…if I hadn't been barren."

I nodded, "That is so…sweet," I said. "Thank you, Aunt Marble."

Marble beamed and shook her head, "Nope, you'll call me Mum."

I nodded to her, "Okay…Mum."

Aunt Marble squealed with delight and hugged me again, "My sweet baby!"

Her tears were falling now. I was overwhelmed. Then I looked at my garment again and was immediately underwhelmed. It was one day, I told myself. I could dress like a sixty year old hippie with a piñata fetish for one day, especially if it was going to make Aunt Marble this happy.

"Should I call ya by yer flower name?" Aunt Marble's magnified eyes grew larger.

"No," I said a little too quickly, "I don't want people who aren't in the know, to know my ritual name. It's very private to me," or at least it should be, I thought.

Aunt Marble tapped the side of her nose, mafia style, "Gotcha, right." she nodded as if we were sharing private business.

Truthfully, it was a joke I wish would have been more private…or maybe just not sound like something that should be.

We all did the wave thing as the ship set sail. I wasn't sure why we were doing this, as none of the people on the dock, knew any of us.

Afterward, Fitz, Barry and I went to our rooms to put on our bathing suits. I slipped into my new black bikini.

Fitz looked at me as I exited our closet bathroom. "Is that what yer wearing?" she asked, furrowing her brow.

I looked down, "Does it look bad?"

"I thought ya got that one piece, the blue and white striped thing?"

"I was, but then decided that I want to tan my stomach. Does it look bad?" I asked again.

"No…it's just more revealin' than what I'm used to seein' on ya," she shook her head.

"Well, maybe you're rubbing off on me," I smiled. "I just figure a tan makes you look slimmer, better to tan the parts that need *slimming* the most, right?" I laughed.

"Yer not gonna wear a shirt over it?" Fitz looked shocked.

I was confused, "All my life you've made fun of me wearing a shirt over my bathing suit, now it seems like you want me to. What's up?"

"Nothin'…it's just, I don't want ya to be uncomfortable that's all."

I hugged her, "I'm fine. It would be different if Cecil was here I'm sure."

"That it would be," she forced a smile.

We headed back up to the outdoor deck to find some lounge chairs. As we approached where we said we would meet Barry, he caught us in his view and stared with a grin.

"Hey, yer not wearin' a shirt over yer suit, this is the most I've ever seen of ya."

"Not exactly true," I said, remembering the night I accidentally flashed him after my first ritual.

Barry let out a chuckle.

"What does that mean," Fitz asked.

Barry and I laughed, "The night…the kiddie-pool ritual night?" I started.

"Yeah," Fitz said.

"I went to go change in the kitchen, and, well, Barry walked in on me," I blushed.

Fitz's eyes rounded, "You didn't see anything?" she asked like she was mortified.

"Well, yeah, she didn't quite turn away fast enough to hide," he looked at my boobs, "well, those," he blushed as well.

"Ah," Fitz said, like she was uncomfortable at the thought.

I took the chaise on one side of him and one was open on the other. Fitz asked, "Barry, ya want to move over and I'll sit next to Janie?"

"Why?" he asked.

I was confused too. It wasn't like we were sitting on opposite sides of the deck.

"I just...never mind," she said. They shared an odd moment that I wasn't included in.

She couldn't still be worried that I was pining over Barry? I knew it had been hard on our friendship, for like two seconds, when she found out that I had had a crush on her brother for 20 plus years. But that was a moot point now that I was wrapped up in Cecil.

As we started to get comfortable, adjusting our chaises, and pulling magazines out of our beach bag, Fitz said she wanted more drinks.

"The bar is right there," Barry pointed to his right.

"Would ya be a dear and go get Janie and me a drink?"

They exchanged weird looks again, but of course Barry said, "What would ya like, sissy?"

Fitz looked at me, "Pina Coladas?"

"Mmmm," I said, making Barry laugh. "Two, comin' up," he grinned at me.

As soon as he stepped away, Fitz moved his towel over to her lounge chair, and took his.

"What are you doing?" I lifted my sunglasses.

"Nothin'," she shook her head.

"Look, is this about the crush I used to have on Barry? Because I can assure you, it's not a problem anymore, okay."

"I don't know what yer on about. I just wanted us to sit together so that we can show each other pictures," she lifted her wedding magazine at me.

When Barry came back, Pina Coladas in hand, he shook his head at Fitz.

As we sat in the sun, baking, I had almost forgotten I was on a ship, heading out into open waters. The fears that had gripped me earlier were sailing away, just like the pretty clouds. I looked at my almost empty Pina Colada. These things really did pack a wallop.

I realized Barry was looking over at me, "Another?" he asked.

"You really are trying to get me drunk," I laughed, "sure."

Fitz butted in, "Are ya sure ya want another?" she inquired.

"Why not, I'm on vacation," I rationalized with a buzzed grin.

"Ya know what, I'm gonna go this time. Be right back," Fitz jumped up and took off in the direction of the bar.

I just watched her go.

"What's up with Fitz?" Barry asked.

"Honestly, I don't know. She's got a lot going on; the wedding, being away from Scotty for a week, something they've never done," I grinned. "Then there's Aunt Marbles wedding…" I trailed off.

"Yeah about that, how did ya become her honorary daughter? And what was all of this stuff about a flower name?" He gave me the palms-up, "Ya don't have to tell me…but then it's left to my imagination, and ya don't want that either," he smiled.

I thought about that for a moment and had to agree. "Fitz and I were accepted into the *Ladies of the Moon*. Well, actually, we're second generation, so we're *Daughters of the Moon*," I corrected.

"Oh Lord," Barry did a slow shake of his head.

"But seeing as how I'm not really a member's daughter, I guess Aunt Marble became my mother by proxy," I explained.

"And the name, if ya don't mind my asking."

At this, I took in a deep breath, "Clematis," I said as straight faced as I could.

"Clematis," Barry repeated with rounded eyes. It took him a moment before he busted up, "Ya do know what that sounds like?"

"How could I not?" I laughed. "It's a horrible cross of Chlamydia and climax."

His eyes rounded, "Oh my God, I didn't even think of Chlamydia. Climax, yes," he offered.

Fitz walked in on the conversation, "What the hell are ya two talkin' about?"

Barry was laughing too hard to tell her, so I piped up, "He's enjoying my flower name."

"Oh," Fitz laughed. "All I heard was…never mind," she said again, and handed me my drink.

I took a sip and made a face.

"What's wrong?" Fitz asked.

"It doesn't taste like there's any alcohol in here," I tried it again.

"Really? Mine tastes fine," Fitz stretched back out on her chaise.

"No, I'm pretty sure mine doesn't. It tastes like a coconut milkshake."

Barry gave Fitz a look before saying, "Here, let me try it."

Handing him the glass, he took a sip, "Yeah, there's no alcohol in this," he gave his sister a look.

She must have forgotten the rum," Fitz offered innocently.

"Well I'm gonna go have her fix it," Barry raised his brows to his sister.

"Fine, fine, go ahead," Fitz told him as he walked away.

When Barry came back, I took a sip of my drink, "Whoa," I shook my head, "Damn!"

"Yeah, the bartender felt bad about the misunderstandin' so she gave ya a hard double," he explained.

'Hard doubles' were the family's way of saying *a triple*.

"Well, this is gonna knock me on my ass. Thank you," I raised my glass to him.

Pauly showed up a few minutes later and took the chaise next to Barry.

We all turned our heads to him, "Where's the wife?" Barry asked.

"I'm gonna guess anywhere where she can avoid me," Pauly answered.

We all shook our heads, "Not getting any better, huh?" I asked.

"Well, she told me she wasn't speaking to me, and then yelled at me for twenty minutes before the *not speakin' to me clock* began tickin'."

"She's not still on about yer stupid childhood crush on Janie, is she?" Fitz made a face.

"Aye, along with everything else I do, or say. I'm afraid I may be breathin' wrong, as well," Pauly answered. "Then again, I should be grateful she hasn't offered to remedy that, as well."

"I'm really sorry," I told him.

"This wasn't yer fault, Janie," Pauly shook his head. "I should have known she would have reacted this way, and never said a damn word."

"But it was when you were kids, right?" Barry asked. "I mean, nothin' new was said that would make her have Janie in her sights?"

"Yes Barry," Pauly said, like he was tired of explaining it. "But Mona's always been so jealous. I really should have told her that I knew no woman before her, and have never looked at another since."

"Well, I'm flattered, just so you know," I added.

"Well, ya were a cute kid. Not so bad now, either," he winked at me.

"See it's things like that, right there, that are gonna land ya on an episode of Snapped," Barry insisted.

"Well brother, the truth shall set ya free," the two brothers stared at each other as Fitz and I furrowed our brows.

"Oh look," Barry changed the subject, "they're starting chicken contests in the pool. That could be fun, right?"

Fitz looked over her shoulder, "They're all elderly people, it seems a little...wrong."

"Well then we better win," Barry laughed. "Janie, be my chicken partner."

"No!" we all stared at Fitz. "I'll be yer partner. Janie can be Pauly's partner."

"Uh, no," Pauly said. "No offense," he said to me, "but I'm not doin' anything with Janie that will fry my ass further if Mona finds out. You be my partner, Fitzy."

Fitz made a face, "Oh, alright then."

The four of us headed to the shallow end of the huge square pool. There were eighty year olds mounting the shoulders of other eighty year olds. I wasn't sure, but this seemed like we had an unfair advantage. Most of their bodies looked fragile, even if their hearts were still young.

Barry got into the water and asked if I needed help mounting him. I told him, "I only need you to go down enough, so I can get my legs around your neck."

Pauly hearing our conversation said, "That sounded way worse than it was intended to...I think," he added, before he sunk into the water so Fitz could get on his shoulders.

There was a group of twenty or so partners. Traditional *chicken* rules applied, last one on the shoulders of their partner, won. A whistle blew, but I can't be sure that everyone heard it. The first couple *out* was when an elderly gentleman yelled, "Charley horse" and tossed his rider into the water, swim cap and all.

Another poor man started walking toward the deep end with a

woman on his shoulders, and just kept…going. We all stopped for a moment to await their rise to the surface of the water.

As Barry turned, I was face to face with Fitz. She came at me with both hands. Unfortunately, her forward lunge caught Pauly off balance, and down she went.

Soon it was just me and a wisp of an elderly woman in a bright pink skirted suit and matching swim cap.

I smiled at her and her gentleman. They were such a cute couple. As we moved closer to each other, she let out what can only be described as a primal yell. Her gentleman was moving directly at us like a torpedo, head down and barreling at unbelievable speed. Barry took a few steps backward at the shock the oncoming duo created. The nice grandma and I, locked arms and she began to howl like a banshee. Her jaw tightened, but her teeth were bared rabid dog style. "Yer goin' down, cupcake," she said with a thick New York accent.

As the men staggered and shifted, I tried not to hurt the woman who was definitely besting the hell out of me. I had her upper arms in my hands and she had the same grip on me. I pushed and pulled trying to knock her from her *old man perch* she seemed to be glued to. Not having any of this, she pinched my bicep, and hard.

"Ouch! Dammit!" I scowled at her.

"That's the least of it, sister," she warned. Her eyes rounded psycho style, "Yer goin' down! YER GOIN' DOWN!" she enunciated, loudly.

"Get her, Janie," Barry said, in a panic. But he didn't see the look in her eyes.

This old lady was gonna have me for breakfast. Her man friend took a step into our personal space. He was almost nose to nose with Barry. The tiny, elderly woman let go of my arms and reached behind my back. Before I knew what the hell she was doing behind my back, her man-friend took three steps, backing away from us. I watched her swinging something black over her head as she howled. I cocked my head, what the hell was she waving around?

The crowd began to holler with her as I shook my head. Cameras were snapping pictures and recording. I could see Fitz's rounded eyes. Pauly's were popping from his skull as he started clapping his hands and whistled. Barry bent his head up at me from between my legs, causing me to look down. My bikini top was gone and once again the girls were on display.

Barry immediately dropped me from his shoulders. I tried frantically to cover the girls with one hand and pinch my nose off with the other. Barry pulled my half naked body against his bare chest, trying to block my girls from the view of the onlookers who were still hooting, hollering and recording. Holding my half naked body against his, Barry yelled to Pauly for a towel.

The old lady was still up on the shoulders of her man, the clear winner. She was surrounded by all the other elders in the pool, shaking my bathing suit top like a war prize. As Barry held me, my checks began to burn with embarrassment. I couldn't even meet his eyes. At that moment I wasn't sure I'd ever be able to look at him again.

Pauly threw a towel to Barry who pushed it between our naked chests and wrapped it around me.

Stepping out of the pool, I finally took stock of the people on the deck: there stood Mum, Da, Aunt Marble, and Benny.

The old lady was still mounted on the shoulders of the old man, as he walked her across the pool to where I stood, "Ya did good kid, but ya lack the killer instinct." Her thick nasally New York accent put me in mind of someone. She handed me back my bathing suit top and winked at me.

Benny laughed and I knew. I could see the resemblance.

Benny held out his hand, "Everyone this is my sister, Tovah."

Everyone in our circle laughed and smiled, shaking her hand,

and welcoming her. Had we all forgotten that this woman just ripped off my bathing suit top and made me the half naked laughing stock of *elder-land*, I wondered.

"Sorry kid," she said to me, "anything to win." She looked at Barry, "I hope yer not offended by me releasing yer girl's fun bags."

"I'm…I'm not her boyfriend," Barry stammered shaking his head, his face still bright red.

"Too bad," she eyed us, "you two would be a gorgeous couple."

Barry looked more than uncomfortable. If he was, he still had a way to go to catch up to my discomfort level.

I thanked Barry for his buffer of my mortifying exposure then went to the bathroom to put my girls away. I decided on a double knot this time.

Standing in the bathroom trying to cool my red cheeks in the sink, Tovah walked in.

"Hey kid, I hope I didn't embarrass ya too much," she put her palms-up.

"Well, I will say that more people saw my girls today than the last ten years combined," I gave her a sarcastic smile.

"Yer the modest one, aren't ya, honey?" she questioned.

"If modesty means not showing EVERYONE *my stuff*, then yes," I replied coolly.

She smiled, "Oh honey, ya don't even know," she waved a hand at me like it was no big deal.

"Excuse me?" I said, starting to let my temper rise.

"Sweetheart," she began, "Ya have a great body. Yer fun-bags made a bunch of men, with one foot in the grave, no less, very happy," she nodded.

I furrowed my brow, was this supposed to be comforting?

"Ya made a bunch of women happy, too, I might add."

I gave her a confused shake of the head. We weren't on an elderly gay cruise, were we?

"Oh, honey, yer Viagra with skin, sweetheart. All the men out there right now, are randy as teenagers."

I closed my eyes, "Yeah, well, I didn't want to be *elder-porn*."

"Oh, yer so sweet," she made a shooing motion with her hand, "completely dressed, you'd be *elder-porn*!" she laughed then snorted. "The truth is, at our age, sometimes the fire needs some kindlin'."

At this I allowed a smirk to crack my angry façade.

"So I know yer the modest one…Marble's daughter, right?" she took off her bathing cap to reveal a short salt and pepper, faux hawk hairdo.

"Honorary daughter," I confirmed.

"Right, Benny's told me all about ya. Yer the artist, yes?" she nodded.

I was surprised that he had mentioned me, "Yeah, that's me, Janie." I smiled and shook her hand.

"Well then, I don't need to tell ya, sweetie, art…is all sex and sexuality."

I gave her a perplexed look.

"Sex, paintin', creatin', they all come from inner passion. Without passion, ya can't really create. Somethin' inside of ya, child," she pointed at me, "is raw passion. It's what drives us," she made a grinding motion with her hips. "My guess is, once you open up…let passion overtake you…set it free…yer whole world is gonna open like a flower bloomin'. Don't be afraid of it, honey," she patted my check then turned to walk out. "Oh, and hopefully ya do it while yer fun-bags still defy gravity."

I was puzzled by being schooled by a complete stranger. What exactly had Benny told her? I'm uptight? And I had been told about needing to let my flower bloom, way too much this week.

I walked back to the chaise lounges with my head held high… er, trying my best not to emit the awkwardness that I felt.

Barry was having a hard time looking me in the eyes, so I put my sunglasses back on.

A cute elderly couple started to pass by then stopped directly in front of me. The gentleman said, "Thank you, by the way."

I bit my lower lip and nodded awkwardly.

Then the woman smiled and said, "I'm really the one who should be thanking you." As they hurried to another destination, I saw the old man grab his wife's butt.

I scrunched up my face, while Barry, Pauly and Fitz busted into roaring laughter.

"Well there ya go Janie, yer boobs have become a public service," Fitz rolled with laughter.

"More like a *pubic service*," Pauly said. "Hey, did ya want to see the video?" Pauly pulled out his phone and started scrolling.

"Seriously?" Barry looked at his brother. "Ya didn't record it?" he shook his head.

"It's not like I expected that to happen. I was just recording our havin' fun," Pauly stared at his brother.

"What did you record?" We all turned to see Mona, her hands on her hips.

Now I was uneasy. The look on her face…for God sakes my boobs were the talk of the pool. What were the chances she didn't already know?

Mona reached down and grabbed Pauly's phone, hitting play. A moment passed where I almost thought she was going to smile. I knew it wouldn't last long. Pauly tried to say, "That's pretty much it," and take the phone away from her, but she pulled it back from his reach.

All we could hear on the video was a banshee howl…followed by applause. Mona turned her dead cold eyes to me, "So I see the attention whore hasn't taken a vacation."

Barry piped up, "It wasn't her fault. She didn't know Benny's sister was gonna rip her top off."

"And yet, you not only chose to record it, you chose to keep it?" the stare she gave her husband was arctic cold. She threw the phone at him and stormed off.

"Well, there's another nail in my coffin," Pauly said.

Barry shook his head, "What the hell were ya thinkin'?"

"I thought it was funny, so sue me," Pauly said.

"I don't think I'll be able to. That woman is gonna take ya fer every cent ya have, and every cent you'll ever make!" he pointed to Mona walking off in the distance.

Fitz shook her head, "Yeah, I think the pooch has been screwed on this one, Pauly. You should go after her, try and smooth this shite over."

"No, ya wait for the wolverine to calm down. Ya don't poke it when it's pissed," Pauly shook his head again.

"I don't think yer ever supposed to poke a wolverine," Barry pointed out.

Danny and Andy arrived at the pool with their wives.

"Hey, ya missed the show," Pauly informed them.

I shook my head, "Pauly, no."

Danny looked down at his extremely relaxed wife, "No I didn't, brother," he kissed her cheek.

We all busted out in grins as she happily blushed.

10

DINNER AND A SHOW

Fitz and I were back in our tiny room dressing for dinner when she got a text from the great Rudolpho.

"Oh, my God, no!" Fitz covered her mouth.

"What? How much worse could it have gotten?" I asked, trying to skirt my bed and not run into the wall. I looked at the phone, "What?" was all I could say.

"Somehow, he managed to add more ruffles? How? It already looked like I was to be wearin an eight year old girl's bed ruffle. "

WHAT THE HELL!" she gave me a pleading face as she shook her phone at me.

"Well now are you gonna say anything? Seriously Fitz, are these the pictures you want of your wedding day…you, in that?" I pointed to the picture.

She let out a sigh, "He's a master," her head swinging back and forth. "How?" she asked me.

I took her phone and clicked it off, "Okay, breathe," I instructed. "Your wedding is over a year away. We can't do anything about this now," I was trying to rationalize the *calamity of fashion* that only seemed to be getting worse. "Let's just go to dinner, enjoy where we are and try not to sweat the small shit, okay?"

Her deep breathing was bringing her back to a more normal self as she nodded to me, "Okay."

We dressed and took the elevator back up to the grand hall. I was in the little black dress with matching heels. What I was going for, was understated (given my new found popularity), and thankfully, next to Fitz, I always would be.

Fitzy was in her emerald green kimono style dress with red pumps and black lacquer chopsticks holding a messy bun of fire red hair. Big red lips made her snow colored skin glow like a porcelain doll.

The beautifully set tables sat eight and we found our place cards. I was to sit next to Barry, who still hadn't arrived. Fitz's place card was on the other side of Barry. Danny and his wife's cards sat on empty place settings. I grinned, but said nothing. Pauly and Mona were also to be at our table but, I wasn't surprised to see their spots empty, as well.

When Barry walked in, I couldn't help but smile. Dressed in a traditional black tux, he was even more shockingly handsome. Women of all ages turned their heads as he walked by. All I could think was: if I was old-man-candy, he was the 'sweet-tooth' for their wives.

Fitz caught my grin and followed my eyes to her brother, "He looks good in a tuxedo," she stared at me.

"Yeah, he always has," I admitted.

As he walked up, he nodded his head to me. Fitz looked from me to him, from me to him, again.

"Ya look lovely," Barry said to me.

"Thank you," Fitz said.

"Yes, you too, sis," Barry kissed her cheek. "So, I see Danny and his wife are still M.I.A.," he laughed. "Maybe we should make them plates and drop it off at the room so they don't die from a lack of protein."

Fitz nodded, "He's makin' up for years of quickies during naptime. From the look on their faces today, our brothers and their wives, will be the only ones to ever lose weight on a cruise" she grinned.

"Would ya ladies care fer a cocktail?" Barry asked, looking at the champagne on the table.

"Please!" said Fitz. "I'm tryin' to avoid a champagne hangover."

I had to agree. I loved champagne, until the next morning. And since it was Fitz's and my tradition to eat black forest cake and drink shitty champagne after a break-up, we had had more than our share over the years. Mostly thanks to me.

"What can I get ya?" Barry asked us.

"Whiskey, straight up," said Fitz.

"Beer for me, please," I said.

Barry turned to me, "A woman after my own heart, ya are."

I smiled, but Fitz's smile seemed forced and tight.

There was a smogishboard of surf, turf and everything else under the sun the stomach could crave. I had just brought back a plate full of shrimp and lobster tails to the table, when Pauly showed up. He was half crocked, and of course, minus one wife.

He sat at the table, cocktail in hand, "Well, it's official, she wants a divorce. I came clean about everything."

"Everything?" I asked.

"Everything," Pauly sighed.

Fitz looked fit to be tied but she held her anger. "It's goin' to be okay, brother," she said, going to his side, and wrapping her arms around him.

Barry nodded, "It really will, Pauly. Things have a way of workin' out," he said and looked at me.

I nodded in agreement, but couldn't help but wonder what else was going on.

Fitz went to go get Pauly a plate of food to hopefully mellow his drunken state.

As the plates were cleared, the lights went down. A spotlight illuminated the podium on the stage where a quite handsome older gentleman stood. He welcomed everyone to the Fun with Seniors Cruise. Suddenly a slide show began to play on the movie sized screen behind him. Each slide showed what the cruise had to offer: there was a picture of a woman enjoying a massage, another of a mud treatment, women getting their nails and hair done, shuffleboard, Monte Carlo gambling, card rooms, great food any time of the day, or night, from room service, yoga, Tai Chi, and swimming in the Olympic sized pool. That's when it happened; there I was on a giant screen, topless on Barry's shoulders.

I was humiliated again, as the crowd applauded and roared with laughter. Off to the side of the stage, I saw Mona. She made the same symbol with her hands, that I now knew wasn't a giant vagina. My eyes slit at her.

The spot light was searching the crowd and I knew it was only a matter of time to find the young people in a sea of elderly. I refused to give her the satisfaction of thinking she damaged me. With my chin held high, I stood and smiled as wide as I could to the roar of applause. I waved at the crowd and bowed. One person was whistling so loud it was almost ear shattering. I looked around to find the *whistler* and there was Tovah, my smile became a real one and I pointed to her.

Turning my head, I caught Barry grinning and clapping hard.

Fitz was beaming with pride at watching me come out of my shell after twenty plus years. "Own it!" she yelled loudly!

I took another bow, put my hands under my boobs and gave them a little lift.

Mum and Aunt Marble, who also saw Mona, stood and beat their hands together furiously. Aunt Marble was screaming to everyone who would listen, "That's my daughter, the one with the healthy rack. Chip off the old block, she is!" she said, lifting up her own funbags.

Da, was trying to be supportive while still looking away from the slide on the screen.

Mona's face squished up with rage, before she stomped off the stage.

As the applause began to die down, I took my seat.

"Did ya catch Mona's face?" Fitz asked me quietly. "That was priceless," she laughed.

Later we were escorted to a giant ballroom by Barry and Pauly. I was enjoying the music and waltzing. Never having been much of a dancer, I envied people who had the rhythm gene. My head bobbed from side to side with the music.

Barry was watching and smiling. Soon, he stood and held his hand out to me, "Would ya care to dance?" his green eyes staring down into mine.

"I really don't dance well," I admitted.

"Sometimes ya just need the right partner," he said.

"They're your feet," I warned.

I let him lead me out onto the dance floor. One arm wrapped around my waist, as his other hand slipped into my palm. We began to move. His hand on my low back, was gently guiding my flow, to and fro. I wanted to see what my feet were doing, so I looked down.

"No," he said, raising my chin slightly with his fingertips, "look here," he motioned to his eyes.

I made his eyes my focal point. At first we shared an innocent smile with fat cheeks, but then his smile began to change as we floated. There was a seriousness I hadn't expected. What was this? Was I imagining the look of…I wasn't sure what. He was staring at my mouth witch made me feel slightly self-conscious. His mouth parted, like he was going to say something…then his teeth bit slowly into his lower lip. I swallowed hard. I was having trouble breathing all of the sudden. Some part of me wanted to look away…needed to look away, but couldn't.

I felt a tap on my shoulder and shook my head like I was coming out of a dream.

Fitz asked, "May I cut in?"

Barry and I still had locked eyes "Of course," he told his sister. "Thank you, Miss Janie," he said in almost a whisper and kissed my hand.

I felt panicky as I made my way back to the table. Downing my beer, I reached for Fitz's shot and downed it, too.

Standing at the bar I ordered another shot for Fitz and one for me. I watched her and Barry dancing. Fitzy was talking to him through a tightened jaw, a fake smile pulled across her face. Whatever he said to her made her green eyes flash.

I looked to my left and saw Mum and Aunt Marble approaching, "You and Barry look really good together," Mum said, raising an eyebrow to me.

"What?" I asked.

"Dancin'," Mum pointed to the dance floor.

"Oh, yeah," I said and downed my shot.

I watched Tovah walk up. She really was a slight thing, with a knee length black dress that came off one shoulder and dripping with diamonds. "Well, hello there, fun bags," she put an arm around me. "You've got yourself a great girl, here," she said to Aunt Marble.

"Well, I can't take all the credit," she shook her head. "Mum's been a big part of her life, too," she hugged me from the other side.

I laughed wondering if my actual mother was going to get any credit.

"Is that boy, one of yours," she asked Mum, pointing to Barry.

"That's my baby boy," Mum cocked her head.

"Quite a handsome lad you have there," Tovah nodded.

"I just wish I could find him a good woman," Mum let out a sigh.

Tovah looked confuse, "I think he already has," she gave me a sidelong look.

Mum was busy watching Barry and Fitz dance, "No. That's his sister."

Tovah was still watching me, as I downed the shot I bought for Fitz, and ordered another.

Mum looked at Tovah, "He's such a good man…it kills me to see him with a broken heart."

"A broken heart?" Tovah repeated.

"Aye, he was dumped, not only a week ago. This one may take him some time to get over," he says.

"Aha," Tovah added.

"I'm not a spiteful woman, but I'd love to have the head of the woman that broke his heart, on a spike," Aunt Marble said.

We all turned concerned looks to Aunt Marble. Mum politely took her cocktail from her.

"So where is your husband?" I asked, looking at Tovah.

"In the ground," she said matter-of-factly.

"I'm so sorry," I stammered, "I just assumed that the gentleman from the pool was your husband."

"That's okay kid, I assumed that guy was yours," she pointed to Barry.

"Oh no," Mum shook her head, "they're like brother and sister."

A smile stretched across Tovah's face, "O-kay!"

I saw Fitz stomp huffily across the dance floor towards us. "Come on," she said, grabbing me by the wrist.

I pulled her closer to me, "Where are we going?"

"I think we best get some sleep. We'll be in Mexico before morning and we don't want to be hung over, do we?"

"It's early," I gave her a questioning look.

"It's almost midnight," she corrected.

"And…you're afraid that my chariot will turn back into a pumpkin?"

I said my goodnight's to the ladies and let Fitz drag me back to our room. She seemed fit to be tied. As we changed into our jammies, my phone rang. A smile stretched across my face.

"Good morning," I said to Cecil.

"Good mornin' to you, luv. How's the cruise goin'?"

"Good," I said. "Not a whole lot happening; drinks, sunbathing, swimming…"

"Flashin' the elderly?" he asked.

My heart dropped, "What?"

"I was lookin' at yer feed, just missin' ya, and there ya were, on Barry's shoulders…topless."

Mona, that horrible wretch! "I can explain…" I started.

"Explain what?" he asked.

"It's not what it looks like…" I stammered.

"God I hope it is…"

I was confused.

"It would have been nice to see ya for the first time in person…and in private," he added, "but I gotta admit, the view is…beautiful."

I gave a half cocked grin, "It's embarrassing," I admitted.

"I knew you'd feel like that. I also knew ya didn't post it, so I thought ya might need a little positive feedback."

I shook my head, "You really are amazing. I just, I…" I was going to say 'like', I swear I was, but "I just love you," came out before I could stop it.

Cecil let out a sigh, "Ah, okay, yeah, I'm comin' right now," he said.

"Ugh, what?" I asked, totally confused.

"I'm sorry, Shelia was sayin' somthin'. I hate to do this, Janie, but I've got to run. I'll talk to ya later, okay?"

"Yeah…okay," I said before the phone went dead.

My heart began to pound, I was having trouble breathing. Oh my God, I told Cecil I loved him, and not only did he not reply… he rushed off the phone. This wasn't, couldn't be, a good sign.

Fitzy peeked out of the bathroom with one hand covering her eyes, "Is it safe to step out?"

When Fitz noticed that I didn't laugh or give her a shitty retort, she asked "What's wrong Janie?"

I explained the call and she came to the same conclusion I did about the video; Mona. But when I told her what I had said, she beamed with happiness…until she heard how Cecil had reacted. The look on her face confirmed how *not good* this was.

"So…he didn't say…anything?" she asked.

"He said his assistant was saying something and he had to go."

"But he wasn't upset about the video?" she shook her head.

"No, on the contrary, he said I looked beautiful."

Fitz bit her bottom lip.

"Say something," I begged of her.

"I'm not sure what to say. I don't know how to read it, but you can be sure… it could be read more than one way," she squeezed my hand.

Nodding, I was desperately hoping she could come up with one other than, *he doesn't feel the same way.*

"So…you do love him?" Fitz cocked her head at me.

It took me a moment to answer, when I did, I came up with, "I think so… maybe."

Sleep sucked as I tossed and turned. In my dream, I was chasing Cecil on an old fashioned bike with a huge front tire and a tiny one in the back. On a unicycle, he worked hard to get away from me, as we kept climbing a never-ending hill. When I woke, I was exhausted.

Fitz threw on a cute blue with white polka dot jumper and a wide brimmed floppy hat. I was seriously wanting my comfort clothes; my 501's, but I threw on a red sundress and pulled my hair into a long ponytail. I was determined not to look how I felt.

We filled our plates with breakfast enchiladas, quiche, bacon, sausage, and fresh fruit accompanied by mimosas.

Normally, when there is a disturbance in the emotional force, I can't eat, but I was ravenous. Finishing my plate, I asked if Fitz was going to eat her sausage. Her brow furrowed at me as she watched me inhale what was left on her plate, too.

"Ya okay, Janie? I'm not used to seein' ya *put it away* like that."

"I'm fine," I insisted, scooping up the last of her quiche.

"Okay," she gave me the eyes. Then it was like a light went on, "Oh," she said.

"Oh what?" I shook my head.

"I think yer comin' down with the five-day-fallopian-flu."

Pauly, who had been coming to sit, heard this and turned around finding another table.

I shook my head. "He has a wife…and kids! Why would he act like this isn't normal?"

"Never mind him, when was yer last menstrual?"

I thought, "In Ireland."

"Ya didn't tell me?" Fitz looked exasperated. "I always tell ya!"

"I know and after all of these years, ya don't have to. I KNOW when you're on your period," my eyes rounded.

"What's that supposed to mean?" she put her hands on her hips.

"Nothing really, you just become…"

"Kitten with a whip?" she questioned, crossing her arms over her chest.

"Kitten with a bazooka," I laughed.

"Well, yer eatin' like it's either yer time, or yer knocked up. One of those things I KNOW isn't a possibility," she gave the *angry fairy* smile.

Barry and Pauly met us at our table just as I had eaten the last morsel of Fitz's food.

"Did ya go back to yer room last night?" Fitz asked Pauly.

Barry gave him an irritated look.

"Well, I did," Pauly started "…then she threw me out. I slept in Barry's room," Pauly said.

"And ya snore like a freight train," Barry shook his head. "I didn't get any sleep, thanks to ya."

"Bitch, bitch, bitch," Pauly shook his head. "At least we get to pal around Mexico. If Mona was coming, we'd have to be on our best behavior."

"I wouldn't," Barry corrected, "because I wouldn't be around the two of ya. Not with all this negativity loomin' about."

"Well, now we don't have to worry about it," Pauly put his arm around Barry's neck, "Let's go show Mexico how the Irish Party."

11

WELCOME, MISS FITZPATRICK

As we made our way to the ferry, we saw Mum, Da, Marble, Benny and Tovah waiting in line.

"Good mornin' luvs," Mum said. Looking about, she asked, "Where's Mona?"

"About that, Mum," Pauly started.

The look on Mum's face said she didn't need to be updated. She knew. "Ya will be behavin' yerself in Mexico, or you'll answer to me, are we clear?"

Although she was talking to Pauly, all four of us nodded our heads.

It was going to be a warm sunny day as our ship docked just outside of Ensenada Mexico. I was doing quite well, until the smaller boat took us hostage. My heart began to pound as we skimmed across what I considered choppy waves (what other people considered the normal rise and fall of a boat riding the water). Fitz saw the look on my face and squeezed my hand.

After a moment she asked, "Are ya okay?"

"Yeah, why?" I tried to be cool in front of the family.

She pulled her hand free of mine, "Because you've almost broken the skin," she showed me my finger nail indents.

"Sorry," I winced.

The boat hit a larger wave than normal causing me to gasp and grab onto the rail for dear life. Barry laughed and wrapped his arm around me, "I got ya," he smiled. All I could do was nod furiously. So much for playing it cool, I thought.

Tovah had been watching me with a cocked head. "Afraid of boats, huh?" she asked.

I shook my head, "No. I'm afraid of the water and what lives in it," I explained.

Tovah smiled at me. "What's the worst that could happen?" she shook her head.

"Off the top of my head? Death," I answered.

She laughed at me, "We're all gonna die, honey. That's just a truth. And just so you know, nothing you do…will keep that from happenin'," she patted my cheek. "Do this with me," she instructed.

I watched her grab the railing with both hands; throwing her head back and closing her eyes, she began to howl. She looked at me, "Come on."

I was shaking my head and grinning, but I did as she said. I grabbed the rail, closed my eyes and turned my chin to the clouds. I let out a quiet, reserved howl.

"No honey," she shook her head at me and then she let go. A primal, goose bump causing, *hair on the back of your neck raising* howl escaped from her soul, I think.

I looked around as people began to notice the old woman in full wolf-mode.

"Come on honey, sing with me," she smiled.

I couldn't help but laugh. I threw back my head again, took a deep breath, and howled like a wolf on a full moon. Something inside of me was releasing. My shoulders were relaxing, I was breathing deep and steady. It almost felt like I was more wild than the waves; like I was their master. Before I knew it, Mum, Aunt Marble, Fitz and Barry all joined in. Then, half of the boat joined in, and even the sound of the engine was drowned out.

As we stepped ashore, I felt...alive and pulsing with an energy I couldn't quite put into words. I hugged Tovah, "Thank you," I beamed.

"Ah, there it is," she inspected my face, "the light's back on," she looked deep into my eyes.

I laughed as she kissed both of my cheeks.

"Now...Bloody Marys anyone?" Tovah asked the crowd.

A handsome older gent asked Tovah if he could pal around with her for the day. He was tall, slender with olive skin, hazel eyes and a full head of salt and pepper hair. She grinned at the Man and said, "If you can keep up!" He introduced himself as Orlando, and he, and the whole family headed to the first bar on the pier.

The Cantina was open air and had a 360 degree view of land and sea. Ten Bloody Marys were ordered as we sat taking in the beauty that was Mexico.

Benny was so happy to have his sister there for his wedding he said, "Tovah, tell us the story about the subway. I love this one," he said to Marble and kissed her cheek.

Tovah began in her thick New York accent; I take the subway to the city from time to time. Ya know, to shop, like ya do," she nodded to all of us. "Well, I was standing on the platform headin' home to New York. They have a Lindt Chocolate Store there," she made mmm noises. "I probably bought them out of their chocolate hazelnut bars. So I'm standin' on the platform, waiting for the subway home. I'm just mindin my own bee's wax, when this guy in a trench coat jumps right in front of me. We're staring at each other, right. I mean, what is he doin, is all that's goin' through my mind. Is he gonna mug me? I mean, he tries to take my chocolate," she raised her palm to us, "I'm gonna fight, right?"

she gave us a palms-up. "All of the sudden, he throws open his coat to display his nakedness to me. Well, I'm sure you can imagine my shock," she grinned, putting her hand to her chest. "I yelled out 'Oh my God, no!' Not that I'm afraid to see the male anatomy," she grinned. "I just figured that was the response he was goin' for, ya know, *shock value*. I didn't want to make the poor guy feel like he hadn't succeeded," she explained. "But being who I am, I did have to take a little peek, ya know, he went through all this trouble. So I gave it the obligatory look while doin' the *I'm so shocked* face. But then I see it and I couldn't help it. I started shaking my head, I had to tell him, 'Oh no, honey'!" she shook her head. "Ya can't go around flashin' that. No honey, I've see bigger wieners come out of a can, sweetheart. Ya don't want to be known for that!" she curled her pinky finger at us. "Well then he starts trying to tell me that it's cold outside and that's causing him to have a bad penis day, and all. I just shook my head and told him, "Sweety, if ya have no braggin' rights, ya don't flaunt. With a penis like that, ya may want to play up yer sense of humor." I felt bad for him, so we split a Lindt dark chocolate bar waitin' on the subway. He needed some Lindt love. Well, honestly, what he needed was a penis enlargement, but, what are ya gonna do?"

The whole family was busting up and I couldn't help but picture this story playing out in my head; Tovah on the subway, sitting next to a man in a trench coat with black socks and sneakers, commiserating over a chocolate bar. After all, Tovah seemed somewhat disheartened by the man's shortcomings, too.

The elders of the group wanted to hit some of the sights, but we youngins wanted to shop. Well, Fitz wanted to shop and wasn't going alone. Barry and Pauly came with, to escape the watchful eye of Mum.

We hit almost every shop within walking distance. I found a ruffled Flamenco style dress and held it up to Fitz, "Look, it's your wedding dress."

She gave me a shit look as she answered her phone. I could tell by the look on her face, that it was Scotty.

I smiled at her as Barry came up beside me, "They're really happy together, aren't they?" he said.

"Yes they are," I told him. "He's a wonderful man and they are just perfect together."

"What about his brother? Is he a good man?" Barry asked. "All I know of him, is that he wears boxers."

I laughed. Barry had dropped by my house to return a sweater to Fitzy, the morning we were set to leave for Ireland. Cecil, who was sleeping on my couch, answered the door half naked, I remembered. "He is a good man," I nodded.

"So are ya two like…an item, now?"

I bit my lower lip. I still wasn't sure what we were. After my *I love you* faux pas, and his *gotta go*, I wasn't real clear where we stood. "It's still new. I'm not sure how he feels," I admitted.

Barry looked concerned, "He hasn't said how he feels about ya?"

I thought about him calling me *his girl*, "Kind of," I said. The truth was I didn't want to read too much into it. Yet, when I thought of how we were my last night in Ireland, I thought we were definitely…something.

"Well, maybe you should ask. Get clarification. I mean…you deserve someone who knows that he wants ya," that look was back, the one that made me swallow hard.

I nodded, "I just don't want to push him," I admitted.

"Ya shouldn't have to," Barry raised his brows. "But it beats the hell out of guessin'."

I nodded and we went back to shopping. Fitz was buying everything in sight. She loaded up on so much at one shop, all four of us had to carry her bags.

After she was all shopped out, we headed to a restaurant for a late lunch. Taking a table out on the patio, the view was spectacular. The sky was so blue and the off shore breeze was perfection. I wasn't sure how people talked themselves into ever leaving Mexico.

Before our food even arrived, I noticed a whole eight top of men, staring. They were speaking in Spanish and kept grinning over at our table.

Pauly seemed concerned, "What the hell are they lookin' at?" he asked, like any of us knew or spoke Spanish. We all shook out heads at him. Finally after about twenty minutes of this, Pauly stood.

"Where are ya goin'?" Barry grabbed his arm as he was passing by.

"I'm gonna find out why the hell they're starin' at us."

"You do know yer in a foreign country, right?" Barry asked.

"So?" Pauly shook his head.

"Decorum may be required. Give it some thought," Barry warned his older brother.

Pauly made a *pfff* sound as he pulled out of Barry's grasp.

We watched Pauly taking to the table of men. His hostility was apparent and Barry looked uneasy at the thought of having to aid his older brother in his stupidity. It was a somewhat broken conversation, since we didn't speak the same language. But soon I heard something that apparently united American and Mexican men alike, "Sarra Fitzpatrick."

Pauly pointed to Fitzy then gave her the come here finger bend. I laughed as Fitzy posed for picture after picture with the young men who all knew her from her bathing suit spread calendar. One man just called her Miss January. Before you knew it, more and more men were showing up and asking for a picture or an autograph. By the time all was said and done, I counted over thirty men who had posed next to the redheaded bombshell that was Fitzy. She kissed cheeks and wrapped her arms around others. Drinks were bought for the table so many times that I knew we'd never be able to use all the coins this bar used as free drink markers.

As I watched Fitzy, a nice elderly couple from the ship passed behind me. I could tell that the wife had hearing problems as her husband spoke loudly, enunciating everything he said.

"Why is everyone taking pictures with that girl?" the wife asked loudly. "Who is she?"

"That's Sarra Fitzpatrick," her husband informed her. "She's a model."

"Oh she's so cute," his wife said. "What about this one?" she pointed to me. "She looks familiar. Is she a model, too?"

"No, that's the boobie girl from the pool on the boat," her husband explained.

"Yer right," the woman said, "she looks different with her clothes on."

My face squished up as I thought, and now I'm the boobie girl. Great.

Waiting for the ferry that would take us to the ship, was the rest of the family. All of them were wearing sombreros and singing. I grinned and shook my head as Tovah presented all four of us with our sombreros.

Back on the ship, we headed to our rooms to get ready for dinner. Fitz asked, "What were you and Barry talkin' about earlier? Ya looked a little…green?"

"He asked me about Cecil…whether or not we're an item," I felt the green returning just talking about it.

She rolled the thought around in her head before asking, "What did ya tell him?"

"The truth…I really don't know." My smile faded away.

"What did he say?" her brows arched.

I let out a sigh, "That I should ask him."

"Maybe ya should. Yer too far away from each other to let miscommunications and assumptions rule ya."

As much as I agreed, I wasn't sure I wanted to know the answer.

Fitz wore her new off the shoulder dress in vibrant red, blue, yellow and green. Her red mane was thrown into a loose bun and her lips were lined a bright coral for Fiesta Night.

I also had an off the shoulder dress in plain white made out of some gauzy material. Fitz insisted on doing my make up since my dress had no *pop* as she put it. She lined my eyes with a dark brown and my lips with a Scarlet Red. I really wasn't much on lipstick, but I indulged her need to fashion me up a bit. As I went to throw my long blonde hair into a clip, she stopped me, "Leave it down. You have beautiful hair," she squeezed my hand.

Dinner was another masterpiece of seafood and traditional Mexican cuisine. I could eat my weight in lobster, crab legs and shrimp, and gave it my best shot. Fitz eyed my plate, "Are ya gonna eat all of that?"

I was a little embarrassed as I looked at my plate and then said, "Every last bite."

"And we're sure yer not fallopian-izin'?"

Pauly, who just was walking up, squished up his face, "Why? I'm tryin' to eat here! Why do ya have to have girly conversations in public?"

"I'm gonna shock the hell out of ya, she and I," Fitz threw a thumb my way, "we're girls!"

"It's just so…unnecessary," he shuddered and shook his head.

"I swear, how did a woman ever marry ya? Much less, have babies with ya. Ya come from a family of strong women, who are respected by strong men. Try and remember that!" she added.

Barry walked up right about that time, "What are we talkin' about?"

"Periods," Fitz told him.

"What about them?" he asked.

"See, I'll ask him," Pauly did a palms-up. "Does it gross ya out to hear about periods? Answer honestly."

Barry shook his head, "No."

"Ah come on, be honest," Pauly insisted.

"You were brought up in a house with Mum! How in God's name could ya act like such a man-child about somethin' natural? It's not like women chose this."

Fitz folded her arms across her chest and nodded, "Exactly."

"It's just...yucky," Pauly squished up his face again.

Barry looked shocked, "It's not like you have to deal with any of the pain, bloatin', nausea...if anything you should be sympathetic and grateful, not a grossed-out, ass."

I smiled. I wasn't a fan on the conversation either, but it was nice to see the monthly hell we go through, be defended by a man.

"Okay, fine," Pauly shook his head, "Can we just change the subject?"

"Here, here," I said.

"So where is Mona?" Barry asked.

Pauly grinned, "Boy the chattin' at this table just sucks. I'm not sure. She wasn't in the room when I grabbed my bag."

"Grabbed yer bag?" Barry repeated.

"Yeah, I hope ya don't mind, Mona wants me out. It's either I bunk with you for the rest of the trip, or on a chaise at the pool."

Barry looked like he was on the fence about the choices.

After I plowed through dinner, the Salsa music started and couples hit the floor.

Before I could even think about how much I would not want to do this dance in public, Benny was at my side.

"May I have this dance?" Benny held out his hand to me.

Looking at the body grinding, just short of humping that was taking place, I wanted to decline. But the look on his face: His tiny stature, bald head and huge square glasses, all dressed up in a child sized tuxedo, I grinned.

"If it's okay with Marble, I mean, Mum," I corrected.

Aunt Marble clutched her chest at me calling her Mum and smiled from ear to ear. "Of course, you go dance with your new papa."

Being honest, normally, I wouldn't do this dance with anyone. Much less someone I was told to refer to as papa, but it's one dance right? That's what I had to tell myself to get on the dance floor.

The first problem with Benny, and I dancing in close proximity, was that I was several inches taller than him. In fact, Benny's nose was just about boob level. Next was less obvious to some, but I was the worst dancer. The Salsa was a sexy dance, done by sexy people. Not to be done by a woman who had two left feet and oozed awkwardness.

Out on the floor he led me. As we found our personal space and joined hands, he wrapped his arm around my waist and pulled me against him, hard. My eyes rounded as I felt his bones slam against my ample curves. So much for that *personal space* thing, I thought. It really wasn't the gyrating that had me concerned; it was the pace of the gyrating. For a moment, I felt like my leg was being speed-humped by a Chihuahua. I couldn't quite keep up with the tiny man who was approaching seventy. As he rounded me, he slammed into my backside and went to town. I'm sure I didn't hide my look of shock and fear. Meanwhile, all of the Fitzpatrick's and Tovah were clapping and bobbing their heads, dancing in place. When the song ended, I couldn't help but give props to Aunt Marble. If Benny still had that kind of energy, those moves, she was a lucky woman.

I was walking back to our table and all the Fitzpatrick's were gawking in my general direction. Of course my first fear was that somehow the *girls* had found an audience again. I searched my dress. Nope, boobs were right where I left them. Then I noticed their stares were a little further off. Turning my head, I saw Mona on the dance floor.

Dressed in her own L.B.D., she took the hand of the handsome young dance instructor. He was tall, dark and gorgeous, to say the least. As their bodies came together, a slow writhing began. Mona's eyes were locked as she and the man's mouth, were within an inch of each other's. His hands holding firmly to her hips as he walked her in a circle, clearing the dance floor. Moving together as one, not a glimmer of light could be seen between their bodies. Holding her around her waist, he dipped her, and swung her from side to side. Her arms reached above her head, giving him full access as he brought his face to her not so ample bosom. They acted out a very sexual dance for all of the onlookers. One onlooker seemed to be flushing red. Mona's red lips parted as she threw her head back, a look of pure ecstasy washed over her face.

Mum's eyes slit at the game Mona was playing.

Pauly was red-faced as he hotly held his hand out to me, "Come on, let's show her how it's done."

My eyes rounded, "First, no! I am not getting in this anymore than I already am. And second, you did see how badly I dance, right?"

He gave a little understanding nod, "Yeah yer not exactly a sexual dynamo, are ya?"

My face squished up at his comment, "You want to make her jealous, you're going to have to find someone else," I put my hands up.

"But everyone else here is a hundred years old," he said.

Tovah, shot him a look, "Excuse me, son, but some of us hundred year olds, can still rip that floor up."

Pauly raised his brows to her, "Ya wanna?"

Benny piped up, "You may wanna pack a lunch, son," his bald head nodded.

As Pauly and Tovah hit the floor, Mona and her partner, stepped back and let the newcomers have spotlight. Mona looked less than threatened by Pauly's dance partner. Tovah started out letting Pauly lead, but then I saw her shake her head at him. All of the sudden, she took over. Talking to him the whole time, I assumed Tovah was giving him directions. There was grinding, gyrating, and the molding of bodies. The whole room was in awe. I found myself wondering, how could that woman, move like that, and make it look so fluid and beautiful? She gave him the come hither eyes. I didn't think a woman her age could still make this look so damn sexy, especially since I couldn't do this at twenty-six. Was Tovah right? Did I need to find my inner sexuality? Was whatever she had, locked inside me, as well? I knew I was awkward in my body, always had been. But was that just *me*, or was that the *me* who hadn't found her inner self? As the room shook with applause, Tovah and Pauly headed back to our table, leaving Mona seething with rage.

Tovah smiled and put a kiss on Pauly's cheek, "Thanks for the dance, kid," she said.

"No, I should thank you," Pauly said, with a dreamy, far off look that we all caught. "Maybe you'd like to get a drink?" he asked. "Or a walk on deck?" he offered.

"You're a sweet kid," she patted his cheek.

Barry, Fitz and I all exchanged looks of concern. Was Pauly… smitten? As Tovah walked back to the adjoining table where Mum, Da, Aunt Marble and Benny sat, Pauly's eyes followed her.

"Um, Pauly?" Fitz began, "Ya okay?"

"Yeah," he said, but never took his eyes off of Tovah. "She's just amazin'. Don't you think she's amazin'?"

With furrowed brows we all just nodded.

"Okay," Barry finally said, "so, um, would you like to dance, Janie?"

I looked at the floor, and shook my head. "No, I've had enough dancing for tonight. Plus, I really don't dance well," I laughed.

"I disagree," Barry grinned. "I think maybe it's the partner that makes the difference."

Back in our room, Fitz said, "Well, that was weird."

I had to agree, "A little bit."

"I know Pauly hasn't had much action lately, Mona refusin' him, and all. But I didn't think he would turn his yearnin' on Tovah," Fitz looked confused.

"Yeah, that look he gave her…kind of threw me," I laughed. "You have to admit, though, there is something about her."

"I agree," she nodded her head. "She is a bombshell, and definitely confidant. Maybe we shouldn't have you trying to *Barrymore*. You may want to be *Tovah-ing*."

I laughed…but Tovah's words did keep coming back to me. Great art is all from sex and passion.

My phone rang, and I was nervous when the screen read 'Cecil'. Our last talk, I had said the *I love you* which was met with the silent *dip out*. Or at least that's the way I took it.

"Hi," I answered.

"I…ows y irl?"

He was breaking up so bad. I could kind of make out what he was saying. "You're breaking up!" I told him. I looked at my phone…full bars.

"I n ane. Ing oo Sct end," he said. "An u hr e?"

"I can make it out a little," I said. "Can you understand me?"

"Arely. I y ter, iss u," he waited.

"I miss you, too," I said loudly into the receiver, before he rang off.

"What the hell was that about?" Fitz asked, coming out of the bathroom.

"Cecil. I think he said he was on the plane heading to Scotland. Phone was breaking up," I made the sad face.

"So, ya didn't get to talk to him, again?"

"Nope," I slumped down on the bed.

"Don't do that," Fitz sat on her bed facing me.

"Do what?" I asked.

"I know exactly what yer thinkin'. You think because the line was breakin' up, it's some kind of a sign," she made air quotations.

I both loved and hated that she knew me so well. I know it was a lot to read into something, so nothing, but it was the way my mind worked. Always, everything meant something. But I'm glad Fitz was there to reel me in from my trip to symbolic hell.

"You're right," I admitted. "Just...so much has happened and I always feel like I'm in the dark, trying to find the light switch."

"I think, you've allowed the dark to creep in," she cocked her head at me. "The switch is in the same place it was before, where it always is. You just have to turn on the light."

"I told him I love him, and he said nothing. Where's the light in that one?" I asked honestly.

She gave me a heavy sigh, "I honestly don't know. But I don't think you should go off half cocked. Wait until you can talk... then talk."

I knew she was right. I was the kind of girl who always let her mind get carried away. It was rarely a good thing. I had done the same thing with Cecil and his ex-girlfriend. I was so sure I knew his intentions, that I almost let myself be run off.

"Look, we'll be in another port tomorrow and I'd love it if you would try to have a good time, instead of worrying. I mean seriously, we're in Mexico," she exclaimed. "You should be having the time of yer life."

I nodded, "You're right. Plus, there's nothing I can do about it now, so why worry about it now, right?"

Fitz nodded, "That's the spirit!" she said and went to take off her make-up.

Half an hour later, she stepped out of the bathroom and I jumped. I never would get used to her green face mask and chin strap.

"Uck ooo," she told me.

12

BAJA-HAHAHAHA

"Welcome to Baja California," said the voice overhead. "Please enjoy the beauty and history of this magnificent port."

Down to breakfast Fitz and I went. Mum, Aunt Marble and Tovah sat at their table meant for eight.

"Can we join ya?" Fitz asked.

"Oh, there are my babies," Mum beamed.

"Our babies," Aunt Marble corrected. "Come give yer Mum a hug," she said to me.

"Hello Mum," I said while hugging her.

Aunt Marble squealed with delight.

"So, what are your plans for today, ladies?" Tovah asked. "Kayaking? Snorkeling?"

Fitz snorted, "Right, like I'm gonna get Janie in the water!"

"You're afraid of the water, I forgot." Tovah looked at me.

Fitz answered for me. "She hates the water, boats, large fish, heights…I could go on, but I think I've made my point."

Aunt Marble began to cry, "Oh no, oh no!" she grabbed her head and shook it.

"What's wrong…Mum," I asked her.

"Some Mum I am! Ya have all of these fears, and I've subjected ya to all of them. What kind of a mother does that?" she sobbed.

I threw Fitz a *you are an asshole* look, before I soothed Aunt Marble. "You didn't know. It's okay! And I'll gladly face all of my fears to be here for your wedding, okay, Mum?" I threw in, so she would smile again.

Tovah was staring at me and nodding.

When my phone began ringing, I went into *search mode* in the bottom of my purse. Looking at the incoming call, I sighed.

Fitz grinned.

"What's with the face," Aunt Marble asked.

"It's her mom," Fitz's grin widened. "Her other mom," Fitz told her aunt.

I walked away from the table, shooting death darts at Fitz with my eyes.

"Hi Mom," I said.

"Hi Janie," she sounded strange. I could only imagine what I did wrong that made her voice overly sweet, yet stressed out sounding.

"What's going on?" I asked.

"Well, honey, I just got off yer PAGE," she said like I wouldn't understand the word.

Mom had been trying new things, and had even stepped into the twentieth century by getting a cell phone. Several nights I had received calls from her home phone because she had locked herself out of her cell and needed help getting back in. I knew it was only a matter of time before she fell victim to the shiny newness of social media.

"Okay," I told her.

"Well, something on your page concerned me…" she said.

I could only guess. Undoubtedly, mom had seen the video of me (or my boobs, rather), that Mona had posted.

"If this is about the video, it's already been removed," I told her.

She was silent.

"Mom?" I called out to her.

"I was just concerned as to why you would have posted something like that?" she was talking very calmly and slowly.

"Mom, I didn't," I explained. "Pauly's wife, Mona, posted it."

"Well, I don't think that's something a FRIEND would do," she pointed out like I was back in kindergarten.

"Believe me, Mona and I are not friends. She did that as kind of a *screw you* to me. In fact, she hates me."

"I guess my question is, why are you going topless in the pool?" she said it like she was afraid that I would admit to being an exhibitionist.

I looked back towards Tovah, "I…had my bathing suit top ripped off during a chicken fight. You know, where you're on someone else's shoulders, and have to push other people off of other people's shoulders. Anyway, Mona got a hold of the video and posted it."

"Well, I would excommunicate her, immediately!" Mom said matter-of-factly.

I knew what I thought she meant, but I had to give her the correct wording so she wasn't saying this to other people.

"Un-friend, mother," I told her. "You un-friend people! The church excommunicates. And I'm pretty sure they don't do it because you posted a video of someone you don't like."

"Well they should," mom huffed. "Do you want me to talk to her mother?" she asked.

I tried not to laugh. It was cute that she still wanted to protect me.

"No mom, I got this."

"I just know how many people have been in your garden…and we want to keep your garden free of…snakes," she added.

There it is, I thought. Some things just didn't change quickly enough for my liking. I shook my head, "Don't worry mom, I'm keeping my garden…free of pests."

"Okay honey, you have fun. And I'm here if you need me."

"Love you, Mom," I told her.

"I love you, too," she rang off.

I stared at the phone, tired of a metaphor being used to discuss things, I didn't want to discuss in the first place. Especially with my mother, I shuddered.

I made my way back to the table and told Fitz, "Great, mom's worried about my garden."

Fitz laughed, but Aunt Marble said, "Oh ya have a garden, tell me all about it."

After picking Fitz up off the floor, we excused ourselves to go finish getting ready for Baja.

"I can't believe yer mom, that's hilarious. She's gonna keep yer garden free of snakes, meanwhile, ya haven't had a snake anywhere near ya in months…and months …and months."

"I got it Fitz," I told her.

"No, I think the point is, ya don't," she laughed.

I put on a new sundress and flip flops. I assumed we'd probably be doing some walking. Fitz, on the other hand, put on a pair of four inch heels.

"Those are going to be uncomfortable to walk in," I warned her.

"Well now that I know I'm famous in Mexico, I can't really go out without dressin' up a bit, now can I?"

"You always look amazing, I'm sure comfortable shoes won't detract from that," I shrugged.

As we waited for the ferry, I noticed that the older brothers and their wives were nowhere to be found. I knew someone's garden had been visited, I grinned.

Tovah, Benny, Aunt Marble, Da and Mum, had taken the

earlier ferry while I waited for Fitz to Fitz-a-fy herself. I looked over at her perfect hair and make-up; like she was going to a photo shoot. Decked out in a white silk dress, she fanned herself with her hand.

"Are you sure you don't want to dress more…comfortably?" I asked.

The heat was turning her face red, "I'm fine," she breathed. Tiny drops of sweat were forming on her upper lip.

Barry and Pauly made it just in time to ride the ferry with us.

"Wow Fitz, ya look great, but aren't ya a bit…hot?" Barry asked, watching a bead of sweat roll from her hairline down the side of her face. "Are ya wearin' fake eyelashes?" he asked.

Fitz put her hand on the rail and let out a deep breath, "I am," she told him.

"Why are ya so dressed up?" Barry asked, "it's gonna be like ninty-five degrees."

"I want to look good," she told her brother.

"Yeah, but ya look like yer gonna pass out," Barry told her.

"It's just the girdle thing, it's a little warm…and hard to breathe," she added.

"Why the hell would you wear a girdle?" I asked.

"I wanted all of the lines of the dress, perfect," she explained.

"But…you're already perfect? That doesn't even make sense!" I tried to reason with her.

This ferry trip didn't bother me at all, I noted. It had to be because my best friend looked like she was about to keel over at any moment. My attention was on the bad thing that was happening; not the bad things that could happen.

As we came off the water, the off shore breeze wasn't as strong as it had been on the ferry.

We walked to a nearby cantina to rehydrate.

"Holy crap, they don't have air conditioning?" Fitz asked.

"The place is open air, Fitzy," Barry extended his hand to the great view.

"Water!" Fitz breathed. Her silk dress starting to show sweat marks under the arms, and between the boobs.

Pounding a whole pitcher of water, Fitz said, "Fer god sakes, cut this damn thing off of me! I'll just wear my bra and panties. I don't care what I look like," she shook her head and did a finger wave to the waitress. "Water, water," her red, sweating face looked up at our waitress.

Out of my bag, I pulled her black romper and a pair of toeless, heelless shoes and handed them to her. "I was worried you'd be uncomfortable," I said.

"Oh Janie, I love ya so much right now," she gave me a salty wet hug. "I'm gonna need ya to remember that, when yer helpin' peel me out of this horrible dress and girdle. Come on!" she pulled me off of my stool and led me to the Senorita's room.

Not gonna lie, there was a time while I was trying to peel the form fitting silk from her sweat riddled body, that I thought it may just be easier to cut the damn thing off.

We got Fitz rehydrated, then started on Margaritas when her color returned to snow white.

"Oh for the love of God," Fitz took a well needed drink. "Take me as I am world, I'll not be roastin' like a hotdog on a grill."

"I think a hotdog's casing is a little looser than that dress was," I told her.

"So what should we do today?" Barry asked.

"Maybe reel Pauly back in," Fitz said, looking past Barry.

Barry turned around, and Pauly was sitting in between two young ladies. Barry let out an agitated sigh, before standing and walking over to where Pauly and his entourage were seated.

"Guess I lost track of ya goin' to the jukebox?" Barry asked.

"Oh, I made some new friends," Pauly said. "This is Lila," he put an arm around the brunette with her tits bulging out of her self-cut band shirt. "And this," he put his arm around the blonde wearing a thong bikini, "is Cherry," he smiled from ear to ear. "They go to school at UCLA. Sorority girls on vacation, doesn't that just make ya happy?" he asked his brother.

"No, actually it doesn't," Barry said. "Maybe we should call yer wife and ask her, if it makes her happy?"

"Such a buzzkill," Pauly told him, and said goodbye to his new lady friends.

Back at our table, Fitz was fit to be tied, "Ya really have no clue, do ya?"

"Oh come on, don't give me the big speech about what a dog I am," Pauly gave all three of us the finger waves. "I wasn't gonna do anything ya know. Ya don't have to treat me like I'm a cheatin' louse."

"Well, I should hope not. Especially since they're prostitutes," Fitz gave him the *evil-fairy-grin.*

"No, they're not. They're collage girls…here on vacation," Pauly shook his head at his sister.

"I'm tellin' ya, they're prostitutes!" Fitz said again.

"And how would ya know that?" Pauly looked smug.

Fitz folded her arms across her chest, "Bacuase…when we were in the bathroom, the blonde asked me for a tampon."

"Okay, it's gross, but it's not prostitute gross," Pauly raised his eyebrows at his sister.

"Then she told her friend, she'd only be able to give *blowies* fer the rest of the weekend." Fitz sat back, confident with her assessment of the ladies.

"Well maybe she's somebody who really prefers to have sex, but is willin' to give *blowies*, instead. Maybe she's just a giver, have ya ever thought of that?" he asked.

"Well," I finally piped up, "There's also the fact that they asked if we were prostitutes, too. They said that we were a little old to pull the college-girl routine, but knew a bar where we could make great money."

"Ya didn't have to tell him that part," Fitz bellowed at me. "I could totally still pass fer a college prostitute!" she argued.

Barry shook his head at his sister, "Please…don't ever say that again."

"Ya act like I was gonna cheat!" Pauly bellowed.

"No," Barry told him, "YOU act like you were gonna cheat!" he told his brother.

Pauly let out a huff, "Let's just get out of here."

We stumbled onto an open air market. There was tent after tent of clothes, home décor, jewelry and curios. I was having the best time picking up some small gifts for mom, dad and Betty. Two small curios of a Dia de los Muertos couple, dressed in wedding attire, made me smile, so I bought a bride and groom for mom and dad. I knew it wasn't her style, but they were too cute to pass up.

I also found one of the tiny dolls for Betty, she was dressed like a dead Mae West, and had that rockin-blonde-do. And tight floor length dress. I knew this was right up her ally. I wondered if I should buy something for her boyfriend, but all I knew about him was that he was from Australia… and his penis size. Because of a bumbled attempt at saving Betty from a horrible fate, I had walked in on her and her boyfriend. He was in her garden. The memory of it, made me wince, but in this instance, it had brought Betty and me closer.

From where I stood, I could see that Pauly had walked down a side road and was talking to a shady looking fellow. I gave a head nod to Fitz so she would see what I was seeing.

Barry, Fitz and I walked down the narrow road and heard Pauly asking about Spanish Fly.

"But how do I know this is the real deal?" he asked the young man.

Watching us approach, the young man took on a look of discomfort and walked quickly away.

"So…now yer trying to find a way to roofie someone?" Barry was trying hard to maintain.

"Not someone," Pauly stared at his brother like the question was rude. "My wife!" he spat.

Barry shook his head at Fitz, "I can't…I can't fuckin' talk to him." Barry walked away.

"Look I don't want anyone else," Pauly explained.

"But ya want to drug yer wife? Have ya thought fer a moment…that buyin' some shady drug, from some shady guy, might be DANGEROUS. Not to mention, unethical!" Fitz yelled. "What the hell are ya thinkin'?"

"I wasn't gonna buy it, I just had questions," Pauly tried to rationalize.

"I've got questions too," Fitz grabbed Pauly by the ear and dragged him back up the street as he howled.

"I'm just horny…it's the way God made me," he screamed.

"Oh, no ya don't," Fitz let go of his ear, "Don't ya for a minute blame God for yer stupidity!" her eyes bugged out of her head.

"I don't know what else to try to get her to want me," Pauly gave her a shrug.

"Try booze like everybody else," Fitz stormed off.

"Ha, like that's gonna to work! She hates me more when she's drunk!" Pauly yelled after Fitz.

The four of us sat at lunch in a beautiful restaurant on the bay. A window looking out to the ocean, stretched across one whole wall, giving us a spectacular view. As I looked from one Fitzpatrick to the next, I became fidgety. Picking at my nails, I tried to find something that would break the uncomfortable silence. Pauly was busy pouting about being schooled by his younger siblings. The younger siblings were pissed off at having to school their older brother. Fitz's jaw was clenched so tight, I was afraid it would spasm.

"Look," I began, "can we just…let today…go? I mean this is supposed to be a great vacation. Look at the view! We shouldn't be spending our time fighting," I reasoned.

Barry reached out his hand to my fidgeting ones. "Yer right." He gave my hand a squeeze.

"Pauly," Barry said, "I'm sorry I got so angry with ya."

Fitz released her jaw, "Me too. I'm sorry Pauly."

"Well if yer admittin' you were wrong…" Pauly started.

Fitz and Barry's eyes rounded.

"I'm just kiddin'," Pauly told them. "I'm sorry if I acted like an ass."

I let out the breath I had been holding, as conversation moved on to other things.

A beautiful woman, in her forties, I would guess, took the stage; microphone in hand.

She introduced the song she would sing, Amarte es un Placer, as the music began. I had no idea what any of the words meant, but her voice captivated me. Something deep inside of me, stirred. I could see the passion she felt. Every breath she exhaled seemed to carry words straight from her soul. Somehow, she soothed the savage beasts in all of us.

Soon, we headed back to the ferry.

"What's goin' on back at the ship tonight?" Fitz asked.

I think tonight is a murder mystery dinner," Barry said. "We're supposed to dress forties style."

"Easy fer you, all you men have to do is wear a tux. We're the ones that have to put together a classic outfit," Fitz pointed to herself and me.

Back in our little tiny room, Fitz pulled out a flapper style dress.

"You brought a flapper dress?" I asked.

"Yeah, I looked over the nightly events in the brochure Benny gave us. What did you bring for the Dinner and Death show?" she looked down into my suitcase.

Um, I riffled through, already knowing the answer, "Nothing, I got nothing." I shrugged.

Fitz curled her long red hair then tucked it under, to give her the appearance of a bob. She put on some kind of beaded headband with a feather. Pulling out a long black cigarette filter, she put a cigarette in the end.

"What are you doing with a cigarette?" I practically yelled at her.

We had both quit smoking months and months ago. We had a relapse a little over a month ago, and went through the hell of quitting, again.

"We swore we wouldn't do this to ourselves again!" I gave her the crazy eyes.

"I'm not gonna smoke it, it's a prop. Nothing more," she said, smelling the cigarette and going misty eyed.

I gave her my best *bullshit* look.

Having not gone over the itinerary, I went through my suitcase one more time.

Fitz stood next to me and looked down into my case, "Ya don't think women in the forties wore muumuus, do ya?" she asked.

"I have a black pencil skirt, but the top I brought to wear with it, won't quite fit the bill," my face scrunched up.

"Why, is it a Don Ho shirt?" she lifted some questionable outfits from my bag and shook her head at me. "I have a red silk button up shirt you can wear," Fitz suggested.

I looked down at my *girls*, "We're not exactly the same size, Fitzy."

Yeah, but ya can wear a camisole and leave the buttons across the bust, open! Come on, let me play dress up with ya," she begged.

"I thought we grew out of this," I said, defeated.

"Yay," Fitz clapped her hands.

I had to hand it to her, this might actually work. I looked at myself in the mirror.

"The arms are a little tight," I admitted, trying to pull them down.

"So don't flex," was Fitz's solution.

As we headed down to dinner, Fitz was the smoldering flapper, and I was Mary Astor from the Maltese Falcon…with better hair, thanks to Fitzy.

As we sat, a nice older gentleman in a tuxedo with a green rose in his lapel came to our table.

"I hate to ask you ladies this, but two of our cast members… won't be able to do the show tonight. Would either of you, or both of you, like to help us out?"

"Are they sick?" I showed visible concern about some kind of mad cow breakout.

"Drunk," he said under his breath. "Not everyone can handle Mexico."

I wasn't really the performer type. I liked the idea of just sitting back and watching the show.

"Um, I'm not good at being me," I smiled. "Much less, someone else."

"Ah come on Janie," Fitz folder her hands in pleading manner, "no one knows ya, here. You can just relax and have fun!"

I didn't put *relax* and *in the lime light* in the same category. I was most relaxed being a wallflower.

Fitz jumped up and down with folded hands, her flapper dress doing the *shimmy shimmy* shake.

"You can be the dead girl…no lines?" the nice gentleman shrugged to me.

"Fine," I said, like I was walking to my death.

"You'll be great," Barry said.

Back in the dressing room, we were handed our costumes.

"This is going to be awesome," Fitz said, walking into a private stall. "I've always wanted to try my hand at actin'."

"I have to pee," I shook my head. "I'll be right back."

"You and yer nervous bladder," Fitz mocked.

When I came back to the dressing room, I finally saw my outfit and shook my head.

"Fitz?" I called.

"Yeah," she called from the next stall.

"I don't wanna do this anymore!"

"Why? What's the big deal?"she whined.

"He didn't tell me I would be dressed as a French maid!"

Fitz was quiet for a moment "Ooh, that's gonna look great on ya!" she said looking at the costume I was holding up.

"Not exactly incognito, Fitz! Not to mention, not made for a woman my size."

"Get over it. Who's gonna care?" she asked. "I'm up first. Yer gonna be set on the stage after I make my debut."

I heavy sighed, "Fine."

I could hear Fitz. She only had a few lines. I had to get dressed quickly.

I waited backstage or in this case, behind a curtain on a Seniors Cruise Ship.

"Talk loud," an older gentleman said to me.

"I'm the dead girl," I told him.

"You ate a squirrel?" he cupped his ear, and stared at me like I had gone crazy. "There you go, curtain's down, hurry. Your mark is a big black X," he told me. "Lay down on it!" he yelled, like I was hard of hearing.

I found the big black X and tried to lie down in my tiny skirt. Closing my eyes, I heard the show start again.

"Oh my God, is she dead?" I heard Fitz yell. I tried not to smile at how loud she was talking for the crowd.

An old woman from the crowd, yelled, "What'd she say?"

This wasn't so bad, I thought. I mean all I have to do is…ouch! I thought. It felt like something bit me. I lay still thinking I had imagined the sensation when…ouch! I tried not to call out loud and just lie still. Ouch! I thought as something bit my ass. I needed to scratch, but all eyes were on the stage. I had that feeling, all over my body…an itch-itch here and an itch-itch there. Oh my God, I was going crazy. My face winced as I tried to focus on anything else. Finally, I very discretely rubbed my back, in slow motion, on the ground. It wasn't working, but I had drawn attention…from Fitz.

"It's so hard to believe she's really dead," she scowled down at me, "I almost imagined she moved," she said through a clenched jaw, as the crowd laughed.

The itching was getting worse. A million possibilities ran through my head. Was the costume dirty? Was the last person who wore it, dirty? My face scrunched up at the thought. Did they have bugs? Was I covered in bugs right now?

Fitz gave me a stern warning again, "I'd hate to have to shoot her again, just to make sure," her eyes bugged out at me, as the audience howled and applauded.

"Janie," I heard my name whispered from backstage. I moved my head ever so slightly, and there was Mona…holding a bottle of itching powder. My eyes rounded as she made an itching motion, smiling. She took off running, as I came up off the floor. I scratched a million different body parts, all at once and shivered with the delight only scratching could bring. The crowd roared, thinking that this was all in the script.

"Well, I guess there was no murder after all," Fitz said loudly and angrily, putting her hands on her hips.

"Wanna bet?" I said, and took off after Mona.

She was long gone when I made it to the elevator. Hurrying to my room, I peeled off the costume and jumped in the shower, washing every square inch of my body.

"What the hell happened down there?" Fitz busted through the door.

"Mona," I growled! "She put itching powder in my costume!"

"Are ya kiddin' me? That must have been who I thought was you. I called out yer name, but no one answered. I wonder how she got itching powder?" Fitz queried.

"We're in Mexico," I screamed. "I'm pretty sure if you can get Spanish Fly, you can get itching powder," I roared. "I'm gonna kill her!"

Barry was kind enough to retrieve my clothes from the dressing room and bag up the costume.

"So, she really got ya with itchin' powder? I'll give her this, she's inventive," Barry shook his head.

"Inventive?" Fitz screeched, "It's somethin' a ten year old boy would do!" she paced the three feet of floor she had to move around.

"Yeah, well that woman with the imagination of a ten year old boy just shook my world," I was still itching out of habit.

After the itching stopped, Fitz asked if I wanted to get dinner. I was in a foul mood and had lost my appetite.

As she and Barry left, I thought about calling Cecil, but I hated to call him when I knew I would rant. Plus there was always the chance that HE wouldn't be answering the phone.

An hour later, there was a knock at the door. I wondered if when I opened it, I would get a pie to the face or seltzer water sprayed at me. Cautiously I opened the door, just a sliver.

There was cake. Barry stood before me with a slice of Tiramisu.

"I know ya said ya weren't hungry, but…" he offered me the plate.

Smiling I took the cake from him, "It's my favorite," I said.

"I know," he smiled and walked away.

Morning came and the next port was announced: Cabo San Lucas. I knew Cabo to be a party town, by reputation, alone. Fitz had been here before on a bathing suit shoot, and loved it.

Fitz and Scotty were on the phone doing the *I love and miss you* thing. She even did the baby talk thing that I so seldom heard her do. I couldn't help but laugh when she referred to him as her big-cuddly-wuddly. Every part of me enjoyed who she was with Scotty.

Never being a shorts wearing kind of girl, I opted for another Venice strand find. As I stepped out of the bathroom, Fitz's face squished up, "Are ya gonna wear that?"

I looked down at my dress, "What's wrong with it?" I asked.

"It goes to yer ankles."

"Yeah? So what?" I gave her the palms-up.

"I don't know. I guess I thought you would want to sexy it up a bit, ya know, show off yer legs…or something."

"I don't understand. The other day, at the pool no less, you wanted me to have on more clothes. Now you what? Want me to wear a thong and nipple tape?"

Her eyes rounded "That's not what I'm talkin' about. It's just… Cabo is a sexy town."

My brow raised, "And this is not sexy?" I asked. "Why, what are you wearing?"

When Fitz stepped out of the bathroom, I caught my breath. She always had that pin-up look about her, and knew how to play it up. Fitz had on a skin tight red romper with a thick white belt, cinched at the waist to accentuate her curves, white platform toeless pumps, and big shiny red lips. Yep, next to her, my wardrobe said, "I've had three kids and don't need the added skin damage."

After Fitz applied sunscreen 1000 for her whiter than white skin, we headed down to find something to eat.

Another great spread was on three huge buffet tables. Everything from egg dishes and sides to French pastries and fresh fruit, served with coffee, tea, milk, orange juice or mimosas.

Before we even got seated, here came the rest of the crew. Still minus Mona, no one even asked Pauly how things were going between them. I was happy to see that when Pauly looked at Tovah today, the look was more normal than the weird yearning look he had last night. Maybe the spell had worn off?

Back on the little boat that was to take us to Cabo, I stood trying to breathe again. I was almost ready to start howling, but knew that would alert everyone to my slight panic attack. I quietly howled under my breath and it was enough to get me to the dock.

The shoreline was unbelievable. This was a resort town the way I had always pictured one. Beautifully tanned and half naked bodies walked on the sand. Everyone looked like they were models with perfect hair, glowing white teeth, and hard bodies. I did feel a little squishy, even though I had lost ten pounds since I'd been home from Ireland.

Fitz, of course, got so many head turns, men were getting the *look* from girlfriends. Smart men, still looked, but where quick about it.

As we made our way to the first stop, a bar, Bloody Marys were again ordered for the whole clan.

As I scanned the people walking by, Pauly started pointing out women to Barry.

Barry seemed less than interested in Pauly's picks, though.

"That one," Pauly would say and point.

This was followed by Barry saying, "Nope."

Over and over again, this went on before Pauly said, "Well, ya can't have the one ya want, so ya better pick another."

Fitz's eyes shifted and Barry stared at Pauly. This comment would have been just pushed under the table, if it weren't for the fact that Mum had heard it.

"Who do ya want, son?" Mum asked, raising her glasses to reveal her questioning green eyes.

"No one," Barry said and kicked Pauly under the table.

"No," Mum said, "tell me who he's talkin' about?"

Barry gave a look to Pauly that threatened death.

Pauly catching himself, knowing that this would start Mum's quest to find Barry a mate for his broken heart, said, "That girl" and pointed. A gorgeous Latin woman, in a white thong bikini, was walking up the beach with her huge steroid-created boyfriend.

Mum looked at the woman and said to Barry, "Maybe ya should find one that doesn't have a man," in a tone of warning.

"Ya Barry, maybe ya should," Pauly said.

Fitz's eyes narrowed at both of her brothers.

"Put yer eyes back in yer head," Mum said to Pauly who was still ogling the woman in the white bikini.

"They wear stuff like this because they want ya to look. Plus, it doesn't matter where I get my appetite as long as I eat at home," he told his mother.

"Yeah, and that kind of thinkin' right there, is why ya haven't eaten in months," Mum flared back.

Everyone at the table winced and averted their eyes.

"I still don't get what the big deal is. It's not like I'm gonna cheat," Pauly reasoned.

"Ah, son," Da shook his head, knowing that silence would have been a better option for Pauly to have employed.

"Let me explain it to ya," Mum began. "Every woman, hell, every person…deserves to think that THEY are their partner's appetite. Saying 'I'm a good boy because I eat at home,' is saying nothing more than 'It's okay to cheat in my mind and heart, as long as I don't cheat with my body'. Well, if the mind and heart are where love is made and felt…are ya cheatin' yer partner then?"

None of us said a damn thing.

"Plus, I have to ask," Da turned to Pauly. "Why would you be with someone...who isn't your appetite? Who isn't the one who stirs desire inside of ya? If ya need to look to someone else to find your appetite, doesn't it mean that yer partner is no longer what ya crave?" Da rationalized. "I know that over years, bodies change, we can get overly comfortable, but if you really love someone, for them, for who they are...ya never lose yer appetite for them. And if ya love yer partner, they should never have to question that." Da grabbed Mum's hand and brought it to his lips for a kiss.

Mum's smile sparkled as she returned the kiss to her husband's hand.

Da looked Mum dead in the eye, "Everybody looks...but YOU have always been...and will ALWAYS be...my appetite."

Da wasn't much of a talker, that was true enough, but when he spoke, all ears listened.

I couldn't help but wonder about the "months" comment, Mum had made. If it was in fact "months", there had to be more to the story of him and Mona than I knew.

Cabo had so many fun things to do. It was morning, but it was still hard to think of what we wanted to do, vs. what we had time to do. Fitz wanted to go shopping, this was a given. I couldn't help but wonder if one of the things she should purchase was another suitcase, for all of her new clothes. I was burnt out on shopping and wanted to do something I didn't usually do at home.

Barry and Pauly went to go get more drinks, while the rest of us looked over brochures. Looking at one for horseback riding, I couldn't help but think of Cecil and his horse, Babygirl. She had taken me on quite a ride while I was in Ireland (a ride that ended with me doing a *Superman* impression, into the lake). We did finally create a bond, and I got to ride her with no scary-ending. I missed her, almost as much as I missed Cecil.

I pondered what I would look like, riding down the beach. In my mind, I saw myself, riding in slow motion as the wind whipped through my hair and the sun shined down on my golden skin: a picture I would love to send to Cecil. But then reality broke in and I saw myself again in slow motion falling off the horse, face down in sand, then spitting out a mouthful of mud. Let's just say that vision wasn't one I wanted him to see…again.

Tovah piped up from down at the end of the table, "Well, that's what I'm doin'," she said.

Mum and Aunt Marble both made oohing sounds.

"What are ya doin," Benny asked his sister. She turned the brochure to us: Boat Parasailing.

My eyes rounded, "Really?" I asked.

"Sure, why not. It looks like a blast, doesn't it?" she finished her drink.

I didn't enjoy flying…or the ocean, and wasn't huge on heights. It seemed like this would be a phobia tri-fecta for me. "I can't wait to watch you," I said.

"Watch?" Tovah questioned.

"Um, yeah," I offered.

"Oh kid, you're not gonna do it with me?" she looked confused.

"I'm not really big on…everything that entails," I pointed to the paper in her hand.

Tovah laughed, "What are you afraid of, kid?"

I thought about it then said, "Same as the last time you asked…dying."

"Is that all?" Tovah laughed. "Look, if you were to croak, it would be over. No big deal, done. There would be nothing more to worry about then, right?"

I nodded to her with rounded eyes.

"Well, if you're gonna be afraid…be afraid of breaking a leg, or your back. Be afraid of the things you'd have to live with, if ya didn't die. Dying is easy," she gave me a wave of her hand, "plus, no side effects from death," she laughed.

I was trying to see the logic in her thinking, to apply it to my fears. Nope, still didn't want to die and I said as much.

Her reply actually made me think, "But do you want to live?" she asked. "I told you before, fear of death, only keeps you from living…you're still going to die."

This rolled around in my head. What good would it do me, to live to be ninety-nine, but not have any stories to tell?

Tovah was watching me think, "Remember kid, it's the things we live through that make us strong. And what you choose to do, to achieve, to conquer, is as strong as you'll ever be. You can spend your time safe, rocking on a front porch, or you can go for the strength that only adventure brings. Your choice."

It wasn't really a dare, per say, posed by Tovah that got my ass put in a harness. It was me testing myself. As my dress was hiked up to fasten the crotch and leg straps, my insides were turning to mush. I found myself thinking about the horseback riding that I had thought was too unsafe for me to indulge in.

I heard the boat engine start and was just about to back out, as it sped away from the dock. Open water was right before us. The gentleman who had made sure all my harnessing was correct was standing near giving last minute instructions. I remember him saying, "Do you understand?" I nodded, but really hadn't heard anything other than the blood pounding in my ears. I wasn't alone, though. Tovah and I were going tandem. As my breathing started to feel shallow and panicked, she reached her hand out to mine and said, "You got this, kid!"

Off the end of the boat, we were released. Up into the air the parachute pulled us. In my mind, I screamed FUCK, but all that emitted from me was a stifled squeak. I closed my eyes and tried to think of everything but plummeting to my death. I still had Tovah's hand in mine and realized that I was applying a great amount of pressure, and I tried to release her from my death grip.

"Squeeze as much as you need to, kid," she yelled. "But you need to you open your eyes. You're missing this!"

I slowly opened my eyes and saw the whole coastline; green trees that looked like tiny emerald dots, ships in the distance, huge rocks that were now dwarfed and people no bigger than ants on the beach. If I turned my head, I could just make out the whole brood of Fitzpatrick's, on the dock, cheering us on. A smile stretched my mouth back as tears filled my eyes. I was still scared; my heart was still pounding out of my chest. But I also had this amazing feeling of facing a great fear, and kicking its ass. Not quite fearlessly, mind you, but I was doing it none the less.

I turned my smiling face to Tovah, and she beamed with pride. As we descended, being pulled back to the boat, I was a little worried. I had a vision of JAWS jumping out of the water, and grabbing us like we were squeaky toys. But once I was back in the boat, all I could think of was what I had seen and done. The mental image would stay with me forever.

Tovah gave my hand a squeeze, "Feels good to live, doesn't it?"

I had to agree…and I had to pee.

As the boat returned us to the dock, all eyes were smiling.

"I can't believe ya fuckin' did it," Fitz grabbed me and put a kiss on my cheek.

"Like a pro," Tovah offered, not showing anyone my fingernail indents in the back of her hand.

The Fitzpatrick's had known me for over twenty years. And for as long as they had, I had been the overly modest, phobia-bridled girl they loved. It was nice to have them with me while I faced some of my biggest fears. Maybe, they were part of the reason I could? Well, them and Tovah, who had quickly become one of my favorite people, I thought as I watched her.

Barry was grinning from ear to ear as he took me into a bear hug, and spun me around. "You are amazin'," he said, and kissed my cheek.

Putting me back on my feet, I noticed that all the Fitzpatrick women seemed to be looking at me differently. Fitz, Mum and Aunt Marble, cocked their heads, while Tovah gave me a one sided grin.

After I peed, Fitz wanted to do some shopping. I wanted to wrestle grizzly bears and spit in a rattlesnake's face, I felt so empowered! But I figured clothes shopping with Fitzy, took some big balls, too.

Fitz's phone rang as she, Barry, Pauly and I walked up the boardwalk. Squealing with delight, I didn't even have to ask her who it was. I tried not to feel the green-eyed-monster creep in. As happy as I was for Fitzy, I missed Cecil badly. I also had so many questions that I didn't get a chance to clear up. For someone whose brain was always going, this just kept it well fed.

"I love you, more!" Fitz said with a cute grin. "I want that more, too!" she added to his comment, raising her brow.

Barry saw me give a heavy sigh.

"Ya still haven't talked to Cecil?" he asked.

"Not really," I admitted.

"What's the problem? I mean, why aren't you two connectin'?"

I hated that he put it that way. It wasn't that we weren't connected…was it?

"We're just having a hard time between our schedules, for us to get some time to really speak."

"Hmm," Barry, bit his bottom lip. "Well, ya better make the time. It's important in a relationship," he nodded.

It wasn't that I wasn't making the time, or him for that matter. It just seemed like a lot of things went crazy every time we spoke. "I know."

"I hate to see you sad," when he said this, he avoided eye contact.

I knew this was true. He wasn't like Pauly, where everything was a joking matter. Barry was the sensitive one, the one who had always been my protector, even if I had never actually given him the title. Since we were young, this was who he was to me.

"It'll be okay," I gave him a weak smile. "We just need to find our groove."

"I don't mean to be nosey…and you can tell me if it's none of my business…" he shook his head at me.

My eyes slit at him, "Hmm, starting a sentence that way is designed to put someone on guard," I laughed.

"Well, Pauly said somethin'…and I never know with Pauly if what he heard is really what happened…or even if he has half the story correct…"

He was rambling and nervous, "Just go ahead and ask," I told him.

"Well, Pauly told me…that Cecil and you…haven't…been intimate," he turned his eyes to mine. "I know it's none of my business, but…" he shook his head some more.

Fitz was about ten steps behind us, still talking to Scotty. I looked back, knowing she was the only one who would have told Pauly about my *lack of*, but why?

Barry wallowed in my silence for a moment then said, "Ya know what, it was wrong of me to ask ya. I'm sorry, Janie."

"No, it's not that. It's just," my face squished up, "I wish sometimes that I had…had just had thrown caution to the wind and allowed myself to let the moment take me."

"But ya didn't?" Barry looked sidelong at me.

I shook my head, "No…I didn't."

"Can I ask why?" Barry stopped walking, so I did as well.

I sighed again, "It has to mean something to me, is what I would have told you."

"And…it wouldn't have?" he was trying to understand.

"No, I believe it would have…I know it would have," I admitted. "But…?"

"But what?" he wanted to know.

"But, I was leaving the next morning."

"Right?"

"Honestly…I think I was afraid it would…make me miss him more." I now knew that this was what I was really afraid of. I had at one point thought that I didn't because I was still the girl who needed it to mean something. Now I was sure, between Cecil and I it would always mean something.

"Ah," Barry nodded his head. "So…you regret not…ya know?"

It took me a moment, "Actually…I do. I mean, even if nothing ever came from our night…together…I don't think I would have regretted it,…more than I regret not doing…it."

Barry let out his own sigh, "So…ya are happy, then? I mean, with the way things are goin'?"

I had to laugh, "Well, not at the moment, but I'm hopeful it will get better, soon. When our timing is on, I'm happier."

"Timin'…everything comes down to timin'," Barry nodded.

Fitz came up between us, "What's goin' on?" Her eyes bounced from Barry to me to Barry again.

"Barry was just asking how things were going on the Cecil front," I told her.

"Were ya now?" she asked her brother. Her tone was one of concern, as she gave Barry's shoulder a squeeze. "I'm sure Janie and Cecil are fine, brother. Don't ya worry yerself about it," she added.

I furrowed my brow.

"I was just catching up…checkin' on her. It's what I do," Barry told his little sister.

Fitz nodded, "Yes…it is."

After a couple hours of shopping, we were supposed to meet the rest of the Fitzpatrick's, Benny and Tovah for lunch at a place named El Corazon. Walking in, the brood was not only seated and waiting for us but appeared to be on their second or possibly even third round of drinks.

We joined the family at two long tables that had been put

together to make one large one. The family was listening to another one of Tovah's stories and they were laughing out loud.

"So then when the police arrived, I told em', 'You can either let us grab our clothes, or you can put us in the back of your patrol car naked, your choice'. I'm sure that usually when they get these calls, it's teenagers," Tovah grinned. "Not this time though. Scared the hell out of 'em."

I was filled in on how Tovah and a few other people from her retired living community had gone down to a private pond and done some skinny dipping.

"New York's hot in the summer," she explained. "I made it through hot flashes for eight years. If I don't ever have to feel that way again, I won't."

I couldn't help but laugh. Her facial expression and explanation were so matter-of-fact. It was like she just didn't care what anyone thought of her. Not even what I'm sure was a pretty caught-off-guard police officer.

Benny was beaming. You could see how much he loved and enjoyed his sister.

Aunt Marble following suit, also told her own skinny dipping story, which included Mum. I snorted as I pictured the two of them, holding onto their *girls* and running down the beach at night, being chased by a horny seal.

Covering my mouth, I noticed the way Fitz was staring at me. I cocked my head at her, then gave a small shake, 'no'.

Fitz began to grin, "We have a story about skinny dippin', too, don't we Janie?" she laughed.

My cheeks began to flush just thinking about it. "Oh they don't want to hear about that!" I assured everyone.

"The hell I don't," Pauly said.

Barry nudged his brother.

Mum's brows lifted to me, "You went skinny-dippin'?" she asked with an astonished look on her face.

"Tell yer Mum all about it!" Aunt Marble said.

Tovah leaned back and locked her fingers behind her head, "You have my full attention, kid," she gave me a wide smile.

"Well, actually," Fitz began, "Janie didn't plan on skinny-dippin." Fitz's evil red-headed-fairy grin was in full effect.

I let out a sigh. "No…I really didn't."

"So what happened?" Pauly asked.

"Go ahead, Fitz," I told her.

"It was during Indian Summer," Fitz recalled. "It was so hot that even after the sun set it was still sticky miserable outside. Janie and I were still in high school and were drivin' back from a party."

I nodded, yep, this was how it started.

"Well, we decided to stop at Hermosa Beach…to cool off, like ya do," Fitz grinned at Tovah, using her wording.

Everyone nodded.

"Well we already had our suits on, because the party we had been at was a pool party. So, in our suits, we ran down the shore. I told Janie that I was gonna go skinny-dippin', but she wasn't havin' any part of that," Fitz laughed.

I shook my head.

"We were probably in the water for all of ten minutes, when a huge wave, that of course we didn't really see in the dark," she winked, "smashed and slammed us both. When we floated to the top…well I was supposed to be topless. Janie on the other hand, didn't expect to be."

I nodded at the memory.

"Ya have a hard time keepin' yer *girls* in check, don't ya?" Pauly asked.

I shot him a shitty grin. "Not by choice," I added.

Tovah raised her glass to me.

Fitz kept going, "So, I was headin' back to the sand; I figured I'd run back to the car and grab her shirt. She's so modest, that even on a barren beach she wouldn't hold the *girls*, and just walk back to the car with me. So I got to the car, and a cop stopped me. I guess I was out after curfew and he threatened to either give me a ticket, or follow me home and rat me out to my parents. Either way, he wanted me off the beach and right now!"

My head was shaking faster.

"Well, I figured I'd pull away, he'd follow, I'd lose him and come back for Janie," Fitz was beginning to laugh.

"I take it that's not what happened?" Da said.

"Oh no," Fitz shook her head. "I pulled away, but the cop didn't move. When I got a block away and still no headlights behind me, I parked on a side street and spied on him. I guessed he was takin' his lunch break. And this whole time, Janie's down in the dark water, just floatin her half-naked self."

I had to giggle at the memory. "I remembered thinking the whole time, 'where the hell is she'?"

"Well, an hour goes by and the cop hasn't moved. But then I realize, he really hasn't moved!" her eyes rounded. "Like not at all. He was asleep! Poor Janie is still stuck in the water," Fitz is rolling with laughter now. "So I get back to my car and grab her shirt. My intention is to creep past the cop, by goin' around the next block over…avoid him all together. The problem is, from where his car is parked, he'd be able to see us on the sand for at least a block or two down shore. If he woke, there was no way he wouldn't see us."

"So you were just floatin' in the water the whole time?" Barry was trying not to laugh.

"Not exactly," Fitz smiled. "Turns out, I walk back down to the shoreline, as stealthily as I could, to go save her, ya know? But I can't find her! I can't very well yell out, or the cop will hear me, right?"

Now my cheeks began to burn.

"So I catch her in my sights, and she's stompin' up the shore, so pissed it shows in her walk. She stomps straight toward the cop car. I'm runnin' as fast as I can, in sand, to try and stop her. Right before she walks directly at the police car, I get to her and very quickly and very quietly, try to explain why she had been left bobbin' in the water for well over an hour."

Now, I shook my head and covered my face with my hands

"So ya have to picture her," Fitz is forcing her words through her laughter, "the most modest girl in the world. She's all pruned-up and PISSED OFF. She stomps over to the cop car and yells, 'Wake the fuck up'!"

I started laughing at Fitz's impression of a pissed-off me. She stood and stomped for the family.

"The cop looks stunned, but then there's a young woman, holdin' her tits, angry-screamin at him. "You and your damn nap", she yells. "I've been floatin' in the fuckin' water, screamin' for help! But no, yer fast asleep, and on the fuckin' job, no less!" Fitz could barely breathe. "She yelled SO LOUD," Fitz recalled.

"You didn't!" Barry was shocked.

Fitz continued, "So then, Janie stomps off. She doesn't take the shirt from me. She doesn't even know where I parked the car and doesn't even care. I think she was gonna walk back to Manhattan."

"What did the officer do?" Da asked.

"Well, he turns his shocked face to me, and I tell him, 'We may both want to forget this ever happened'. I skirted his car and ran after Janie. When I caught up to her, half a block away or so, I tried to apologize and explained that the cop had threatened me with a ticket fer curfew. So what does Janie do?"

"Oh God," I said

She looks back at the cop, who was still starin', right? She grabs the ties on the bottom's of her suit and does this," she made a pulling motion.

"Nah, ya did not!" Barry was grinning.

"Oh, but she did! Janie turned around, bent clean over and B.A.'d the cop," Fitz was almost crying. "Even from as far away as we were, we could see his body stiffen and his head snap back. We started runnin' our asses off, thinkin' he was comin' after us. And Janie…Janie was buck-ass naked! But she was SOOO PISSED, she didn't care."

The whole table was cracking up and clapping.

"I'm startin' to like ya more and more," Pauly said. "I would have paid to see that!"

To this comment, Barry shot Pauly a look.

"It wasn't one of my finer moments," I put my palms up.

"I beg to differ," Tovah raised her glass to me.

"He's a Hermosa cop?" Mum asked. "Didn't ya ever see him again?"

"Oh yeah," I nodded my head. "He gave some kind of anti-drug assembly at the school. We looked at each other and there was a clear moment of recognition," I remembered. "We both kind of bobbed our heads at each other and then looked away quickly. He's retired now."

"I don't know," Pauly started, "sounds like I would enjoy pissed-off-Janie."

"Unless she's pissed off at you," Fitz made it sound more like a warning than an observation.

The sun was well past high noon. We were trying to decide whether to eat dinner on the ship or hit a restaurant off of the boardwalk. It was so beautiful in Cabo and I kind of wanted to see one of the many nightclubs it had to offer. Not that I was a huge nightclub kind of person, but when in Rome…?

All of us decided to go to the nightclub and at least check it out. It was pretty much like all the nightclubs in Hollywood (except half of the music was in Spanish and half was in English.) Drinks were the same, and judging by the looks Fitzy was getting, men were the same.

Benny, Aunt Marble, Tovah and Mum, all hit the dance floor, while the rest of us camped at our table. Mum danced her way over, giving Da the eyes. When she held out her hand to him, there was no hesitation. Into the middle of the dance floor they walked. As if by divine intervention, a slow song began to play. I couldn't understand the words but it didn't matter. I was more interested in watching one of my favorite couples.

Da held Mum close then spun her out only to pull her back into his arms. The look on their faces as they stared deeply into each other's eyes, to me…that was what true love looked like. I saw Fitzy dab the corner of her eye. She felt it, too.

"Oh, this shit is so mushy!" Pauly whined. "I see enough of this at home."

"Let me see if I get this straight," Barry began, "yer upset because our parents are in love and show the love they have fer each other?"

"No! I'm not a douche!" he shot Barry a look. "It's because it's always been crammed down our throats."

Fitz furrowed her brow, "What the hell are ya talkin' about?"

"Not everyone is goin' to have that kind of love in their life," Pauly shook his head. "Tell me I'm wrong?" he said to Barry.

"Maybe not. So?" he did a palms-up.

"So…because of Mum and Da, we've been programmed to think that whoever we choose…we'll have that!" he pointed to Da dipping Mum.

"So…you are unhappy…that our parents ARE happy?" Fitz squinted at her brother.

"No, dammit! I'm upset because we all deserve that. I may never have that and I want that! Because of them, I know it exists. How come it exists for them…but not me?" he slurred a little.

None of us had been babysitting Pauly and right now, it seemed like maybe we should have been.

"How come I couldn't have found a woman like Mum?" he asked.

All of our eyes rounded at him.

"Ya know what I mean! Why couldn't I find a woman who was

secure in herself? Why couldn't I find a woman who just…went with the flow?" he shook his head.

"I'm gonna say this," Barry began, "and if it needs repeatin' when yer sober, so be it."

"Go ahead," Pauly raised his chin.

"Are ya like Da?" Barry asked.

"What do you mean? In what way?" Pauly looked a little slow on the follow.

"I mean, do ya treat Mona, the way Da treats Mum?" Barry gave him questioning eyes, "Do ya give her the same respect, Da gives Mum? Do ya do the same things fer her? Do ya think of her as yer best friend? Do ya put her before all others?"

"Well, not all the time," Pauly admitted and rolled his eyes.

"But Da does!" Barry nodded to his drunk brother. "Part of the reason she's such a good woman, is because Da has been such a good man. And it works both ways. Ya can't expect a woman to give ya her all, the very best of herself, while yer puttin' her on the back burner, and makin' her think she doesn't matter."

"Here here," Fitz raised her glass.

Pauly thought about it before saying, "It's just exhausting."

"Then she's not worth ya being exhausted? Ya want yer woman to feel and act secure…make her feel that way!" Barry offered. "Give her no reason to question. If ya want a relationship like them," he pointed to his parents, "ya have to put in the work…the effort. And, it shouldn't be such an 'EFFORT', if you really love each other."

Barry said all of this with more passion than an outsider with an opinion. He knew something about the *Mona thing* that I didn't. For that matter, so did Mum, I assumed from her comments today. That whole 'where you get your appetite' thing? She was schooling her boy. This whole conversation had gotten a little too deep for a nightclub in Mexico.

Mum headed back to the table and whispered something in

Barry's ear. Pointing, she directed his attention to a beautiful woman on the dance floor. I couldn't hear what Barry was saying to her, but he shook his head, 'no'. I guessed that Mum's set-ups were already rearing their ugly head.

When Mum kissed Barry's cheek and walked away, Fitz cocked her head at him, "She's pretty."

"Yep," Barry nodded.

"Maybe ya should at least go dance with her," Fitz reasoned. "I mean it's just a dance."

"Yer right," Barry said. He turned to me and offered me his hand. "Would ya like to?"

"Wouldn't ya rather dance with the lady who apparently doesn't have a man?" Fitz said through clenched teeth.

Barry smiled, "Nope."

As I stood, Fitz gave me a weird look. "What? Like you said, it's just a dance."

As we headed to the dance floor, I couldn't help but wonder what the hell was wrong with Fitzy. Did she really think I was still carrying a torch for Barry? Yes, he was still an attractive man, but that ship (that had never even been pulled in to port), had sailed. I needed to make her see that I could spend time with Barry, be close to him, and it wasn't an issue for me.

On the floor, we did a little boogie. I basically bopped along and tried not to make finger guns. The fact that I was surrounded by no one who knew me, or would ever see me again, helped me cut loose a little. I was relaxed, not just from the Margaritas, but by anonymity.

When the song ended and another began, I started off the dance floor. Barry reached out and caught my hand and my attention. Turning, he motioned me back toward him with a grin. A slow song was playing as I grinned back and stepped into his space.

Smiling, he pulled me closer. Taking my hand in his, he

moved his body against mine. I could smell his Polo cologne, always a favorite of mine. My eyes closed, while we rocked back and forth. Laying my head on his shoulder, I sighed. It was nice to be close to him and not have that awkward feeling. I had been a nervous wreck around him for almost as long as I could remember, but now? Now I was comfortable, not the bumbling idiot I had been.

When the song ended, I pulled back and he kissed my cheek. It wasn't a quick kiss. It lingered a bit, but was still innocent, just two old friends. I wrapped my arms around him and gave him a squeeze, "Thank you for the dance," I said.

I turned to walk back to the table and there was Mum, Marble and Fitz, mouths gaping. Tovah stood nearby with that same look as before. Kind of a half smile pulling up one cheek.

"What?" I asked the ladies.

Fitz gave Mum a weak smile.

"Nothin' darling," Mum said and then walked around the table to hug me.

Soon enough it was time to head back to the ship. Pauly was leaning heavily on Barry and Da for support. Mumbling, he said something about 'not bein' a good man', to his father. I tried not to overhear the conversation. But Pauly had drunk man's volume happening.

"She had every right," Pauly slurred. "Those other women… they meant nothin'," he shook his head.

I hoped it sounded worse than it was, because it sounded like Pauly had cheated. And it sounded like it was several different women. I have to say, that would make any woman crazy and most women would have been long gone. I liked disliking Mona better when I didn't feel sorry for her.

I shot a questioning look to Fitz.

"Later," she said under her breath.

Back in our room, I gave her the palm up, "What the hell?" I asked.

"From what Pauly told me…"

I cut her off, "You mean what you should have told me?" I flared.

"You," her face squished up. "What do you have to do with it?"

My eyes rounded, "I think because his wife has threatened to make my life a living hell, because of whatever he's done or she thinks he'll do!"

Fitz thought about it, "Yer right. You probably should have been told."

I nodded, "Ya think?"

"Okay, I'll tell ya. Calm yerself down! I guess Mona was gaining weight…" she began.

"Where? When?" I asked surprised.

"I know, I couldn't tell either, but she was feeling less than attractive the last few months."

"Okay," I said.

"Well, every time Pauly tried to, ya know, get intimate, Mona would shoot him down."

I nodded.

"I guess he started…" she looked away.

"What? An affair?" I asked.

"No, of course not! He started watchin' porn," her eyes widened.

"O-kay," I was trying to understand. "Was it weird porn?"

"What do ya mean weird porn?" Fitz shook her head.

"I don't know," I shrugged. "I mean was it like, animal porn?"

"What?" Fitz made the disgusted face.

"Was it gay porn?" my eyes rounded. "Because I would think her husband watching gay porn, might freak her out a little."

"What the hell are ya talkin' about? It was porn, normal porn!" her brow furrowed.

Of all the ways a man could get off on another woman, porn was the least to worry about in my opinion. So I wasn't following the problem, unless it was excessive. "Did he become like an addict, or something? I'm really not getting the big deal."

"That's cause ya won't let me finish the damn story!" she huffed.

"Sorry, go on."

"Well, ya knew Mona went back to work at the advertizing agency…"

Actually I didn't, but wasn't about to interrupt her again, so I nodded.

"Well, she had her presentation on her computer. At a huge business meeting for her company, trying to land an account…she queued up her computer," Fitz's mouth puckered.

It only took me a moment before my eyes rounded, "No!"

Fitz nodded, "Yep. On a screen damn near as big as a movie theater. The porno played…right where he left off apparently."

"Oh shit!" I added.

"So…she was humiliated…in a room full of colleagues and a potential client, which they didn't get, of course," she shook her head. "But that was only the half of it."

"Damn, there's more?"

"She was fired! The company said that they didn't need, or want anyone who could make a mistake like that."

"But he said, 'all those other women'? What did he mean by that?"

"Well, not only was she humiliated about what happened, she went to the dark place inside, thinkin' she wasn't as hot as the women on the screen, or he'd be findin' ways to be with her. So now…all of those other women that he gawks at like a prepubescent boy, no less, now they're a threat in her eyes. Every woman he looks at, is looked at as a threat."

"Wow. That must have been really embarrassing." As horrible as Mona had been to me...I still felt kind of sorry for her.

"Right?" Fitz said. "It's one thing to know your man has to look *outside* to get turned on. That in itself can be a woundin' thought. But it's a slap in the face for everyone else to know it, too. So, then the crush thing with you, and then him stayin' at yer house..." she let the sentence just hang there in the air.

I nodded. I got it. Even though Pauly had never been anything thing but an obnoxious brother toward me, I could see where her mind went. "Maybe I should talk to her tomorrow? Try and clear the air?"

"I don't see how it could hurt. I mean what's she gonna do, hate ya more?" Fitz grinned.

13

IT COULD ALWAYS BE WORSE

I called Cecil first thing in the morning, but he didn't answer. Listening to his voice message made my heart ache. I left the generic message of "I miss you".

Fitz's conversation with Scotty was getting a little risqué, so I decided to go down to breakfast without her.

In the dining hall, I searched out Mona. I wasn't looking forward to talking to her, but figured if there was even a slight chance it could make things better, it was worth a try.

In front of the fresh fruit (which I noticed was the only thing on her plate) she stood. In her gauzy white dress with her small stature she could have been mistaken for a child. The thought of revenge, was *creeping in* as I remembered all the crap I *owed* her. I tempered my vindictiveness with a renewed attempt at understanding her personal hell.

As she turned, we were face to boob. Her glare was unmistakable. If she could have killed me with her eyes, she would have.

"Can we talk?" I asked.

"I don't see what we have to talk about? You do know I hate

you, right?" Her facial expression never changed. She said this the way someone might say they hated broccoli. Not really passionately, but definite.

"Believe me, you've made that very obvious over the years," I told her.

"So what exactly do we need to talk about?"

"Look, you have the wrong idea about me," I told her.

"You're an attention whore who likes to show people your boobs," she gave me a forced smile and a head shake.

"I assure you, I am no whore," I said honestly, as passersby glanced at me. "And the boob thing…that was an accident."

"Right, I'm sure it was," she said straight faced. "I heard you also flashed Barry. Should I let the other Fitzpatrick men know when they can expect to see your tits?"

I forced a smile, "Well, thanks to you posting that video on my feed, I'm sure they already have," I had to reel back my anger. "Look, it was an accident. Both of them!" I blushed, thinking about the Barry thing. "You've never taken the time to get to know me but I'm really modest," I told her.

Mona's eyes rolled so hard, I thought they could see behind her for a moment.

"I'm not lying. I am extremely modest…and a little more insecure than I'd like to be. Okay, a lot more insecure than I'd like to be," I admitted. "Seriously, try and imagine what it feels like for me…standing next to Fitz all the time. For God sakes," I shook my head, "I feel…invisible sometimes."

She looked like she was considering everything I had said. "You're a little too tall to be invisible, don't you think?"

"Believe me, I'm aware," I told her. "It's another one of those things that used to make me really uncomfortable in my own skin."

A moment passed as she thought about what I was saying. I could only hope she could see my sincerity.

"Well…Pauly did say the same thing…that is was an accident," she let out a heavy breath.

"Seriously, he didn't know I was in the shower. And he was just as shocked when he walked in, as I was," I explained.

I watched her eyes slit and her head snap back, "What are you talking about?"

Oh shit, was what went through my head. Abort! Abort! When Pauly said he CAME CLEAN about EVERYTHING, what the hell had he meant?

"Ummm," I stalled.

"Did this happen…when he stayed the night with you?" Mona questioned.

She was only five foot tall, but the look on her face, made me a little scared. *Hell hath no fury*, was booming in my head. "When he stayed the night AT my house," I corrected.

"What happened, now?" she stepped forward and turned her ear to me. I took a step back. "He walked in on you…in the shower," she raised her voice.

"It really wasn't his fault," I tried to defend her husband.

"No, I'm sure it wasn't," she took another step. "Why didn't you lock the door?"

"I, ugh, didn't think about it at the time," I stepped back again as well. If I wasn't mistaking, her right eye was twitching.

"So," all kinds of crazy was showing, as her eye and now her cheek, twitched uncontrollably, "you, tits galore," she took another step toward me, "you didn't even think about locking the door?"

"I didn't. I…" I shook my head, "I rarely have company that isn't Fitz or my mother!" I stared down into the face that was contorting with rage. Both of her fists were curled into white knuckled balls.

"You," she hissed, "you have NO IDEA…how much hell I will rain down upon you!" She made the weird hand symbol again then twitched away from me back toward her room.

As I stared after her all I could think was, that went way better in my head.

I found my seat and poured myself a cup of coffee. I had been willing to forgive and forget how awful Mona had treated me for years. I had been so close, that I could almost feel her changing her opinion of me. Or at least she seemed to be considering the possibility that I wasn't a complete whore who wanted her husband. What the hell had Pauly meant when he said he 'came clean about everything', WTF was he talking about, if not the shower thing?

Fitzy walked up, but I didn't even notice, I was so lost in my thoughts.

"Why the hell do ya look like that?"

"Huh?" I noticed Fitz was there and speaking.

"You look…weird. What's wrong with ya?"

"I think I just signed my death warrant. And not just mine," my eyes were huge, "Pauly's too."

"What are ya babblin' about?" Fitz sat next to me.

"I tried to talk to Mona," I stared straight ahead.

"Oh shit, we better find Pauly," she said. But just as she did, Barry and Pauly, wearing a pair of very dark glasses, entered the dining hall.

As they got closer to the table, Barry stopped in front of me and waved his hand in my path of vision. "Janie? Ya okay? You don't look so good."

Fitz answered, "She just talked to Mona."

Pauly pulled his glasses down, "What the hell did ya say?" he asked, panicked.

"You said you came clean…about everything," I added.

"Oh shit," Pauly shook his head. "What did ya tell her?"

"I told her that you walking in on me in the shower…was an accident," I still stared at nothing.

"Ya didn't tell Mona about the shower incident?" Barry questioned his brother.

"No, and I didn't think she'd be dumb enough to say anything about it either," he pointed at me.

Fitz was about to come to my defense, when Barry popped out of his seat.

"Don't ya dare call her that! Especially when ya made it sound like ya came clean, when ya obviously didn't. This is on you," his voice raised. "This is all on you. And until ya accept responsibility for the shit you've done, ya have no right to say a damn thing to anyone. And ya better never say a bad thing about Janie again."

Barry was hot under the collar, and it drew my attention away from the abyss. I turned my stare to Barry. His face was flushed and his eyes glistened with fire.

Fitz stared at Barry like she had been scolded, too.

I wasn't sure if I should say anything, but I told Barry, "Thank you."

Barry and Pauly stared at each other. It looked like Pauly was going to say something smart assed, but then he said, "Yer right," Pauly held his hung-over head as he took a seat. "This is my fault. I should have told her…and I shouldn't have made it sound like I had told her everything she needed to know. Fuck," he shook his head.

"She's gonna kill us," I concluded.

"She's not gonna do a damn thing to ya," Fitz said, "because Pauly, is goin' to go and take ya out of the equation."

"So it's okay if she kills me?" Pauly asked.

"There is a difference," Fitz practically yelled. Eyes shot in our direction. "You are the only one who did anything wrong…and the rest of us, are sufferin' for yer bad decisions. Personally, I don't appreciate it. And to be honest, I'm not prepared to continue to be so damned understandin'!"

"I have a question, what did you come clean about?" I asked.

"About filmin' ya in the pool. It was an accident," he said.

"But walkin' in on her in the shower wasn't?" Barry was still breathing through his nose like a bull.

"It…was," Pauly recalled the moment and looked off into space, grinning.

Fitz's eyes narrowed at her brother, "You do get that this is probably not the best time to be jokin', right?"

"Jesus…you two are so uptight," he said to Fitz and Barry. "Yes, it was an accident," he smiled at Barry. "A really lovely accident," he added.

"See, stuff right there, is gonna get ya popped in the mouth!" Barry warned his brother.

I turned questioning eyes to Barry, but Fitz looked away.

Pauly smiled from ear to ear, "Now why would ya want to do that, little brother?"

Barry wasn't quick to answer, "Because it's rude…and unnecessary."

"Who's it rude to? My wife isn't here…Janie knows I'm kidding. Even Fitzy didn't say a thing. Was it rude to you, little brother? Why does my jokin' bother ya so?" he taunted.

"Never ya mind," Barry eyes flashed again.

Pauly downed a shot of Bushmills and headed off to find Mona. Barry, Fitz and I said a silent prayer for him. I would have prayed to a patron saint, if I knew which one was in charge of protecting assholes.

Barry took the seat next to me and reached out his hand to mine, "Everything will be okay," he smiled and gave my hand a squeeze.

"Yeah, like Fitz said, Mona already hates me. How much worse can that get, right?" I let out a long held breath, remembering the itching powder and video. Had she already done her worst?

I couldn't help but notice that Barry didn't remove his hand from on top of mine. I wasn't the only one who noticed, either.

Fitz made a face and then asked Barry if he'd like to get in the buffet line.

"No, I'm gonna stay here," he removed his hand. "I want Janie to see the video of her parasailing."

"You took a video," I perked up.

Barry's smile stretched across his face, "Aye," he nodded and moved closer so we could both stare into his phone screen.

Fitz stood, just staring at us.

"Aren't you going to go get food?" I asked.

"I ugh, I ugh…" she looked across the room to the three long buffet tables. "Um, yeah," she walked away.

Barry had the video all ready, "Ya can't tell it's you, except for when ya pull away and return to the dock."

I smiled, "I'm just surprised I actually did it!"

Barry turned his eyes to me, "I'm not. Yer braver than ya give yerself credit for."

I'm not sure why (he's always been sweet to me), but the way he was looking at me, reminded me of the time I almost kissed him. That feeling I remembered, that lost moment in time, replayed. I had been so close. All I had to do was find my balls and just do it. Just lean in…and throw caution to the wind. Right before I could, I was attacked by a crazed woman, a *setup* Mum had arranged against Barry's will.

At the time I was in shock. Later, I told myself that it was a sign. I wasn't supposed to kiss Barry. I wasn't supposed to lay our friendship, not to mention Fitz's and the whole family's, on the line. I let out a sigh. Truth was I was just grateful I hadn't put him in the uncomfortable position of having to say, "I don't feel that way about you." I was also glad he didn't know how I once felt. That would be utter humiliation.

I dropped my eyes to the screen and he pressed play. There I was, high in the sky, wondering if that was how birds felt on their first flight; scared, but elated…free.

"There's no sound?" I asked. "I wasn't sure, but I thought I screamed at one point."

"Oh, I don't think my audio was workin', I'm sorry," he told me.

I shook my head, "No, it's great. That was a great day! Hey, can you send it to me. I'd like to post it or my mother will never believe I did it," I laughed.

"Umm...yeah, or I could post it to yer page? That would probably be easier," he suggested.

"I'd love that! Thank you."

Barry worked it all out on his phone and posted it for me. I was happy to let him do this, since I was technologically impaired. Even a smart phone wasn't smart enough for the likes of me.

Fitz came back with a full plate and saw my smile, "I see yer feelin better," she gave me a weird look.

"I am, Barry helped me take my mind off all the B.S.," I winked at him.

"That's just great," Fitz forced a painted smile.

"What's that face?" I asked.

"Nothin'!" she answered. "They were out of bacon...ya know how I love bacon."

Our next port rang out over the ship's loudspeaker: "Ferries will be leaving for our next port, Mazatlan, every two hours. Enjoy the beaches, shopping, food and history of this great city. For things to do while in Mazatlan, check out the brochures in our gift shops."

I knew it would happen at some point; the family would have to do a walk-through for Benny and Aunt Marble's wedding plans. Secretly, I hoped it would be done another day. I even wished it as we walked to the upper deck. It was such a beautiful day, with the big white puffy clouds over a vibrant blue sky I loved so much... and we were in Mazatlan!

Standing in place were Danny and Andy with their wives. We

had barely and scarcely seen them on this trip. But by the looks on all four of their faces, they weren't missing anything. I had never seen all of them look so…relaxed (especially poor Danny. He was a police sergeant and was going for Detective Fitzpatrick). I had to grin.

Tovah was present and I found out that she would be performing the ceremony. Mum and Da came next to join the group and give hugs. I didn't see Pauly or Mona and wasn't sure if I should be happy or worried about this. After all, all you could see for miles was water. Mona had plenty of places to discard her husband's body, if their talk went badly.

"Where are Benny and Marble," I heard Mum ask everyone. "Has anyone seen them this morn'?"

Everyone shook their heads

"It's not like Benny to be late," Tovah pointed out. None of us could say this about Aunt Marble. It was always a tossup with her. It's not like she didn't care about other people's time, she just got sidetracked…a lot.

Soon Benny and Marble showed up, both of them grinning from ear to ear. I couldn't help but notice that the small amount of hair Benny still had was standing straight out the back of his head. I also caught all of the grins the family gave the two of them.

Tovah showed everyone where to stand, and how we were to start down the aisle. I had been unaware that I was to walk with Barry. Mum and Da would walk together, then Barry and me. Why I was picked, was that whole adopted daughter role I had unwittingly accepted. But Barry, I wasn't sure. I assumed Da was the best man. The rest of the family took their places, standing outside of the aisle. Aunt Marble wanted the men on one side facing their women, on the other. She explained that she wanted them to face each other, so the love in the space between them would be magnified. I actually thought this was a brilliant idea.

Plus, if they got tired of staring at me and Aunt Marble's muumuus, they could stare into each other's eyes.

Barry and I walked to the end of the aisle and awaited our cue. Aunt Marble was staring at us, oddly.

"Ya know, I think I'd like it better, if the two of ya held hands while walkin' down the aisle."

I turned to Barry, "I hope you don't mind hand sweat. It's a little too warm for me to assure you that it won't happen," I giggled.

"I'm pretty sure my hand will be sweatin' too," he smiled.

Fitz piped up, "Didn't ya want Janie to carry a bouquet? I mean, how is she to hold a bouquet and Barry's hand?"

This statement received blank stares. Finally Danny said, "I'm pretty sure Janie could hold a bouquet in one hand and Barry's hand with her other."

I scrunched up my face at Fitz. Did she really think I was so clumsy I couldn't hold onto some flowers with one hand?

As Barry reached out his hand, I smiled. Grabbing his hand with mine, we began to walk down the aisle. Every step was in perfect sync as the family watched us approach. Mum dabbed at the corner of her eyes with a tissue. She had always been so easily stirred by emotion. Fitz, I noticed, wasn't looking at me. She was staring at Barry with the hint of a smile. She loved him so much. I knew she wanted to see him happy and married every bit as much as Mum did. She just wouldn't try to force the issue the way Mum had. As we made our way up to Tovah, I released Barry's hand and took my place facing him.

"No, No," said Aunt Marble, running up the path from behind us. "I want ya to face each other and hold each other's hands…yes Fitz," Marble said when Fitz started in again about the bouquet. "Janie will hand the flowers off to ya, okay?" she asked her niece. "Anyway, you two," she faced us. "I want ya to hold hands and just take a moment to think about everything you wish for the other," she closed her eyes and nodded.

Neither of us was really surprised by her request. Aunt Marble had that whole, hippie, love, star-catcher, witch-crafting thing happening. We nodded to her, took each other's hands and stared into each other's eyes. I smiled at him, as his grin widened.

Even though I knew we would be in casual attire on the big day (casual being the polite way to say ugly as hell muumuu), I couldn't help but picture Barry in his Tuxedo. He was such a handsome man. The years of *crush* that I had had on him weren't wasted. The relationship I had with him for the last twenty plus years, was still the best relationship I had had with any man, save for my father alone. He was my protector, someone I felt safe with. I loved his humor, family values, morals and his integrity. There was always the fact that he was drop dead gorgeous, but that wasn't even secondary to why I thought he was so amazing. Our smiles turned into laughter as we continued to look at each other.

"How long are they supposed to do this?" Fitz piped up.

Aunt Marble, who had been canoodling with soon to be husband at the other end of the aisle, snapped to, "Oh, right, that should be plenty."

We took our place, and let the mock-wedding continue.

"And now," Tovah finished the ceremony, "we go to Mazatlan!"

Everyone hooted and hollered their approval.

All of us, even the older brothers and their wives, were going ashore. I looked around and still didn't see Pauly.

"Do you think he's okay?" I asked Fitz.

Fitz shook her head, "I don't know, but this is somethin' he's gonna have to face. He created the problem, he better find a way to fix it," she gave me a stern look.

I hated it when she made that face, but I was glad it wasn't I who had planted it there.

As we stepped onto the ferry, I was knocked sideways by an

older gentleman who lost his balance. Just when I thought the ground was an inevitable landing place, I felt strong arms catch me.

I turned my head to see who was holding me, I saw Barry. "I may have to hold on to ya…keep ya safe."

I smiled, but Fitz told her brother, "Janie's capable of holdin' herself up."

"Yeah…I'm just not capable of holding a bouquet with one hand," I laughed at her.

This time the ferry ride didn't bother me at all. In fact, I leaned over the edge of the boat to watch a school of dolphins who had decided to chaperone us to the dock.

As it would always be with the Fitzpatrick's, drinks were first on the list.

Before we filed into the cantina, my phone rang. Excitedly, I grabbed for it in the bottom of my purse. It was Cecil! My heart began to pound out of my chest.

"Hi," I said into the receiver.

"There's my girl!" his voice rang out. "Jeez I feel like I haven't talked to ya in forever."

"That's because we really haven't," I told him.

"I know and I'm so sorry! Things here have been nothin' short of a nightmare. And my new assistant…, Jesus, Mary and Joseph," he cried out.

"She's not working out so well, huh?" Some part of me enjoyed hearing this.

"Well, she's a good example of why ya should never hire family."

This comment caught my attention, "Family?" I asked.

"Yeah, she's our cousin's daughter, so my second cousin, I think," he chuckled. "She's a sweet girl, but…"

I could tell he was going for a diplomatic description.

"No polite way to put it, she's as worthless as perfume on a corpse," he admitted. "No one got paid because she erased some files she shouldn't have even been able to access. She doesn't even know how she did it!"

"I've actually never heard that expression," I said, "perfume on a corpse."

"Neither have I, but it fits none the less. Enough about the problems…how are you?"

"Good. Missing you horribly," I sighed.

"Yeah, about that, I was thinkin'…"

"Oh yeah, what were you thinking?" I smiled, hoping for some inspiration for masturbation.

"I absolutely NEED to see ya, Janie!"

I laughed out loud. This was the best news I had heard in a while.

"I'm not kiddin'. I can't go much longer."

My smile faded. Did he mean he couldn't go much longer without me…or without sex? Did I really want to hear the answer to this question? He was a man-whore in recovery, I reminded myself. And I knew that before me, he didn't go long between releases.

"Janie, are ya there? Did I say something wrong?"

I wasn't sure, had he? "I'm gonna need clarification on that one," I blurted out.

He laughed, "What do ya mean?"

"I mean…you need sex, or do you need me?"

"Oh, I get ya. The short answer is both. But sex with you, is what I need, and the ONLY thing I desire."

"Good answer," I told him. "I want that too, and pretty badly," I admitted.

"Are ya still dreamin' about us?" he whispered.

"Dreaming…day dreaming…fantasizing," I bit my bottom lip.

"Really? I'd love to hear about some of these fantasies ya have. Maybe you can tell me about one?"

I looked around, there was no privacy anywhere, "I can't right now. Too many ears, and I'm going to want to be…in a comfortable position when I tell you all about it," I could feel my cheeks blushing.

He made an 'mmm' sound, "Yeah, I'd like ya to be…comfortable…when ya tell me about what you'd like me to do to ya."

"Janie, are ya comin'?" Fitz yelled.

"Yeah, Janie, are ya?" Cecil asked.

"It wouldn't take much," I laughed. "I hate to do this, but I have to keep up with the group," I sighed.

"I understand, soon?" he asked.

"Yes."

"Soon then, my girl," he rang off.

I had to stand still for a moment and try and encourage my legs to move. They had turned to rubber just hearing how much he wanted me.

I missed drinks at the first Cantina (and it was well worth it), so I ordered a double margarita at the second.

"Wow, Janie, yer glowin'," Fitz winked at me. "I haven't seen ya look like this in a while."

"It was a good talk," I couldn't stop smiling. "And, he let me know that his new assistant, the one that answered his phone, is his cousin."

"So no more stressin' for ya? That'll be a nice, unheard of, change," she nodded.

"Asshole," I put my tongue in my cheek.

"Tell me I'm wrong?" she looked sidelong at me.

I just shook my head.

Barry's stare caught my eye from down at the other end of the table. He lifted his glass to me. I smiled and returned the glass raise.

I knew Fitz wanted to shop, but I really wanted to see some of the history. I wanted to see the Historic Center and learn all about the founding of Mazatlan. I wanted to see the Municipal Arts Centre and the Temple of San Jose. But if I knew Fitz, none of this stuff would excite her as much as an open air market and a pitcher of Margaritas.

All of the sudden, Tovah said that she was going to check out some of the historic sites, and asked who wanted to go with her.

I put up my hand, "I'd love to!"

Fitz snorted, "Be my guest. I'm goin' to shop, eat and drink my way through today," she announced.

Barry piped up, "I'd like to go with you two," he looked from Tovah to me.

"The more the merrier, Kid!" Tovah nodded then gave me that same one sided grin.

After one more drink, we headed out saying that we would meet everyone right back here for dinner at 6:00.

The three of us jumped on a bus that took us to our first stop, The Cathedral Basilica De La Concepcion. Walking in, I was in awe. The ceiling was stories high, with amazing arches and an octagonal dome. I read about how the construction on this marvelous structure was started in 1856. Barry smiled as my eyes filled with wonder.

"It's so beautiful," I said with a hint of the amazement I felt.

"Con todo mi Corazon," Tovah said, with her hand over her heart.

"What does that mean?" Barry asked her.

"With my whole heart," she responded, looking at the ceiling.

"You speak Spanish," I asked.

"I speak French, Spanish, Italian, and Yiddish. I understand Bullshit," her brows lifted, "but I don't speak it," she grinned.

Barry and I both laughed.

Next up was the Museo de Arte. For me, being a painter, well this was heaven. Twentieth and twenty-first century Mexican artists adorned the walls. I looked closely at the mediums used, brush stokes, watched light and shadow play. As I stood looking at one painting, tears came to my eyes. Barry looked concerned as he put his arm around me.

"Are ya okay?" he asked.

I nodded, "I'm a little embarrassed," I admitted.

"Why?" he lifted my chin so he could look me in the eyes.

"Because…beauty makes me cry," I answered. "And this, is beautiful," I looked back at the painting.

His expression warmed, "It's one of the things I…I like about you the most." I looked back to him, "Don't ever be embarrassed in front of me, please."

I laughed then sniffled and nodded my head.

Tovah's eyes drew mine, "I have to urinate. Do you have to urinate, Janie?"

"Actually I do," I laughed again. "Thank you," I told Barry before I joined Tovah.

Tovah and I were washing our hands when she looked at me in the mirror, "What are the tears for, kid?"

"Everything is so…beautiful," I answered. "It moves me…all of the work that went into creating the church. All the prayers that have been whispered…all of the artwork here," my eyes watered again. "I must sound ridiculous," I shook my head.

Tovah stared at me, "No. To not see the beauty of these places, to not FEEL the history, to not see the work, to not be amazed," she stressed, "that to me is a sign of a ridiculous person."

I smiled at her.

"You have a boyfriend?" she asked.

"Who? Me?" I asked.

"No the wall…yeah you!" she grinned.

"Kind of," I gave her the 50/50 hand sign.

"Kind of?" Tovah did the hand sign back at me.

"Well, I'm still trying to figure out WHAT we are," I admitted.

Tovah waited for me to elaborate with a questioning look.

"He lives in Ireland, and we never had the 'what this means, what we mean' discussion."

"Hmm," Tovah said.

"Why?" I asked.

Tovah did a slow head shake, "Just nosey. Plus I like ya."

After the museum, we hit a few more places on the list and a restaurant in a historical building. The food was incredible, but it left me with the desire to nap, not walk.

As we made it back to meet the rest of our group, I was ready for a mojito, and a place to put my feet up. I laughed out loud as I spied Fitz coming up the walk. She had bought a red, wide brimmed hat that looked like it doubled as a space ship in a previous life.

"What the hell are you wearing?" I rolled.

"I forgot my damn sunscreen in my other purse, so I had to buy this," she tore it off her head to reveal a bad hair fro.

"Why didn't you just buy sunscreen?" Barry asked his sister.

"Well, she tried," Mum was trying to keep from laughing.

Fitz gave her Mum a scowl.

"What does that mean, ya tried?" Barry's eyes squinted.

"I didn't want to buy a full bottle. I have a full bottle on the ship," she explained.

"And," I said.

"So I bought what I thought was a small bottle, in one of those travel sized bins," she added.

"And?" I kept laughing.

"And it turned out to be Mexico's version of Desitin, okay! I thought it would sink in like sunscreen and I was wrong. I walked around, white faced, for over an hour!"

"My question is how could anyone tell the difference?" Barry chuckled.

"Ha, ha, so funny! Just because ya tan instead of burn, for

some unholy reason, doesn't mean ya should make fun of the tannin' impaired. Tell him the truth Mum, ya had a one nighter with a Latin man!"

"Oh, baby sister," Barry put his arms around her and pulled her unwillingly into an embrace, "If I buy ya a cocktail, will ya forgive me?"

"Ya better make it two. I had to use a degreaser from a restaurant kitchen to get that gunk off my face. I just know my skin is gonna to breakout from that crap!"

"I'll buy ya three," Barry told her.

"Doubles?" Fitz asked.

"Anything ya want," Barry kissed her temple.

"You two are pretty close, huh?" Tovah pointed to Barry and Fitz.

Barry looked at Danny and Andy like he was weighing his words.

"Don't ya worry about it, little brother," Danny told Barry. "It's no secret that yer closer to Fitzy and I'm closer to Andy. It's just an age thing."

"Yeah," Barry squeezed Fitz, "she's the one I'm closest to."

"See, Benny and I are like that. All our lives," she nodded to Benny who sat nodding back. "Does that ever make datin' hard for either of ya?"

Barry looked confused, "Why would it?"

"Well, I know that I couldn't handle dating someone Benny didn't like. It wouldn't happen," she shook her head. "And he's the same way with me."

Benny piped up, "Family is most important. At the end, no matter what, you're there for each other when others might not be."

Mum and Aunt Marble nodded at this comment.

"What about you, Janie?" Tovah turned to me.

"I don't have any siblings," I shook my head. "But Fitzy has been like a sister to me for over twenty years, so I never feel like I didn't have one," I explained.

"How about the other brothers, do they treat you like a sister, too?" Tovah wanted to know.

"Well, they sure as hell tortured me like I was one," I laughed and pointed at Andy and Danny.

"We just didn't want ya to feel left out," Andy nodded to Danny.

"What about you?" she asked Barry. "Did you torture this sweet girl, too?" she grinned.

"No!" Fitz spat. "Barry always came to Janie's rescue. He tortured the hell out of me, though. Hidin' in my closet until I fell asleep, then he'd jump out, growlin'. Scared the crap out of me! Or, he'd wait until I was in the shower then pour ice water over the top of the shower curtain, the jerk," she slapped him in the arm.

Tovah sat back and folded her arms across her chest.

Mum took the conversation from there, "Remember when Barry put green food colorin' in yer shampoo?" she pointed to Fitz.

Barry was stifling a laugh.

"That's right, ya little shit! Now ya owe me four drinks," she nudged her brother again.

The rest of the night, we all laughed, ate and enjoyed great company.

Back on the ship, Barry pounded on our door.

"What the hell, what's with the frantic knock?" Fitz asked when she opened the door.

"Pauly's missin'," Barry told us. "Get dressed! We have to find him before the boat leaves port."

As quickly as we could, we ran down the stairs and met up the rest of the family. Mum had convinced the Captain to let us go ashore and look for him.

"Look, he left a message on my phone sayin' he was comin'

ashore not more than an hour ago," Mum showed the message to the Captain. "We have to find him. He's been distraught..."

"And most likely drunk," Danny added.

Mum did the palms-up, "Yeah probably that, too. Please you've gotta help us. He doesn't speak the language and he's gonna get himself in trouble."

The Captain gave us two hours, "It's as long as I can stall."

"We'll take it, thank ya," Da said.

It was much colder on the water once the sun went down. I stood at the bow of the boat, shivering.

"Here," Barry said, pulling off his sweater and handing it to me.

"I don't want you to be cold," I shook my head.

"I'm fine, I wore a long sleeve, too," he held it out to me again.

I was shivering so hard, my teeth were chattering, "Okay," I took it. "Thank you."

The smell of Polo filled my senses. God I loved that smell.

"Okay," Da got us all together. "Were gonna team up in groups of two, got it. Now he can't have gone far, probably no further than the pier. But every place needs to be searched."

"I'll go with ya, Janie," Fitz said.

"I think you should go with me," Tovah told her. "You're the kickboxer, right?"

Fitz nodded, "I am."

"Yep, you should be with the old broad that can't defend herself so well," she played the geriatric card.

"Fine," Fitz told her.

"And you, Janie, you should go with Barry. I know you're not the kick boxer, so he'll protect ya," Tovah rationalized.

"Yeah, that's fine," I told her.

Mum's voice rang out, "We have to be back here, no later than 1:30. Everyone have their phones?"

The group nodded in unison.

As soon as we docked, each two person group headed off to find Pauly.

Barry grabbed my hand and we speed-walked through people to the first cantina. We each took a side, and Barry checked the men's room. No sign. Meeting back at the entrance, we headed to the next bar, then the next one, then the next one.

"I hope someone is having better luck than we are?" Barry looked worried.

"We're gonna find him. It's gonna be okay," I rubbed his back.

"Great, and when we do, I'm gonna kill him."

"Yeah, I figured," I said as he grabbed my hand and pulled me through the crowd of drunks.

Two more bars, and time was running out. We looked around but didn't see him anywhere. Just as we turned to leave, we heard the drunken Irish rendition of 'You Were Always On My Mind,' being slurred out.

As we turned, there on the stage was a very drunk Pauly, belting out the words he could remember.

Barry sent a group text that we had found him and were bringing him back to the boat.

I walked up to the stage and waved until I got Pauly's attention.

"Janie," he said into the microphone, "how ya doin?"

"Great, we gotta go," I told him.

"Bar friends," he slurred out to the crowd, "This is Janie…and she has great tits."

I let out a sigh of pure exhaustion while the drunk American college crowd applauded.

"Show em' yer tits, Janie. They can't be takin' my word fer it… I'm drunk."

Barry had just sent the text and wasn't amused by his brother's disrespectful request.

"Oh look, there's my little brother Barry," he told everyone. "Hi Barry," he looked down from the stage.

Barry's head shook, "We need to go, NOW!"

"I don't have any reason to go. I'm gonna stay here," he nodded to the crowd.

"WE NEED TO GO, NOW!" Barry repeated.

"Ya do know I'm older than ya, right?" his visions jumped around. "I don't take yer advice…yer opinions…and damn sure… not yer orders."

All of the Fitzpatrick boys could more than hold their own. This was no secret. But to my knowledge, only one Fitzpatrick could best Barry, and that was Da, himself. It seems Da's pugilistic prowess, in its entire splendor, was passed down to his last begotten son.

Barry took a step forward, but I caught him by the arm, "This time, I'm going to remind you, we're in a foreign country," I looked around.

Barry was doing his bull-nose-breathing again, "What the hell do we do then? Short of rippin' him off that stage and fireman carryin' his drunk-ass back to the boat, I mean?"

I grabbed my phone. Within minutes, I saw the crowd moving out of the way for an angry red head. Mum's face was the epitome of what *don't fuck with me* looks like.

As she approached the stage, Pauly's eyes widened. Without a word spoken, she pointed down to the space directly in front of her.

Pauly knew better. He put the mic down and walked to his mother. As he looked into her eyes, his head dropped and tears began to flow. "She doesn't love me, Mum," he sobbed.

Mum took him into an embrace and shushed him, "Come on, son."

As Mum turned, the crowd once again parted.

Back on the ferry, Barry kept his distance from Pauly. I could tell he was still fuming pissed.

I walked over to Barry, "You okay?"

Barry grabbed his head, "I just wish he would grow the fuck up. It's his man-child attitude that has caused all of this in the first place."

I wasn't sure if Barry knew about the porn and Mona's firing, or if he was just talking about Pauly's lack of maturity in general.

"I mean, seriously, who gets his wife fired, then tells her, it's her fault for not having sex with him? No 'I'm sorry', no 'I screwed up', nothin'."

Okay, so he knew, I thought.

"I'm not a fan of Mona's, not even a little," he shook his head. "But she wasn't this bad, until he made her this bad. And he still doesn't get it?"

I could definitely understand her anger…and even her insecurity, on some level. But who did she think Pauly was when she married him? I had known Pauly all of my life, damn near, and one of his big drawbacks, was that he HADN'T changed since Jr. High.

"Well, she had to know what she was getting into, right?" I reasoned.

Barry made a funny sound and shook his head.

"What? They were childhood sweethearts, weren't they?"

Barry looked to where Pauly lay curled in his mother's arms. "Not exactly."

"I guess I was under the wrong impression."

Barry sighed, "Ya see, Mona had a crush on Pauly, since Jr. High. Years later he was seeing some other girl, but they had a fallin' out. He asked Mona out as a way to make the other girl jealous."

I winced, "Oh no."

"Of course his deep desire for this other woman, didn't stop him from shaggin' Mona in the back of Da's wagon. Ya may not want to repeat that, I'm pretty sure Da doesn't know that part."

I nodded my acceptance of the secret.

"Anyway, it was a one-time thing...that led to a pregnancy."

My eyes rounded, "Oh my God,"

"Yep." Barry did the slow nod. "He's fallen in love with her. He really has. But she knew that she wasn't the one he wanted when he married her."

"How?"

"He got drunk one night and told her all about it. Said how he was in love with another woman when he bedded her...and got her pregnant."

"Oh my God," my eyes were huge. I could imagine how painful that would have been to hear. "Well no wonder she's such a bitch," I looked off in the distance.

"Aye. Please don't say anything to Fitzy? Da and we boys only found out at his bachelor party. Hell I'm not even sure Mum knows."

"I don't know...it may make the women...be more understanding?" I searched for a possibility. Given the fact that she had given Fitz an anal roofie, well, this may not be true.

We were quiet for a few moments before I asked, "Why did you tell me about all of this?"

Barry mulled before saying, "I trust ya with my secrets, I guess."

Back on the ship, we were all worn out. Barry took Pauly to bed with him, where I prayed he would pass out before Barry knocked him out.

As I curled up, content with the thought of sleep, Fitz asked, "What were you and Barry talkin' about on the boat?"

I hated to have secrets from Fitz and had even promised I wouldn't keep a secret from her again. But, this secret wasn't mine to tell. "He was just upset with Pauly's antics."

"Well, I can certainly understand that," she stared at the ceiling. "So, you and Cecil…" she began.

I grinned, the same stupid grin I always did when his name was mentioned.

"…you two are okay?"

"Yeah. I think I was just over worrying. The distance between us, just makes my mind go crazy. I still can't believe that he wants…me," I said in awe.

Fitz sat up in her bed, "What do ya mean?"

I let out a sigh, "I just think he has so much to offer. He's handsome, smart, funny…he could have anybody he wants."

"Yeah?" Fitz nodded.

"It's not like I'm down on myself…it's just…I feel lucky to have someone like him…like me."

"You confuse me sometimes. Ya act like ya aren't worthy. When in all truthfulness, he's lucky to have someone like you."

"But, he could have anyone he wants!" I stressed my point.

"I think that's the point yer missin'. He could have anyone he wants. He could have a rich woman. He could have the most accomplished woman in the world. Fer God sakes, he could have a lingerie model who studies neurosurgery in her free time, while saving dolphins. But he wants you! Doesn't that mean that on some level, you are the woman he thinks is perfect? Perfect for him…perfect for his needs and wants. And don't forget, he's a man-whore in recovery, and yer the one who has made him *want* to recover!"

"Well, I'm not sure he hasn't…relapsed at some point."

"I don't think he's cheated on ya," Fitz's brow furrowed at the thought.

"I'm not sure it would be considered cheating. I mean, we never discussed being in any kind of relationship, much less being committed."

Fitz thought about this and shook her head, "I still can't see him thinkin' it wouldn't ruin his chances with ya, to go whorin'. I think he knows ya better than that. And, I think he cares fer ya more than that, too."

I smiled at her, "You always make me feel better."

"I'm not even tryin' to do that. I'm tryin' to make ya think. There are so many men out there that would love to have a woman like you," her eyes bored into mine. "Yer smart, talented, loving, loyal and honest…these things still mean EVERYTHING to some men. These things are hard to find. Some people only care about the packagin'. Then they're disappointed when the packagin' doesn't reflect what's inside. He knows ya, inside…and out, and he thinks yer the perfect one fer him!" she stressed the last sentence.

I nodded to her. It was going take some more self convincing to really make myself feel this way, but that was worth the effort, whereas tearing myself down was not.

"And ya know, yer pretty hot, too. When yer not lettin' unnecessary insecurities flood every cell in yer body, and work yer poor brain to the point of insanity," she laid back down.

I loved her so much. She had done what she always did for me; pulled me up and put me in check. "I love you, Fitzy."

"I love ya, too, Janie. Now shut up and go to bed."

I smiled at the ceiling as she turned off the light.

Something she had said left me thinking. It wasn't so long ago, that I thought I wasn't worthy of my ex, John. I thought he was so accomplished, so driven. He had done so much more with his life than I had. Back then, I was a barista and he worked for a huge publishing company. I couldn't believe that someone like him would want someone like me. At the end of this relationship, this man that saw myself as *less than*, turned out to be a cheater and a liar. He wasn't loyal or honest. Admittedly, those two things do mean the world to me. How had I ever tricked myself into believing that I was unworthy of him? If I really thought about our relationship, I knew I put myself on the backburner. And going a step further, I had allowed him to put me on his backburner, too. Maybe I shouldn't be nearly as worried about the way someone else sees me and my worth, but how I see myself and my worth.

After a long wrestling match with my inner demons, I fell asleep.

14

MAMA MIA

My cell phone was going off as I came-to just enough to riffle through my bag. It was 6:00am.

"Hello," I said groggily.

"Hi Puddin, it's Betty."

I always grinned when she followed Puddin, with 'it's Betty'. No one else called me Puddin. "Good morning, Miss Betty."

"Yer mama wanted to talk to ya, Sugar."

I thought out loud, "Why didn't she call me, then?"

"Well, Puddin, she's still a little too embarrassed."

Now my interest was piqued, "Why? What happened?"

"Well, Walter and I took yer mama and daddy out fer dinner the other night," Betty began.

"Okay," I was coming to. "What happened?"

"Well after dinner, we went to a karaoke bar on the pier. Blow off a little steam and just cut loose."

"Uh huh, and," I was just wishing she'd get to the point on this one.

"There's a youtube video of yer mama…givin' yer daddy a lap dance."

No sound emitted from me.

"Puddin? Honey…are ya there?" Betty wanted to know.

"Umm, yeah. I'm here," then I went silent for another moment. "Why are you telling me this?" I finally asked.

"Yer mama was just sure you were gonna see it. I told her that the chances of you seein' it were slim, if you weren't lookin' for it."

I nodded, once again wondering why she woke me up to tell me all of this.

"The problem is, Puddin, you may find it whether you want to, or not."

This had me worried, and I sat up, "Why?"

Betty let out a sigh, "Damn thing went viral."

My eyes rounded, "WHAT?" I was fully awake now.

"Someone at the bar posted it, and within a day, well, it had over a million hits.

"Are you serious?" was what shot out of my mouth.

"Yes. Now look, yer mama's real embarrassed thinkin' that the video is gonna embarrass you. I told her not to worry about it, but you know how she is," Betty added.

I knew how she was, I thought to myself. But the mother I knew for the last twenty-six years didn't give lap dances at bars. "So…what do I do here? Do I tell her not to worry, and I won't watch it. Or do I tell her 'atta girl'?"

"That, I'm gonna leave up to you. But she wanted you to know before you stumble on to it, that's all."

"Well, I do appreciate the heads-up, and you can just tell her, I'm not embarrassed, at all, and I won't watch it if it pops up."

"That'll work, I think, Puddin. So sorry I woke ya, but yer mom has just made herself sick over this."

"It's okay. Thank you for being such a good friend to her. By the way, what's the name of the video, so I can try and block it, or try to avoid it at least," I asked.

Betty went quiet for a moment, "Betty?" I called.

Her sigh told me I probably didn't want to know, "Sexy MILF gives lap dance…to boner poppin' husband."

I went dead silent. Neither of us said a thing. Finally I said, "Yeah, with a title like that, I won't find it too hard to avoid. I'm gonna go lobotomize myself now. Tell my mom I love her."

"Yeah, I figured. I'll tell her. And remember I love you, Puddin."

"I love you, too, Betty." I hung up.

Fitz who had her eyes closed but had been following my half of the conversation, asked, "What's going on?"

My head shook, "Apparently, my mother is an internet sensation."

Fitz sat up slowly, "What?" she rubbed her eyes.

As I explained the phone call from Betty, Fitz grinned from ear to ear, "That's hilarious. Go Mrs. O," she bobbed her head up and down.

"Yeah," I sounded less than thrilled.

"What? Yer Mom is finally comin' out of her shell. You may want to take a cue from her," Fitz walked to the bathroom.

"All these years, she's made me afraid to embarrass her," I gave Fitz the palms-up. "She practically shoved me into a shell. And now that she's having some great awakening, I shouldn't be embarrassed by her…while she does things, she would have been embarrassed by…if I had done them?"

"Look, I know what yer sayin', and yer not wrong. Yer Mom worked OVERTIME making ya afraid of not always bein' seen as a proper young lady, never raisin' yer voice, never goin' against popular opinion, never showin' the wild side of yer nature…"

"You're not exactly giving her a very good defense," I told her.

"Actually, I am!"

"How so?" I shook my head.

"I think maybe now, yer mom knows that what she did was wrong. She was wrong to constantly worry about the opinions of others. She was wrong to stifle ya. She was wrong to make ya second guess everything ya said, thought and felt. She was wrong. Period!"

"Yeah, I'm not sure that helps me now."

"How could it not? You weren't the only one she stifled. She did it to herself, too. At one time, she believed this was the right way. And now, it's like her admitten' that it's okay to be you. It's okay to have opinions, feelins, and not care who doesn't think ya *fit into* everyone else's version of who they think ya should be!"

I hated it sometimes when Fitz was right. I did have to admit that mom had been happier in the last two months than she had been in the last God only knows how many years. I thought again about her being friendless, her only link to the outside world, dad and me. She had made us, trips to the grocery store, cleaning the house and Sunday pot roast, her whole life.

I let out a very heavy sigh that made Fitzy nod her head at me.

Down at breakfast, I poured myself a cup of black coffee. Usually I would have at least put cream in it, but I was too tired to even care. Our night out, finding Pauly, then my early morning wake-up from Betty, left me exhausted.

During my second cup, Pauly and Barry entered the dining hall. From across the room, I could see that Pauly was donning a shiner. My brows went up as the two of them approached.

Ftz noticed and looked at Barry with questioning eyes.

"Don't look at me like that," Pauly said as he sat.

"Where'd ya get the black eye?" Fitz asked.

Pauly poured himself a cup of coffee, "The wife gave it to me."

Fitz's eyes flashed the dark green of her pissed off Irish ancestors, "Did she, now?"

Knowing what I now knew, I would be surprised if this was the first.

Barry folded his arms across his chest, "Tell her why!"

Fitz's eyes narrowed, "What did ya do?"

Pauly was taking his time. I figured he was trying to find a way to swing a bad situation, in his favor.

"Well it's like this…"

Pauly had gone to Mona's room after Barry kicked him out for singing Irish drinking songs at the top of his lungs.

"I gave him a choice," Barry said. "He could either shut the hell up, or go sleep on deck."

Pauly chose neither. As he told the story, he went to Mona's room and banged on the door until she opened it. He moved inside the room and told Mona to 'ready yerself'. As he stripped naked, he told her, 'I said now, woman! I'll hear no more of this divorce nonsense, and you WILL do what I say, because I AM THE MAN'! "I also may have…honked her boob. That was right about the time she threw a right hook."

I winced, Fitz dropped her jaw and shook her head. Barry just stared at him, with his tongue in his cheek.

"Ya pulled that *I am the man* bullshit on her…while standing, naked…and drunk off yer ass, in the room she kicked ya out of, and then ya HONKED HER BOOB?" Fitz asked with a straight face.

"I did," Pauly raised his jaw.

"Do ya know now…how stupid that was?" Fitz questioned.

"I do now," Pauly said.

"Just bein' honest, if a man had done that to me, I wouldn't stop until he was cryin' his eyes out like a little bitch," Fitz's stare was white hot.

"Well, if it makes ya feel better, I did cry. I got hit in the eye, for Pete's sake!"

"I think ya should be grateful," Barry told his brother.

"Grateful? Fer what?" Pauly pointed to his black-eye.

"Ya still have yer penis, don't ya?" Barry inquired.

Fitz, Barry and I were all trying hard not to laugh.

Fitz nodded, "Yea, I would have taken that thing, clean off."

Pauly looked around the table, "Well, thanks everyone fer havin' my back," he stormed off.

I cannot believe that boy is so stupid, sometimes. It's like he was made from a *low tide* in Da's semen," Fitz pointed out.

Mum, Marble and Tovah came in next. Mum hadn't seen Pauly, so she had no idea what was going on. When she was first told about the black eye, the mama in her was fit to be tied. Then when she heard the rest of the story, she said, "If yer dumb enough to dare the devil, ya better be ready for the fight of yer life."

Three cups of coffee, and I was still exhausted. Barry looked at me, "Yer awfully quiet."

"I'm just tired," I explained. "The last week has been more than I bargained for."

Fitz's phone dinged. I watched her just stare at the screen. It looked like she had slipped into a coma with her eyes open.

"Fitzy, you okay?" I leaned towards her.

A slow shake of her head was barely visible. It was like she had gone into a trance.

"What is it?" Barry's concern was obvious.

She handed me the phone and Barry moved closer so he could see what had muted his sister.

The Great Rudolpho had sent a picture with a message, "What about this?"

My eyes rounded.

Barry chuckled, "What the hell is that?"

"That's my weddin' dress," Fitz said in a whispered.

Barry's eyes shot back to the picture. "That?" he looked at me for confirmation.

I winced and nodded a 'yes'.

"Ya…can't wear…that!" he pointed at the screen.

There is was. The ugliest thing I had ever seen. It was a calypso dress. That, I had expected. What I didn't expect, was the gold Lamay ruffles that were put on top of already puffed up sleeves, making it look as though there were two extra heads. More ruffles continued down the bodice, to just past the waistline, where two more big poofs, made 34 inch hips, widen to 50. It looked like saddlebags hung from the sides. A giant silver heart was sewn in between where I assumed her boobs were supposed to be.

I tried and tried to find something, anything, positive to say. In the end, all I could do was shake my head.

"Yer not really gonna wear that, are ya?" Barry couldn't take his eyes from the train wreck before him.

"I begged him," Fitz said. "I begged him to create for me." She was still staring off into the nothingness.

"This isn't creatin'," Barry told her. "This is what happens when ya leave a nine-year-old alone with fabric, and a sewing machine."

"He's one of the best," Fitz mumbled.

"The best at what?" Barry was losing his mind. "What the hell is hangin' off the hips? Are those gold saddlebags?"

"Oh my God, I thought that exact thing," I said excitedly.

"Ya didn't?" Barry grinned at me.

"I did too, I was just thinking that," I laughed.

"You and I are on the same wavelength about a lot of things," Barry told me.

"I guess so. That is so…weird, right?" I asked.

"Right," Barry nodded.

Fitz finally found her voice, "Umm, problem over here," she pointed to herself.

"You're right, I am so sorry," I patted her shoulder.

"I don't see the problem?" Barry offered.

Fitz and I both shot looks to him.

"No, I mean, I see the problem, obviously," he looked at the dress again and his whole body shook. "What I mean is, why not just wear somethin' else?"

"The Great Rudolpho is comin' to the weddin'. I don't want to offend him," Fitz told her brother.

"Women are so strange sometimes. The only thing offensive is the fact that ya'd even entertain wearin'…that," he pointed again.

I nodded, "I have to agree, Fitz. This is going to be the best day of your life. Do you really want that memory, photographed in this," I turned the screen back to her.

"Turn, it away," she said dramatically. "I can't bear to look at it."

Overhead the announcement for Puerto Vallarta rang out.

Barry put a hand on my shoulder, "Ya goin' ashore?"

As badly as I wanted to see as much of Mexico as possible, I also just wanted to relax. "I think I just want to lie around and veg-out today," I told him.

"Or, ya could come into port, lie on the beach, work on yer tan," he grinned.

He did have a point.

Fitz and I changed into our suits, threw on some cover-ups and headed for the ferry. Her wide brimmed hat cast a three foot shadow around her.

Barry and Pauly met us in line. I had to give Mona credit, Pauly's shiner was impressive. It was also a good warning for Fitz and me to watch her right hook, if it ever came down to that.

I was so tired that I sat for the whole ride inland. The sun was warm, the sky was blue and I was anticipating taking a nap on one of the most beautiful beaches in Mexico. We were racing toward a green mountain and what looked like sandy beaches pocked with palm trees. I made the *MMM* sound.

The beach wasn't packed like I had expected. We walked the shore a little before staking our claim. I unrolled my oversized towel and lay down. The sound of the waves, the warmth of the sun, the smell of the ocean, this was heaven. I was woken up a bit later when Barry said that I was starting to burn.

"Can I put some sunscreen on yer back," he asked?

I turned to look for Fitz, but she was gone. "Where did Fitz and Pauly go?" I asked.

"They went to go get us drinks. I told them to bring you back a pina colada."

"Mmm, that does sound wonderful," I nodded.

"Yes, it does," Barry laughed.

I turned my head to look at my shoulder, "Oh, I am getting red. What does the rest of my back look like?"

"Pretty much in between Janie as we know her and a cooked lobster," he answered.

"If you wouldn't mind, that would be great."

Just as Barry uncapped the tube, Fitz yelled from fifty yards away, "Barry! What are ya doin'?"

My face spun to Fitz, "He's on sunscreen duty," I laughed.

"No, here, take the drinks. I'll put her sunscreen on," Fitz rushed to my side.

"I do know how to put on sunscreen," Barry informed her.

"Yeah, but…ya don't want this stuff all over yer hands. I have to put more on anyway. No reason for ya to get all icky," she took the bottle from him.

"Okay Fitz," he said and put his palms up, submissively.

After Fitz finished my back, Barry asked her if he could speak to her alone for a minute.

Off they walked. I hoped he was talking her out of that horrible wedding dress. I had never seen anything so gaudy, or poofy in all of my life. Pauly and I sat, enjoying our drinks. Every once in a while, I glanced over to where the two of them stood. Fitz's body language was agitated. Her arms kept going in the air like she was trying to shoo birds. Barry's wasn't much better.

"What do you suppose is going on?" I asked Pauly.

Pauly looked over at his siblings, "Nothin' fer you to worry about."

After a few more minutes, Barry took Fitzy into a huge hug and swung her around a bit.

"Hmm, I guess you were right," I told Pauly.

All of the sudden, I heard Rod Stuart singing through Pauly's phone. It didn't sound like the original version, too much background noise. "Is that a live show?" I asked.

"I'll say," Pauly's eyes were huge.

"What," I laughed.

"Well, bein' polite, I'll just say…yer mom has moves…and yer dad is really enjoyin' them," he nodded.

"Oh my God, NO!" I shook my head.

Fitz and Barry were walking back up and saw the stupid look on Pauly's face. "Get it girl," he yelled, and bopped along to the music.

"What the hell are ya watchin'?" Fitz walked around behind him, so she could see the screen. Soon, Fitz said, "Oh my God!"

"It can't be all of that," Barry moved so he could see what had his brother and sister so blown away.

Rod Stuart was drowned out by hoots and hollers from the bar audience.

"Is that…?" Barry's eyes shot to me, "…yer mom…and dad?"

I didn't have to look at the video. I was pretty sure. I gave a slow nod.

A close to 50 (if she was a day), woman in a bright yellow floral muumuu, with Princess Leah buns on the side of her head, just happened by Pauly and looked down at his screen, "That's disgusting!"

Fitz turned to the woman, "Last I checked, no one invited ya to look," Fitz pointed out.

The woman looked taken aback by the logic Fitz had posed, "Well…this is a public beach…and I'm offended. I have the RIGHT to be offended!" she yelled at Fitz, her cheeks flush with anger.

Fitz shrugged, "Ya also have the RIGHT to remain silent. See how this is really about the choices yer makin'?" Fitz grinned as the woman stormed off. "Yer also makin' the CHOICE to be pissed off! Ya have that right, too!" Fitz called after her.

I couldn't even look up.

"Yer mom's got moves, Janie," Pauly said to me, while still dancing on his butt.

"Oh," Fitz's eyes rounded, and her head snapped back "Good fer you, Mrs. O!"

"Yeah, I guess Janie's dad is packin'!" Pauly winked.

"Oh…oh my God. Please turn it off," I begged.

"What's the big deal? I've seen Mum do worse to Da," Pauly admitted. "And I turned out fine," he did a palms-up.

With that comment, Barry and Fitz looked at each other, then back at Pauly, "Shut it off!" they said in unison.

"Janie? Ya look like yer gonna be sick. Are ya okay?" Barry asked.

"I'm fine," I said, not feeling fine at all.

"Why don't ya get her another drink, Barry, and some water," Fitz told him.

Barry stood and turned to walk back to the bar, when Pauly started to try and make me feel better. "At least yer mom is a MILF," he nodded. "That's good news fer ya."

With that, Barry came back and grabbed Pauly by the collar. "And…you'll be comin' with me."

"It's really not a big deal," Pauly shook his head at me. "So yer mother expressed her desire fer yer dad, and well…yer dad returned that desire…fully," At this point Barry pulled Pauly away.

"Eww," I shook my hands like that would clear the icky from my thoughts.

"We've been over this," Fitz started when the boys got out of earshot, "There is NO stork, there is NO cabbage patch. You are only livin' and breathin' because yer parents love each other…a lot…and often," she added wide eyed.

I let out a sigh.

"You should be happy, they're so in love. I'm grateful everyday that my parents are the way they are together. It gives me hope that forever does exist. And for a few of those people, it's filled with passion as well. I wouldn't be getting married, if I hadn't seen the possibility of this first hand."

"Do you worry about…losing passion?" I wasn't sure why I was surprised. I guess Fitz had always seemed so certain.

"Of course I do. There are a lot more couples that lose passion, and fall out of love, then there are ones that don't. And no one goes into marriage thinkin' it will end. They all think they're different. But for a huge percent…divorce does happen."

"Well, it's work to stay together. Or at least I've been told," I laughed, knowing that none of my relationships had ever been the *forever* kind.

"It is," Fitz nodded. "The hard part is to find a partner who thinks yer worth the work, and really tries, just as hard as you will. That's the ONLY way any marriage has a shot in hell. I think I've found him. But the slight chance of him givin' up on me, on us, still scares me sometimes."

I thought about it, "I think it should."

"Ya think I have a reason to worry?" her eyes rounded.

"No," I hugged her. "I just think…everyone should be worried about losing the one they love. Maybe that fear…is what keeps people from taking each other for granted. What keeps the passion alive," I added.

Fitz nodded, "I believe it does."

I got serious, "You're going to have a beautiful life," I kissed her cheek.

"WE'RE gonna have beautiful lives," she corrected me.

"You do know that Scotty looks at you, the way Da looks at Mum?"

Fitz's smile stretched across her face, "You see it?"

I nodded, "I do…like you hung the stars with your smile."

The guys came back a few minutes later and I was surprised Pauly didn't have another black eye. "I'm just sayin', her mom is hot," he said right before Barry slapped him up the back side of his head.

"It's Monte Carlo tonight on the ship," Fitz shot me a grin. "And I plan on bein' dressed to the nines."

I laughed. I was never a gambler. I figured I worked too hard for every cent I made, to risk it on games of chance. I'd rather spend my hard-earned money on practical things, like electricity. Though, since my painting had *taken off* some, I had a little money I might not lose sleep over throwing away.

Back on the ship, Fitz slipped into a form hugging, off the shoulder, red dress that tapered its way from her hips to the floor, with a slit up the center. Her legs peeked out as she walked. A big, ornate silver clip held her messy bun of flaming red hair. As always, she looked incredible.

I had brought a maroon strapless gown, and I was happy not to have any fabric rubbing on my slightly sunburned shoulders. I went to go put my hair in a ponytail, and Fitz stopped me.

"Enough with the damn ponytails," she shrieked. "Ya have great hair, why does it always have to be tied?"

She came at me with a big curling iron. My eyes popped with fear. Twenty minutes later, she had given me a classic Rita Hayworth do, with big waves and side parted bangs, covering one eye. I choked: between how much hairspray she used, and the confined space in the bathroom, I was asphyxiating. She told me to take a look in the mirror, but I was dizzy as hell.

"Ya look amazing!" she rang out.

"I'll just take your word for it," I told her.

15

MIND . . . BLOWN

Fitz and I made it to dinner. When we entered the hall, heads snapped and eyes bugged out. Realistically, I knew we were on a seniors cruise. But the looks we got knew no age. Plus, gentlemen of a certain age remembered when women still dressed classy instead of trashy.

Tovah saw us before anyone else at the tables. It was the first time I had seen her smile instead of a one sided grin. Her smile caught the attention of the others at her table and they turned.

Mum grabbed her heart, "You two, look incredible!"

Da nodded, "Such beautiful women, gorgeous."

I beamed. Usually I was happy to be the one who faded into the background. But I had to admit, getting this reaction was wonderful. Now if I could only control my blushing.

Fitz did a turn, letting the crowd take her all in. I tried to figure out what to do with the hand not clutching a clutch. I went to put it on my hip, but it felt totally awkward. Like I was posing for a picture no one was taking.

From behind us, I heard, "Wow," said in a whisper.

I turned to see Barry looking me up and down. "You…look… wow!" his green eyes sparkled.

He was in his black tuxedo that was cut to show his broad shoulders and tapered waist. He always looked incredible. A handsome man by all standards, but in a tux, he was a breath taker.

"You don't look too bad yourself," I said.

We got in the buffet line and filled our plates. Mum and Da had bought champagne to toast to Aunt Marble and Benny's nuptials tomorrow. We all raised our glasses, and Tovah gave a beautiful speech about how happy she was to have a new sister.

After dinner we headed to a room that had been transformed into a casino. I felt like I was in an old movie as I walked to the craps table. I watched for a while trying to figure out the game. Barry leaned in and explained why the winners were winning. The young man running the table asked if I would like to shoot. I bit my lower lip. It didn't look too hard.

Taking the dice in my hand and walking to the end of the table, the young man smiled and said, "You're going to try and roll a seven, okay?"

This really was a game of chance, I thought. How could you TRY to roll anything? Seemed to me this was in the dice's hands. Barry, who understood the game, was in charge of placing my bets and his own. I pulled back my hand and let them dice fly. And fly they did, straight past the table, and bounced off some poor woman's beehive.

I covered my mouth with my hand. "I'm so sorry," I told her as the young man retrieved the dice.

She gave me a stern look and I winced. "Sorry," I said, again.

Barry tried not to laugh, "It's more of a *feedin' the chicken* movement, than it is a *throwin' the Frisbee*, move."

"Right," I bit my lower lip and took the dice again. As I

released them this time, they hit the back of the table, and bounced back to reveal a seven.

"Seven, a winner!" yelled the young man, and handed the dice back to me.

"Now what do I do?" I asked Barry.

"Ya roll again," he nodded.

I rolled again, and again and again. As stacks of chips were put in front of me and Barry, we drew a crowd.

A poor old man at the other side of the table was apparently betting against me and losing. Unhappy and grumbling under his breath, he walked to my side of the table, grabbed mine and Barry's chips then threw them into the air.

"What the hell are ya doin'?" Barry looked at him, shocked.

The old man never missed a beat and just…walked away.

Barry got down on the floor and started retrieving our winnings. I took them in my hand and reset the piles.

"Wait," Barry had his hand in mine as he raised himself up on one knee. "One more," he said, stretching to grab the runaway chip.

I helped him stand and said, "I think I've done enough gambling for one night."

Barry nodded, "Not too shabby," he looked at the chips.

I had no idea how much we won. As we cashed out, we had each won two thousand dollars. I was so excited, but assumed that I was one of those first-time winners I had always been told about. I was done gambling. Happily, I watched others and had a few cocktails.

We were having the best time, when my phone rang. It was Cecil. I beamed and headed outside to get a little queit.

"Hi," I said.

"Ugh, hi."

"How are you?" I asked.

"Ugh…I'm fine. How are you?" he asked.

"I'm good! I just won two thousand dollars!" I said excitedly.

"Good," he said, flatly.

I knew Cecil's family was richer than rich, but two-thousand dollars was exciting to me.

"So…I saw yer video," he started.

"You did?" I beamed. "I still can't believe I did it!"

"Yeah, uh, neither can I," he admitted.

"Well, I was scared at first…but then I just thought…what the hell, right?"

"Yeah, 'what the hell' is what ran through my mind, too. So, are ya happy…I mean about this?"

"I am! I really am," I laughed. "It's like I'm finally coming alive, ya know?"

"Well, just so ya know, that IS what I wish fer ya. I have to go now. Goodbye Janie," he rang off.

I stared at the phone. His side of the conversation seemed so weird and I hadn't even asked if everything was alright. Dialing him right back, the call went to voicemail. When it beeped, I told him, "I hope you're okay."

Stepping back into the ship casino, I pulled Fitz aside. "I just got a call from Cecil and he didn't sound…right."

"Well, did ya call him back?"

"I did, but it went to voice mail."

Fitz thought about it, "It's pretty early in the morn there. Maybe he just hasn't fully woken up. Did he sound tired?"

I thought about the time difference. Well, it was 5am there. Maybe he was just waking.

Throughout the night, I called a few more times. I didn't leave another message, scared that I was bothering him.

Fitz was working the room, telling jokes and posing for pictures with the older men who had her bathing suit calendar.

I found the restroom and had just shut the stall door, when I heard two familiar voices.

"I still can't believe Janie doesn't KNOW. How can she not? I mean, did you see the way he looked at her?" said Andy's wife, Mary.

I looked through the little crack in the door and could see Mary was talking to Danny's wife, Anna.

"I know. I feel kind of bad for him. He's so in love, and all these years…" Anna said. "I still can't believe he never tried."

"Would you have?" Mary asked. "Think about it. If it had gone badly…she wouldn't be *family* anymore. That's got to be the reason Fitz hasn't told her."

"That's true," Anna agreed.

"They would make such a cute couple though, wouldn't they," Mary said. "Did you see them dancing?"

"Can you even imagine how cute she and Barry's kids would be?" As they walked out I realized that I was panic breathing.

I took a few deep breaths as my mind replayed the last few days. Fitz taking his chaise…her not wanting Barry to be my partner for the *Chicken* game…not letting Barry put sunscreen on me. Fitz knew…Fitz knew and she didn't tell me.

My stomach started spinning. I was pretty sure I was going to throw up or pass out. I dropped down on the toilet and put my head between my legs. I was getting the mouth waters. My thoughts, and feelings, were so overwhelming that I started to cry. But this wasn't a single tear running down my cheek. No this was ugly crying at its finest. How could she not tell me? Years…Anna said ***years***. These two thoughts kept replaying in my mind. "Oh my God," I rocked back and forth.

The door opened again and I heard Tovah's voice. "Janie? Kid, ya in here?"

I sobbed harder, not finding actual words.

Tovah bent down to make sure the dress touching the floor was mine.

"Hey Kid, I watched ya walk in here…that was a while ago. I'd ask if you're okay, but with the sobbin' and all, it seems like an unnecessary question."

I stood and opened the door. The look on my face made Tovah's drop. "Honey, what's wrong?" she searched my eyes. "Oh…you didn't know."

I stared at her, "You knew? Who told you?"

"Oh honey, no one had to tell me," she put a hand to my cheek. "I don't know how you didn't…know."

I cried harder, and covered my sobs with my hand.

"Oh honey," Tovah said again, taking me in an embrace. "It's okay, kid, it's okay," she soothed me.

A few moments passed before she pulled back and asked, "How do you feel…about Barry?"

I shook my head, "I…I…love him," I whispered.

Tovah continued to stare.

"But…I'm in love…with Cecil," the realization of what I just said, made my heart pound hard again.

"Is that the first time you've said that out loud?" Tovah watched my reaction.

"It's the first I've ever really admitted it to anyone…including myself," the tears rolled again.

Tovah had tears in her eyes as she smiled. "Everything is gonna okay, kid." She squeezed me again.

I blew my nose and cleaned up my face. Hugging Tovah, I thanked her for being there for me. I walked back to my room and collapsed on the bed. I was in shock with what I had accidentally found out. I was even more stunned that my feelings for Cecil, in such a short time, trumped a lifelong crush.

A while later Fitz came in, "What the hell! Ya just up-and-left without a word! What's wrong, why are ya cryin'?"

"Why didn't you tell me?" I whispered, unable to look her in the eyes.

"You know?" her voice trembled.

"WHY DIDN'T YOU TELL ME?" I asked again.

"Because," she set her purse down.

"Because what? You were the one...who was so pissed at me, when you found out about my crush on Barry. You made me feel horrible! And now, you know that he feels, has felt," I corrected, "the same way for years, and you say nothing?"

"It's not like that, Janie," she sat on her bed facing me. "I only found out at my engagement party. I swear. I went to find Barry when he stormed off. I found him in the parkin' lot talkin' to Pauly. When I walked up, Barry was sayin' that Pauly had to fix this shit between you and Mona."

I raised my eyes to her.

"What he said next, I wasn't supposed to hear. Pauly said he was doin' his best to fix it. But Barry said," Fitz's eyes began to well. She took a deep breath and said, "He said, 'I won't have the woman I love, treated this way'. Pauly noticed me, so Barry turned around, and I was standin' there...had heard the whole thing," she sobbed.

"Why didn't you tell me?" I asked again.

Fitz shook her head, "Because...I know yer in love with Cecil. I didn't want ya knowin'...I didn't want to screw that up. I thought it would just be better...if ya never knew. And I told Barry as much," she admitted.

I shook my head and gave her a deranged laugh, "And why do you get to decide that? What if you're wrong? How could you do that to me?"

"Look, if I'm wrong, and yer not in love with Cecil...I'll go find Barry this very minute..." her voice was shaking, "and I'll tell him that ya want him...and ya love him and I just want the two of ya to be happy. If ya can tell me, it IS my brother ya want, I'll do it in a heartbeat," she sobbed.

I crumbled as tears streamed harder.

"Can ya say...it's Barry?"

I shook my head, "No…I can't."

Fitz moved over to my bed, wrapping her arms around me, both of us crying our eyes out.

After a while, the crying subsided and Fitz said, "Ya do know, I would have been very happy if it had been Barry."

"Really?" I asked.

"I really think…you could have been happy together. I don't think anyone could have been as good fer my favorite brother…as my favorite person. I love ya, Janie, and I hope ya understand. I really was tryin' to protect ya."

`I nodded, and sniffled, "I know you were, Fitzy." I put my head on her shoulder and let out a sigh.

Emotionally exhausted, I went to bed. Some part of my heart hurt for Barry, and for me. I had always believed that everything happened for a reason. Signs were everywhere. If I still believed this, Barry and I never had a chance, according to timing.

6am and my phone rang. I was starting to wonder if the *sleep gods* had it out for me. I would have ignored it, but it may be Cecil. He sounded so weird last night that I just needed to know he was okay. I wondered if I should tell him about my newfound realization; that I was in love with him.

Mom was flashing on the screen. I let out a sigh and debated hitting ignore. But always the good daughter, I answered.

"Hi mom!"

'Don't you 'hi mom' me!" she raged.

"Okay," I said.

"What in God's name, would make you think what you did was okay?" she sounded fit to be tethered.

If I remembered correctly, she was the one who was doing some stuff that was considered not okay. "What are you talking about?" I sat up and rubbed my eyes.

"Don't you play dumb with me! It's all over your feed. I guess you thought I never went on social media…?"

I knew she had in-fact been on social media as of late, but not the way I would hope for. "Mom, I haven't been on social media since I've been on the ship."

"Oh, so you didn't upload a video?" She was giving me the *I dare you to lie to me* mom attitude.

"I had Barry upload the video of me parasailing. Did you see it?"

"No, I saw the other video, and I can't believe you did that without telling me, having me there. What were you thinking? Your father is beside himself."

I was coming around, but still not following, "Dad's upset?"

"Why wouldn't he be? Seriously, every father wants to walk his little girl down the aisle!" she yelled.

My head cocked, had mom had a stroke? Was she drunk? "What are you talking about, crazy lady? I didn't get married!" Fitz woke when I said this and gave me a quizzical look.

"Well then why am I watching a video of your wedding pictures?" mom screamed again.

"Fitz, bring up my page on your phone," I instructed.

It took a few moments while my mother went over every piece of Irish mother's guilt she could think of. "Mom, please, I'm not married!" I finally yelled back at her.

Fitz sat next to me and cued up a video I hadn't seen. The first photo was Barry on his knees picking up my craps winnings when the old man lost his shit. I shook my head.

There, was a picture of Barry and me, standing at the altar holding hands. "That was rehearsal for Aunt Marble's wedding," I looked at Fitz.

The next was of Barry getting ready to put sunscreen on my back before Fitz stopped him.

The pictures were captioned: He proposed! Our wedding abroad! And not a bad way to spend our honeymoon! All of the pictures had been taken from close-up. How was this possible and who had posted it to my page? It had been posted last night. About an hour before Cecil called me.

"Oh My God!" my eyes rounded. So did Fitz's when I explained that Cecil had said he had seen the video on my feed.

"Helloooo," my mother cried out.

"Mom, I'm NOT married. This is a cruel joke someone has played on me!" and I had a pretty good idea who it was.

"Well thank God for that. I can calm your father down now!"

"Great," I said into the receiver. "But right now I gotta go, mom," I hung up.

I had never dressed so quickly in all of my life. This was it, she had gone too damn far. Fitz was pulling up her pants when I darted out of the room.

I headed to Mona's room and banged on the door. "Are you in there? Open the door, Mona," I yelled.

A very frightened maid opened the door and stepped back when she saw my face.

"Is the person staying in this room, here?" I asked her.

"No ma'am," said the maid.

"Thank you," I said angrily and stomped off.

Fitz had caught up with me, "That low class bitch is about to wish fer death."

We made our way to the dining hall, and looked around. Mum was there with Aunt Marble. We were told that they hadn't seen Mona, either.

"What's goin' on?" Mum asked. "Ya look like yer on the warpath!"

"Oh, I am," I played the video for them.

Both of their eyes rounded as they watched.

"I'm pretty sure Cecil saw it…he thinks I married Barry," I panicked.

"Oh no," Aunt Marble said. "You should call him!"

Mum, Fitz and I just stared at her. "I did," I told her. "He won't answer."

I pulled out my phone and called the Callaghan manor in Ireland. Briggs answered the phone and I asked to talk to Cecil.

"He's not here, Miss," Briggs told me.

"May I speak with Elanor?" I asked frantically.

"One moment, Miss," he said.

It was a lot of moments later, when Miss Elanor answered the phone.

"Janie," she said.

"Hi Miss Elanor," I said.

"Just Elanor, my dear," she said.

Boy had she changed since our visit. Before, she loathed me and Fitz. But by the end of our trip, I finally understood why Elanor was, the way Elanor was.

"Look, I think Cecil saw a video that…"

Miss Elanor cut me off, "He did."

"I'm not married!" I told her.

"I said as much to him," she told me. "I knew there had to be another explanation."

"Oh thank God," I breathed.

"Well, I'm not sure my sayin' that put his mind to rest. He got in his car and drove away. I haven't seen him since."

"Dammit!" I said through a tightend jaw. Normally, Miss Elanor would have chastised me for cursing, but not this time.

"I called the distillery, he hadn't been there either," she offered.

"Okay…well if you see him, please tell him that I'm not married and need to talk to him. Please." I said again.

"I will do that. Try not to worry, Janie. I'm pullin' fer the two of ya," she added.

I thanked her and got off the phone.

I spent the next twenty minutes searching the ship. I searched the gym, the craft room, the elder yoga class, the shuffleboard area, the card room. Finally, I searched the pool. There she was, floating on a raft in the deep end.

I walked to the edge, "Get out of the pool!" I told her.

Fitz ran off to find Mum.

"Oh Janie, there you are. I didn't expect to see you, you being on your honeymoon, and all," her grin dripped with sarcasm.

"GET **OUT** OF THE POOL," I said again.

"No…I'm quite content here…just floating around," she paddled with one hand. "This I think…has been the best part of my trip to Mexico. Well this, and ruining you…the way you ruined me," she raised her voice.

"I'm going to tell you one more time, GET OUT OF THE WATER!"

She laughed. "Or what?"

The whole family came running to the pool.

"Or I'm comin' in after ya," my own Irish was coming out. "Either way, I'm gettin' a hold of ya."

Mona smiled from ear to ear, "Well come on in, Janie. The water's fine," she hissed.

Kicking off my shoes, I dove toward her.

Mona let out a scream and rolled off her raft, swimming for the ladder, with me right behind her.

Some of the old people in the pool moved out of the water, and began asking others what was going on.

Mona had just reached the ladder when I caught up to her. I grabbed her by her shoulder and pulled her down, backward. Panicked, she tried to swim away as I followed **Jaws** style. Mona lost sight of me for a moment and looked around. Her eyes skimmed the water as I surfaced. She screamed again, realizing that I was coming at her like a torpedo. Turning away, she ran around the shallow end slapping at the water behind her. When I came up for air she pushed my head down, then started trying to run again. She was panting hard, with huge bulging eyes.

The old people she passed by, watched with looks of confusion and head shakes.

The Fitzpatrick brood ran around the pool chasing after us.

I stood up in the shallow end, "Get back here and fight me!" I yelled.

I wasn't exactly in my right mind, when I heard Pauly screaming in the distance, "Janie…no!"

Diving back under, I kicked off the side of the pool in her direction, grabbing for her as I swam.

We were back in the deep end now and she was flailing her arms. Holding onto the wall, she was like a kid who was in the water for the first time. She pushed her legs out behind her, trying to kick at me. I grabbed her leg and pulled her away from the wall. Under the water she went. I could see air bubbles follow in a stream as I yanked her to me. Mona kicked out, hitting me in the boob. I let out bubbles of my own and said the F-word as she flapped away. Resurfacing again, I yelled, "Stay still, you little grommet!"

Mona let out a wide eyed squeal and paddled for her life.

I made a leaping motion and grabbed at her again.

An elderly couple we passed for the second time, gave us a dirty look, like we were rambunctious children with no parental supervision.

I heard Danny say, "Twenty bucks on Janie."

Then Andy said, "Really? Whose gonna take that bet? Are ya givin' odds?"

Mum yelled at them, "Quiet yerselves boys!"

Pulling Mona backward again by the leg I had latched onto, I grabbed her hair as she floated past me. When I pulled Mona up, she spit water in my face. Down, I shoved her under. She tried to kick away from me and out of my grasp. But I didn't feel a thing as I dragged her to the side of the pool.

Far off, in my one track mind, I heard Aunt Marble yell, "Clematis, NO!"

Some part of me that was still holding onto sanity, thought: That's me! I'm Clematis...toxic if used incorrectly.

The next thing I knew, someone caught me underneath both of my arms and pulled me out of the water. One good heave and I was up. Mona, I dragged up with me by her hair.

I wasn't sure who had me, but I knew I had her, so I wasn't fighting. Looking behind me, I saw Da had been the one to drag us out of the pool.

I watched her gasp for breath. I would be a good girl and wait for her to be up to par before I beat her like a piñata. I stood and waited for her breathing to return to normal.

Pauly had made it to the other side of the pool and ran in between Mona and me.

"Step aside," I told him. "This is between me and your batshit crazy bride."

"Janie, I'm not gonna let ya do this," Pauly said.

"Stay the hell out of this," Fitz warned her brother.

"I won't," Pauly shook his head at me.

"Step aside Pauly," I said again, as I watched Mona spit up water she had swallowed, choking.

"I'm not gonna step aside and let you hurt the woman I love. Pauly turned to his wife, "I don't just love ya...I'm in love with ya." He looked back at me, "And I'll get between anyone who comes at her...even you Janie," he squeaked under his breath.

Barry stepped forward, "Ya lay one hand on Janie...I'll kill ya myself."

Mum looked worried. This could get very ugly, very fast.

"Tell Pauly what you did?" I said to Mona. "Tell Pauly what you did to deserve me kickin' your ass."

Mona swallowed hard, "I took your phone," she told him.

"I wondered where the hell it went," Pauly told her. "When?"

"Last night…in the Casino…you went to the restroom," she coughed, "and left it on the bar."

"I may owe the bartender an apology," he raised one eyebrow. "What did ya do with my phone?"

Mona bit her lower lip, "I made a video…one that made it look like Janie and Barry…got married."

Pauly laughed, "Is that all?" he asked me. "We all know ya didn't, Janie, so who would care?"

"Ask her what she hoped, and DID accomplish with the video," I spat, feeling my rage rise again.

Pauly turned his eyes to his wife, "What's Janie talkin' about?"

Mona started to tear, "I wanted to…ruin her relationship… like she ruined ours. I didn't expect…"

Pauly thought for a moment, "Cecil?" he asked.

I nodded to him, "Yeah, Cecil."

"We can fix this," the look on Pauly's face showed worry, "I'm sure if ya just talk to him…"

"He won't talk to me," I cut him off. "Now because of your wife and her ridiculous insecurities, that you created," I pointed out, "now I've lost the man I'm in love with."

Barry gave me a weak smile and a head nod.

Pauly turned to his wife, "I have caused this. I've never been good at bein' serious, always jokin', but I say this to you now, all jokin' aside. I'm in love with ya. I fell for ya, head over heels, years ago. Yer," he gulped, "the most important person…in my whole world. I'm so sorry I didn't treat ya, everyday, like yer the best thing that has ever happened to me…because ya are."

As I watched a tear fall from his eye, I knew I couldn't hit Mona. I knew it would make him try to defend her. Then Barry, and possibly Fitz, would come to my defense, and it would turn into an awful mess.

Mona looked at her husband with tears in her eyes, "I love you so much. I always have," she dropped her head and began to tremble. "I just thought...she was the one who got away."

"I've tried to tell ya a hundred times, I don't think of Janie that way. I never HAVE thought of Janie that way."

And lets just add, that Janie does NOT think of Pauly that way," I added, letting my crazy take me to third person status.

"I just...needed to have a reason, why we are the way we are, now," Mona cried. "I don't understand what changed...and then she fought that woman at the bar ...who attacked you," she did a palms-up.

"Yeah, she did. And I've gotta say, it was a hell of a lot more impressive than this was," he nodded to me.

I gave him a shit look, "Don't fucking temp me!" I told him.

"Yes she did fight that girl, side by side...with my other sister. Janie is a sister to me. She always has been."

"I just don't understand what's wrong with us," her face contorted.

"I know, baby. I know. I'm so sorry," he cried ugly tears.

Instead of fighting Mona: Instead of causing a brood war among the whole Fitzpatrick family. Instead of ruining Aunt Marble and Benny's wedding, I did the only thing I could. I pushed Pauly in the water then reached down toward Mona.

Da's eyes rounded. He was sure I wouldn't be able to control myself.

Grabbing her bikini top, I yanked with all my might. ***Snap***, the top came off, as I stepped backward and shot it like a finger arrow onto the roof of the ship.

Pauly lifted himself out of the water, "So now yer even, right?" he asked me, hopefully.

I stared at Mona as she tried to cover her tiny little boobs. I shook my head, "But for the sake of the family I love, I'm willing to walk away."

Da gave me a nod of appreciation. He knew for a fact that this would have divided the family's loyalties.

As I turned, Pauly grabbed Mona in a hug and they kissed, saying how much they loved each other.

Walking away, Fitz caught up to me, "I know," I said, "you can't believe I didn't kick her ass."

"Actually, after watchin' that, I think it's better that ya don't try."

I shot her a look, "Thanks."

"That was …hard to watch, embarrassin' really," she shook her head.

I found a grin thinking about what it must have looked like: Me chasing Mona, Mona fleeing and screaming her head off, and the rest of the family running around the outside of the pool.

"Seriously, I am surprised ya stopped yerself. Yer a better woman than I," she nodded to me.

"It wouldn't have changed a thing," I said looking back to where Mona and Pauly gushed love for each other. "At least not for me," I said.

Back in our room, I tried again to call Cecil with no answer. I looked at my page and read all of the comments on Barry and my fake wedding. So many people posted things like '*congratulations*', and '*where can we send gifts*? I erased the video and made a post telling everyone that Barry and I weren't married. I didn't offer any other explanation. The truth was, the look Barry had given me when I said I was in love with Cecil, broke my heart. I did love Barry. You can't spend the majority of your life having a crush on someone, and have it not hurt. If I had known, that night at the bar when his crazy ex attacked me, would everything be different now? Some part of me had to wonder, if the timing had been right, if I had known how he felt, if he had known how I felt; would we have been like Mum and Da, or my parents? Would we have been a *forever* couples that grew old together? I guess I wasn't supposed to know the answer to this question.

Fitz had given me some space, but it was time now to get ready for the wedding.

"Ya okay, Janie?" she asked.

"No. I'm really not," I admitted.

"Miss Elanor will get the message to him. She'll fix it," Fitz said. "I called Scotty and told him. But Cecil isn't answerin' for him either. He said he'll keep tryin' and he's already left him a message tellin' him ya didn't get married. I'm sure everything will work out."

"Before or after he goes on a whore-athon?" I wondered out loud.

"I told ya, he wouldn't do that. He knows he'd lose ya," she put an arm around me.

"He already thinks he has," I pointed out. "Seriously, he sounded so weird on the phone last night. Why didn't I ask him what was wrong?" I ran my fingers through my hair.

"Don't ya do that, Janie, ya couldn't have known."

I shook my head, "We need to get ready."

I put on the piñata muumuu, and wasn't at all surprised that I looked exactly how I felt; horrible.

Fitz got to wear her own clothes and looked very boat-wedding-sheik in a blue and white striped dress with a nautical patch embroidered in gold on her chest.

Fitz ran down to the bar and brought me back a shot of Bushmills. We downed them in our tiny room. I needed a little pick me up, if I was going to force a smile. I also needed a little calmer-downer knowing I would have to see Mona. No one expected me make nice-nice with her. But they did expect me not to kill her. In order to do that, I needed to find the buzz-line. Too little, I would seethe. Too much, it would be on. I wasn't a fighter by nature. It just wasn't me. But this time, I had felt a rage I had never felt before. It was a byproduct of knowing someone had ruined your life.

A knock on the door dragged me from another bout with rage inducing thoughts.

When Fitzy opened the door, Barry was standing there. He was wearing a short sleeved Hawaiian shirt, red, with khaki board shorts. He looked like a thirty year old Spring Breaker. "May I have a moment with ya, Janie?" he asked.

Fitz looked back at me, "I'll meet ya upstairs, okay?"

I nodded to her and offered Barry a seat on Fitz's bed.

Barry sat and looked around, "I think yer room is bigger than mine."

"You must be sleeping in a closet, then." I forced a smile.

He sighed, "I wanted to apologize to ya. If Pauly hadn't known…ya know…then Mona wouldn't have gone after ya that way."

"Well, it's sweet of you to try and take responsibility, but you weren't responsible for this," I shook my head at him. "Mona has hated me for years. All she really needed was a WAY to hurt me. And she found it."

"I have a confession to make," his eyes dropped.

I was pretty sure I knew what he was going to say.

"The reason Mona knew how to hurt ya, is because she knows…how I feel about ya."

I assumed this, "Barry you really don't…"

He cut me off, "No I really do have to tell ya this. See, Mona thought your thing with Cecil…was fleeting. You'd be fair game again soon. And of course, she thought Pauly was the one who would try to take advantage of you bein' available. To try and clear Pauly, I went to see her last night before I went to the casino. I told her how I felt about ya. I told her that I was the one who had a lifelong crush on ya, not Pauly. I even let her know that Pauly had known about my feelings…fer years."

I cocked my head.

"She urged me to tell ya, to declare my love. When I told her I wouldn't be part of her spiteful game, she got enraged with me, as well. Said she'd get us both. I didn't know what that meant, or even worry about her empty threat. But it seems she killed two birds with one stone. She made me reveal something I planned on takin' to my grave...and tried to ruin you and Cecil's chances at the same time."

"Oh," I tried to absorb her train of thought. It was crazy. Then again, her thinking that I had ever wanted Pauly, made no sense either.

"The truth is, Janie, I HAVE had a crush on ya, since we were young. I knew it wasn't a good idea. I even tried to stay away from ya as much as possible. Thinkin' it would just, ya know, go away." He sighed again, "But it never did. You've always been..."

I was trying hard not to cry and kept swallowing back tears.

"...the perfect girl to me," he swallowed hard, too. "So, in some way, this is my fault...and I'm so sorry. On so many levels, I'm sorry," he shook his head.

I reached out my hand to his. I wasn't sure saying that I felt the same way until just a couple of months ago, would make this better. "First of all, I refuse to blame you in any way, for Mona's warped imagination. Second, you have to know... you've always been special to me."

He nodded like this didn't help to hear, or I was just trying to let him down easy.

"I wish I would have known sooner. There was a time," I didn't say when, "when I felt the same way about you."

Barry looked up into my eyes, and searched them for my truth.

In my eyes, he saw everything I had kept from him for years. "You were the perfect man to me...for most of my life. I do wish I had told you, then," I nodded. "But I was so afraid of everything that could go wrong. I couldn't handle the thought of losing Fitz…or you."

"I would have never have let that happen. If I had met ya before Fitz…I would have held yer hand in Kindergarten…I would have kissed your cheek in fifth grade…kissed your lips in eighth grade…and I would have asked fer yer hand in twelfth," his eyes held mine. "I would never have let ya go," he brought my hand to his lips and gave it a gentle kiss.

With this, my tears fell.

"That night at the bar…ah God, I wanted to kiss ya, so bad," he said. "I came so close. Then when Shelia went crazy and tried to attack ya, I figured it was a sign, ya know. That it wasn't supposed to happen. That I wasn't supposed to try."

We really were on the same wavelength, I thought. I had this same feeling, read the same thing into the situation.

"I will always love ya, Janie," he stood to leave.

"Barry!" I stood too. Throwing my arms around his neck, I said, "I'll always love you, too."

"Well, we better get to the weddin'," Barry said.

"Yeah, I can't wait to be seen in this," I did a little spin in my piñata ensemble.

"Yeah, I didn't want to say anything, but wow, that's hideous," he laughed.

I broke out laughing, too, and hugged him again.

We held each other until Fitz knocked on the door. She entered with one hand over her eyes, "Are ya descent?" she asked.

Barry and I laughed, "Janie, put yer clothes back on!" Barry said.

"That's not funny," Fitz said, but she never removed her hand. "Yer kiddin' right?" she questioned.

"We're dressed, ya daft girl," he told her.

"Wow that was really fast. Sorry about that, Janie," she moved her hand from her eyes.

Barry shook his head, "Yer an asshole, Fitzy."

"And ya love me," she gave her brother a heartfelt hug. "Is everything okay?" she looked from Barry to me, to Barry again.

Barry took my hand and gave it a squeeze, "We'll be fine," he kissed my cheek then headed for the door.

"Barry," I called after him, "Always," I told him.

"Always," he nodded to me.

As the door shut behind my crush of a lifetime, tears pooled again.

Fitz put her arm around me, "Ya okay?"

"We will be," I put my head on her shoulder.

Standing on the deck, a bouquet in one hand, Barry's hand in my other, I just wanted to make it through the ceremony. Today wasn't about me. Benny stood at the end of the aisle, beaming with pride. I wasn't surprised to see his knobby knees, Velcro shoes and black calf high sox, make their debut. This is who he was and I loved that he was just this.

Tovah stood in front of a white trellis awning in a light pink flowing gown. She had that half grin again, the one that I had become so fond of. The truth was, this amazing woman had barreled her way into my life, my business and my heart. I knew that I would actually miss her, dearly.

Mum and Da stood facing each other: mum in a horrible muumuu that somehow looked great on her, and Da, also showing some knee in his board shorts. I smiled when I spied them stealing a quick kiss before the ceremony began. They really were what it was all about. Mum and Da always gave love openly and to everyone. But what the two of them shared, well, it was one of those, 'I love you…and then some' things.

Without wanting to, I glanced over at Pauly and Mona. Regardless of how I felt, I did hope that Pauly had learned a valuable lesson about how you treat someone you love (even if the one he loved, deserved the ass-kicking of a lifetime). She did look different, though. Like a lost piece of her had been given back. I guess Pauly standing in front of her, protecting her from not only me, but his whole family, was the proof she needed. The look on their faces should have made me happy. After all, he was family to me. I thought about it. Nope, I admitted to myself, still wanted to kick her ass. But I knew what I had backed away from, wasn't about me. It was about the family I loved like they were my own.

As Barry and I started down the aisle hand in hand, I had that sickening feeling, like when something you really don't want to end will anyway. I handed Fitz the bouquet and held out both my hands to Barry. Staring into each other's eyes, I saw my own pain mirrored in his eyes. But, then something strange happened, he began to smile. It was just a hint at first. Before I knew it, we were both smiling broadly. Tears rushed to my eyes as we started laughing. At the end of our moment he pulled me to him, and kissed my cheek.

"I love you, Janie," he told me.

"I love you, too," I told him.

I saw Mum, out of the corner of my eye, put her hand to her heart.

Barry and I stood smiling at each other, as Aunt Marble walked between us to her love.

Something inside of me knew I would always love Barry. It may not be in the same way I had once spent sleepless nights thinking about, but it would be forever. And I knew that I, too, was and would forever be loved by him.

Benny put a glass wrapped in a scarf on the ground and he and Aunt Marble stomped the hell out of it, right before Tovah said, "I now pronounce you husband and wife."

The whole family clapped, whistled and cheered.

We were asked not to throw rice because of the birds, so Mum threw crackers. We had to rush off when the seagulls found out there was a buffet for them on the top deck.

There wasn't a reception, per se, but we all agreed to meet for dinner and toast the wedding. Benny and Marble ran off to *nap* as Benny said with a wink.

The great part about this was that my piñata muumuu wasn't acceptable attire for dinner with the Captain.

Fitz and I went back to our room to shower, change and make sure we were packed. Tomorrow, we would be home.

Fitz's phone rang and she turned away from me. I figured it was Scotty.

"Uh huh, okay," followed by a pause. "Alright," was followed by another pause. "Okay, I'll let her know. Thank ya Miss Elanor."

My head swung in Fitz's direction, "Miss Elanor? What did she say?"

Fitz looked like she had bad news she didn't want to share. "Miss Elanor was worried about Cecil, so she went to inspect his room."

"Yeah? What did she find?"

"Well, his phone was left on his bed, so yer calls..." she shook her head.

I let out a defeated sigh.

"Maybe ya should call that Big Dave fellow? I mean he's Cecil's best friend...and owns a bar...maybe Cecil went there?"

I was just as uncomfortable about trying to hunt Cecil down, as I was scared of not trying. "I don't know. I really don't know what to do. Plus, it's still early there."

Fitz nodded, "Right. Well, you should probably get ready fer dinner."

"I'm not feeling like going to dinner," I admitted to her.

"Well tough, yer the maid of honor and ya are expected to be there."

I made a face.

"And...I'm not leavin' ya layin' around here, torturin' yerself. So get dressed!"

I put on the red dress I had brought for the Captain's Dinner. It was a beautiful garment. I really didn't think I could do it justice, even before I felt like all the happy had been sucked out of me.

Fitz, of course, looked jaw dropping gorgeous in her L.B.D. and high spiked heels.

We made our way to the Captain's Dinner and were the last to arrive. Everyone, all the brothers, all of their wives, Tovah and newly married couple sat at our two tables. I had to admit, it was nice to see the whole family together.

I was seated across from Mona, who averted her eyes when Fitz and I approached the table. But it wasn't that *I'm not looking at you* face I usually got. No, it almost looked like guilt. I was okay with the thought that she may be feeling guilty for everything she put in motion.

This was the only meal that wasn't buffet style. We sat as we were served a choice of fish, pork chops, or prime rib, with all of the fixings.

After dinner, the Captain made a speech about how he was grateful to the people who had joined him on another successful cruise. At the end of his speech, he raised his glass to Benny and Aunt Marble's nuptials. Everyone cheered as they kissed.

Da stood, champagne in hand, and asked us all to lift our glasses. "You two, Benny and Marble, what a wonderful adventure, you've allowed us to have with ya! But, may I say with all certainty, your best adventures are yet to come. Remember to listen, when yer angry…to speak when you are happy…and to love every second." Da smiled, "Slainte!"

We all repeated "Sliante," pushing our glasses toward the couple, before drinking them down.

Barry looked over at me, "Ya doin' okay?"

I wasn't sure how to answer this. He was actually part of the heartache I was feeling, and I couldn't say that. "I'll be alright," I told him. "You?"

"Me too," he told me. "Dance with me?" he asked.

I nodded and let him lead me to the dance floor.

I would usually be happy for a slow song. It was much easier for me to just rock back and forth than try and find my rhythm. This time, I worried that it would be uncomfortable for both of us. But, it wasn't. We rocked, and he spun me a few times, smiling the whole time.

When we left the floor, the Fitzpatrick women were watching and smiling. Now that everyone knew about Barry's lifelong crush, it was easier to be exactly what we were to each other; friends.

Everyone took turns dancing with the bride and groom. Once again, Benny's short stature put him at boob height. He moved me all around the whole floor, ballroom dancing.

"Ya know, kid, I'm really glad ya came," he told me.

"I am too," I said.

"You and me…we're not blood," he nodded toward the brood of Fitzpatrick's.

"No we're not," I looked from Barry to Fitzy."

"We're better," he grinned. "They chose us."

I smiled, "You're right."

As I walked to the bar to get anything that wasn't champagne, Mum followed.

Walking up behind me, she asked, "Can we talk for a moment?"

I was a little confused that she asked, "Of course," I told her.

"I feel ridiculous," she said.

"For what," I asked, putting my hand on her shoulder.

"I never knew…I never saw!" her eyes glistened as she shook her head. "If I had just left Barry alone…if I had just let him CHOOSE…" a tear fell. "Maybe he would have found the courage to *live* what his heart felt for so long."

I looked over at Barry dancing with Aunt Marble and sighed, "It just wasn't meant to be," I told her.

"Fitzy told me…how you felt about him, too."

My eyes dropped to the ground. I didn't know if it was embarrassment I felt or just sadness.

Gently lifting my chin to look me in the eyes, she said, "I would have chosen ya…if I had known. You've always been like a daughter to me. It would have been wonderful," she nodded. "But you'll always be my baby, no matter what," she kissed my cheek.

I nodded and took Mum into an embrace and just held on.

Mum said in my ear, "Some things are meant to be, but timing can be tricky." I pulled away and met her eyes, "One never knows," she smiled.

"Does this mean you intend to meddle?" I cocked my head.

"No, I think from here on out, I'm goin' to let God, fate, whoever's in charge, handle this one," she grinned.

Fitz caught up with me after her dance with Benny, "Guy has moves," she informed me. "I could barely keep up!"

I laughed, "Tell me about it!"

"It's been one hell of a trip," Fitz sighed, watching her whole family on the dance floor.

"Agreed, I'll be very happy to get home and finally relax," I nodded.

Pauly and Mona were spinning around the floor, lost in each other's eyes. I tried to be the bigger person, I thought.

"I still can't believe…everything they put us through…" I shook my head. "Maybe turning the other cheek, was the right thing."

"See and that's where you and I differ," the *evil-fairy-grin*, stretched across her face. "I still believe in an-eye-for-an-eye," Fitz turned her grin towards the dance floor.

I could see Mona and Pauly dancing to a fast song. I cocked my own head when Mona grabbed her tummy. Her eyes rounded, just as Pauly's eyes bulged. Fast as lightening, both of them took off running through the crowd.

Looking at Fitz with questioning eyes, she reached into her hand bag and pulled out a bottle called **Ultra Turbo Go**. "You can get anything in Mexico," she grinned and threw her arm around me.

I laughed, "Pauly too," I asked.

"I just felt it fair to give him back some of the shit, he brought into our lives," she laughed.

As the night wore to a close, I was more than ready to go to sleep; if I was lucky enough to fall asleep.

The next morning we were informed via loud speaker that we would be back in Long Beach by noon.

Fitz got her daily call from Scotty. There was still no news about or from Cecil.

I went down to the dining hall and pretended to eat a muffin, just picking at it, while I drank my coffee.

Tovah came and sat next to me, "So, I'm stayin a few days before I head back to New York."

"Yeah?" I asked.

"Yeah, I haven't seen Benny in so long, I figure, I better get as much time as I can. We're not spring chickens anymore. Every time we say goodbye, it could be the last time," she gave me a palms-up.

I laughed, "I think you'll probably outlive me."

"I was wondering, while I'm here, maybe you'd show me some of yer work?"

"Sure! I would love to hear what you think. Especially since you're an art lover!"

"Somethin' like that," she cocked her head.

"Please, maybe we could do lunch?" I asked.

"I'd like that, kid!" Tovah stood, "Now, I've gotta breakfast date," she nodded toward the gentleman who had joined us at our first port. He raised a Mimosa to her and gave a devilish grin.

"Ah," I said, and smiled at her.

When she left the table, Fitz hurried over, "Do you know who that is?"

My face squished up, "Tovah…Benny's sister?" I looked at her like she had lost her marbles.

"THAT…is Tovah Schumer!" Fitz said excitedly.

"Tovah Schumer, as in…?" I could barely breathe.

"As in the Schumer Gallery in New York," Fitz finished my thought. "Mum just told me."

"But Benny's last name is Schwartz…" I tried to find reason.

Fitz looked at me like I was stupid, "Yeah…but her dead husband's last name was Schumer!"

"Oh my God," my jaw dropped, "she just asked to see my work."

"I guess Benny's been tellin' her about ya, and what an amazin' artist ya are," Fitz's eyes were huge. "Janie this is a big deal. She owns…"

"One of the greatest Galleries in the U.S.," my mind was blown.

Fitz nodded and beamed.

I went over Tovah's conversations with me about how art was *all passion.* I was just willing to take her word for it because she was at the age of the wise woman. I mean, she had obviously lived more than me, had been married and widowed, was a daredevil and had that whole *take life by the balls* energy about her.

In my little room, I wanted to be more excited about Tovah requesting to see my work, but I was still stuck on Cecil. I called again; straight to voicemail.

Back in the U.S.A., we pulled into port. Fitz's limo waited for her. As we approached the driver holding up a **Fitzpatrick** sign,

Scotty jumped out of the backseat. I laughed as Fitz dropped her luggage and ran to her man. They stood, lips locked.

Tovah smiled, "Now that's what real love looks like," she gave me the half grin. "Maybe you should ride with me, Kid? Looks like they've already started to make up for lost time."

Their kiss had become a mauling. I smiled to Tovah, "Yeah that sounds like a good idea," I grinned.

Tovah had a limo waiting for her as well, so we got comfortable for the ride back to my house.

"So, are you staying at a hotel?" I asked her.

"I stay with Benny when I visit," she smiled. "I know that may sound odd at our age, but we're two peas in a pod. It's wonderful that he's met and married a woman who loves her family the same way."

I nodded, "One of the best things about this family is how close they are," I agreed.

"Well, since I'm driving ya home, maybe I could take a quick peek at yer work?"

I mentally went over how clean my studio was, before answering, "Yeah, that would be fine."

There was a little silence while I began to fidget.

"So, that man of yours, have ya heard anything?" her head cocked.

Shaking my own head, "No," I sighed.

"Look, kid, I'm gonna be honest with ya, there are some things, you should never have to force. Work for, yes…force, no. If he feels the same way about you, as you feel about him… everything will be fine," she gave my fidgeting hand a squeeze.

Pulling up in front of my little yellow house, I could see that someone was sitting on my porch swing.

My hand flew to cover my mouth as I spied Cecil. Sitting there, with a bouquet in hand, he stood as the limo pulled up.

I started to sob and laugh.

Tovah looked to the porch where Cecil stood, and smiled. “Maybe I’ll see your paintings tomorrow, she told me. When she gave Cecil another look, she said, “Or maybe the day after that,” she grinned and hugged me. “Go find your passion, kid.”

As I exited the limo, the driver asked Tovah if he should get my luggage out of the trunk.

I heard her tell him, “What, and ruin the ending? We’ll get it back to her later,” the limo pulled away.

16

DESPERATELY SEEKING CECIL

"You're here!" I said as I walked to where he stood.

His face was drawn as he swallowed hard, "I know ya may not want to see me, but I have somethin' I have to say, and I have to say it to ya directly."

"No wait, you don't understand," I pled.

"Please Janie I just need to say it…please just let me say it."

I wanted to blurt out everything…everything that happened… everything that was taken incorrectly…everything I felt, but the look on his face, stopped me.

"All I want…all I'll ever want…is fer ya to be happy. Deep in my heart, it's my truth," his eyes sparkled. "And if ya say ya are," he let out a deep breath, "just let me kiss ya goodbye?"

Tears started to fall, "I'm happy…for the first time…" I was swallowing back sobs.

He began to nod and looked to the ground.

"No, you don't understand…right now, this moment, is the first time I've been happy…since I left you in Ireland!"

His eyes raised, question filling them, "What?"

"I didn't marry Barry!" I laughed through my tears and shook my head furiously.

"Ya didn't?" he asked under his breath.

"No!"

"But the video?" he was searching my eyes.

"I can explain all of that, but first, I have to tell you something." I gulped, be brave, I thought. "I think...no," I corrected myself. Be braver than that, I told myself. "I'm in love with you!"

Cecil's eyes went wide, and I couldn't tell if what I said was a good thing or if it just ruined what could have been.

Cecil grabbed his heart before wrapping his arms around me and pulling me off of my feet. "I love ya, Janie O'Connelly. I'm in love with ya!"

A sob escaped me, one of relief and great joy. We kissed and hugged, until I was sure what he said, what I was feeling...was true.

Smiling up into his happy face I said, "Come inside, I want to show you my garden."

Stepping inside my room, with Cecil's hand in mine, it wasn't the way I had pictured it in my head. In fantasies, sometimes there was candlelight. Sometimes, I was dressed in lingerie and had to seduce him. Other times, my brain had come up with ridiculous scenarios where we are on a plane about to crash, or I was a patient and he was my therapist. And still other times, we lay under the huge willow on the Callaghan property.

In truth, all of these dreams and daydreams had brought us here. There was no candlelight, no lingerie, no props or roll playing. It was just him and me. And I wouldn't have wanted it any other way.

Cecil stayed for another three days, during which time, we only left the house once.

At Aunt Marble's and Uncle Benny's wedding reception held at

Fitzpatrick's Pub, we raised our glasses again and toasted the happy couple.

Late into the evening, Cecil said, "Maybe you should go have a dance with Barry?"

My eyes shot to Cecil. I had never told him that Barry had felt the same way for me, as I had for him for so many years. I figured there was no point. When I raised my brow and asked why, Cecil said, "I think…no, I KNOW, yer a hard one to lose."

I stared at him, wondering what he knew…how he knew.

"Ya can't think I didn't know, Janie," his eyes sparkled. "Women aren't the only ones with a sixth sense. Now go…dance with yer friend. I'll be right here…Clematis."

My eyes shot to him, "I told you that in confidence," my eyes rounded.

Cecil laughed, "Go!"

17

JUST A DANCE

Walking up to where Barry stood, a drink in his hand, he smiled. I didn't say a word, just held out my hand. His hand found mine and we moved to the dancefloor. The feeling I remembered the most growing up with Barry, was absolute nervousness. Always I was worried that I would trip, fall, or my eyes would give me away. That one secret that had lasted almost my whole life, had left me a wreck of sorts. I knew now though, as we moved in a tiny circle, I may trip, but he would never let me fall. And in my eyes, the not-so-secret-secret, it was there…mirrored in his.

We danced quietly for a while before he said, "If ever…he doesn't treat ya right…"

My eyes went to his.

"I'll be here," he whispered then leaned in and kissed my cheek softly.

I smiled and nodded as he pulled away.

The thought of what he said, both warmed and cracked my heart.

18

HEARTACHE AND HOPE

I rode to the hanger with Cecil. We held hands the whole time, my head on his shoulder.

The closer we got, the harder my heart began to pound.

"I hate to leave ya," he kissed that spot between my brows.

"I hate to be left," I kissed him back.

"It won't be fer long. I couldn't handle it if it was," he smiled. "Maybe I'll meet ya in New York, when ya have yer auction at the Schumer Gallery?"

"I would really like that," I sighed.

We kissed and kissed and kissed, until the pilot started to wonder if he was in fact flying Cecil back to Ireland.

We exchanged our *I love you's*, with big sighs and pounding hearts. Waving to me from the top stair of the plane, I blew a kiss. As the plane taxied away, the pain I would have normally felt was mixed with great hope for our future. I smiled, knowing that I, Janie O'Connelly, was finally in love.

19

BACK TO NEW YORK

Fitz yelled into the receiver, "I don't know what to pack!"

"YOU don't know what to pack?" I asked her, staring at ten pairs of 501's. "You've had almost a month to pack," I pointed out.

"Well, that's the problem. I've been packin' and unpackin' and repackin' for weeks! I do better when I pack at the last minute."

"So, dump everything out of your suitcase, and pretend you're packing for the first time," I suggested.

There was silence for a moment then Fitz said, "That just might work. What time are we leavin', anyway?"

"We have to be at the airport by 10am, and then we meet Marne for drinks at 7pm."

"I can't believe we're gonna see Marne, I'm so excited!" Fitz announced.

"Me too," I told her.

"Now the flight is first class, right?" Fitz asked for verification.

"Yes Fitz," I confirmed for the hundredth time.

"What can I say, riding on private planes has spoiled me," she laughed.

"I'm aware," I laughed. "Now can I get off the phone and finish packing!"

"Mum's tonight fer dinner and our blessin', don't forget," she warned.

"I'll be there," I assured her, and hung up.

Looking at my luggage, I couldn't help but worry. Last time I rode the friendly skies on a commercial flight, my baggage went on its own holiday without me. Not to mention, my first visit to the Big Apple, was a train wreck, where I wound up in a dominatrix outfit in the back of a cop car. As I zipped my bag and said a small prayer over it, I told it, "I need you to be on your best behavior. We're going back to New York."

THE END

THANK YOU

Thank you: to Louise Zanotto for editing, support and love.
Thank you: to Sarra (Fitzy) Hu, for inspiration and being my favorite head-shaker. I love you.

Don't miss JANIE vs. THE BIG APPLE.
Available Now

The fourth entry in the quirky, poignant* Janie Chronicles *finds Janie O'Connelly's feet back on blessed dry land… until an unexpected opportunity has her jetting to the Big Apple. What do broken plans, bad drivers, unexpected visitors, and a psycho stalker have in common? Yep, that would be Janie.

Janie has been invited to be a featured artist at the prestigious Schumer Gallery in New York City. It's the offer of a lifetime. But as she knows, nothing ever goes exactly as planned.

Horrible taxi rides and Fitzy's over-the-top Halloween plans have nothing on an involuntary spiritual shift that leaves Janie more awakened but no less confused about the craziness of her quickly changing life.

Turn the page for an excerpt from *Janie vs. The Big Apple*.

1

THE TERMINAL: TAKE TWO

"Run dammit!" I yelled when Fitz turned to come help me off the floor. "Hold the damn plane!" I yelled again as she turned away and headed for our boarding gate.

Picking up my lightning-bolt shaped rune, that had become a part of my everyday wardrobe, I wondered if its defection from my pocket was the *stone* trying to give me a sign; don't go back to New York!

"I got this!" Fitz yelled back to me as she ran.

I knew this would happen, I thought to myself as I stood and grabbed my carry-on. Limping, I soldiered on.

Historically, airports haven't been a great place for me. In fact, several months ago, I had been dumped at LAX. Not just dumped, I reminded myself; but dumped in public right before our flight to Hawaii, while his mistress stood waiting for my ticket so she could go and bask on the beach in my place with my boyfriend of almost two years. My luggage, sensing it was actually going nowhere, had gone on a trip without me. Actually, my luggage has seen more of the world than I have.

I began to hobble my way forward, somewhat Quasimdo-ish, as I threw my bag over my shoulder and limped onward.

Approaching my terminal, I heard Fitz say, “There she is, she’s here!”

The desk attendant, 40-ish, ample in every way, with the biggest over-bleached hair helmet I had ever seen, turned her eyes to me, “That’s not an eighty-year-old-woman on life support!”

“Did I say eighty?” Fitz asked with innocently rounded eyes. “I meant *crazy woman* who needs *mental support.*” Fitz blamed her Irish accent, “A lot of people find me hard to understand.”

I noticed she really Irish’d it up for effect.

The attendant gave Fitz the stern mother look I knew only too well.

As we were directed to first class, the flight attendant said, “Well, now that you two have arrived, I guess the plane can finally take off.” The attendant flashed that painted on smile that all of them must be trained to do.

Fitz smiled at her and said, “Can ya teach me that?”

“And what exactly are we talking about?” the attendant asked with big rounded eyes over the forced toothy smile.

“How ya can say catty things while smiling like that,” Fitz pointed to her face. “I’d like to learn how to do that instead of just telling people to fuck-off.” Fitz made an attempt to give the attendant the same smile. “I feel like I’m not doin’ it right.” Fitz and the woman fake smiled at each other until the attendant walked away.

“I can’t believe we almost missed the flight,” I buckled my lap belt. “And an eighty-year-old-woman…on life support?” I questioned her.

“Ya said if we missed the flight, ya’d kill me. So really, ya left me little choice in the matter,” Fitz gave me the fake attendant grin she was working on.

"You could have been packed and ready to go like I asked you to be," I threw the thought out there with my own fake smile.

"Ya know Janie, I'm sorry, but when Scotty hits that spot on my neck, I lose all track of the rest of the world. I think I may be a sex addict," she said like she was admitting a feared flaw.

"Yeah, I don't think you should try that as a defense," I shook my head.

"Anyway, we made the flight, with a little creative wording, and we're off to New York. And then…we'll get to see Marne!" she beamed.

This did bring a smile to my face. Fitz was my best friend since kindergarten, that's the truth. But once upon a time, we weren't just Lucy and Ethel. Once upon a time, our twosome was a threesome. Kind of like *The Three Amigos*. Or in our case, *The Three Stooges*.

Marne had also grown up to be a supermodel but lived and worked mostly in Europe. Her long legs, dark caramel skin and perfect smile had made her the toast of the industry more than once. She graced the covers of magazine after magazine and was the spokesmodel for everything sultry; from five star restaurants and luxury cars, to five star hotels, resorts and a Scotch that was twice my age.

I hadn't seen Marne in over five years. Her arrival at my twenty-first birthday had been my gift from Fitz. I don't remember some parts of that visit since between Fitz and Marne, everywhere we went drinks were paid for by people who loved the gorgeous duo.

Fitz had seen Marne a little more recently since they had done a few runway shows and photo shoots together. I'd see pictures of them on social media, hugging, sitting down to a fancy meal or at the opening of a new nightclub, while I made complicated coffee drinks for the early risers at *Spilled the Beans*. Some part of me had always been a little jealous. Not of their lifestyle, just the thought they got to see each other more often than I did. And now that I was a little freer to roam, I was afforded the time to reconnect with my old friend.

As the plane raced down the airstrip, I began my panic breathing. Flying had never been my cup of anything, but I thought I had left those fears behind in Mexico. Turns out, I hadn't.

"Remember what Tovah taught ya…for panic," Fitz squeezed my hand.

Tovah, the sister of Benny, who married Fitz's bat-shit crazy Aunt Marble, was who I was going to see. She owned a huge art gallery in New York and asked if I'd like to display (and possibly sell), some of my paintings.

When I met her on the wedding cruise to Mexico, I was a wreck. I wasn't fond of the ocean (or being up close and personal with any of its inhabitants). I didn't like flying, or boats, or heights…let's just say, feet firmly planted on the Earth's surface, I'm good with. Tovah, though, a sixty-ish widow with a zest for everything wonderful, was under the impression that you had to *LIVE* life, swallow it whole. She told me this was the only way to find my passion. And as I dangled next to her in a harness, high above the ocean, I had to agree with her…once I stopped digging my fingernails into the back of her hand and cursing loudly, that is. I still wasn't sure if I had actually said the stream of curse words out loud, or if they were just screamed in my own mind. Either way, landing, feet back on the ground, I felt lighter…like I had faced one very real fear and kicked its ass. Yet here I was again, wringing my hands and fidgeting.

I looked around the first-class cabin. Passengers in Armani suits and Prada pumps lounged in their own luxury bubble.

"I don't think me howling like Tovah would be considered appropriate, Fitz."

Fitz looked around, "Ya care what these strangers think of yer copin' mechanisms?"

"I just don't want to disturb anyone," I told her.

"So, do it low! Does it not work if ya do it low?"

"I don't know," I admitted.

"Yer gonna have to get past worryin' all the time about what other people think of ya," Fitz shook her head.

"I told you, I just don't want to be a bother, that's all."

"Okay," she humored me with a sigh and head shake.

"I'm being serious," I lifted my brows to her.

"Fine," she said condescendingly.

"Why are you being so condescending?" I flared.

"I'm not," she gave the palms-up and had that new damned flight attendant's smile plastered across her face again.

"Oh my God, you are so infuriating sometimes," I clenched my teeth.

"And yet," Fitz pointed to the window Vanna White style.

Looking out, we were not only in the air; we had leveled off and were just cruising along.

I smiled at her, "Thank you…asshole."

"Yer welcome…asshole," she grinned.

2

BUMP

"What the hell!" I grabbed at the armrests.

"Calm yerself, luv," Fitz told me. "It's just turbulence. It's like we're just hittin' an air pocket, no big deal."

"How does air have pockets?" I asked in a slightly panicked tone.

"What am I, Mr. Science? I don't know it's just what I've been told."

"Great! That's helpful!" my sarcasm reared its ugly head.

"No need to get lippy," Fitz said. "Maybe we should have some champagne?"

"Why? Will that help?" I looked at her.

"I think what we should be askin' is, could it hurt?" Fitz gave me a palms-up.

Three glasses, or a bottle of champagne later, I wasn't nearly as aware or concerned by the periodic bumps. Fitz and I turned our attention to more important things.

"So, Cecil's gonna come out to see ya in New York?" Fitz grinned at me.

"He is," my cheeks immediately pulled up into a fat smile. "I really miss him," I said feeling the effects of the champagne.

Cecil and I had a rocky road getting to where we are now. My first impression of him was a spoiled rotten man-whoring playboy with no ambition who had been fortunate enough to have been born into a very rich family. It wasn't exactly love at first sight. But after Cecil decided to show me the real him, I was reluctantly won over.

He had actually come to my rescue like a knight in shining armor when my ex (the airport dumper, John), knocked me out while trying to win me back. Then I was hired by Cecil's father, Martin Callaghan, to do two paintings for him…in Ireland…at the family's manor. A lot of misunderstandings and screw-ups happened there, too, as his ex tried to sabotage whatever was budding between us. I'm happy to say, though, neither of our exes succeeded in pushing us apart. But oddly enough, if I thought about it, both of them had brought us closer together. We knew what we didn't want.

"Yer in love," Fitz's eyes sparkled.

I wasn't sure if this was from emotion, or champagne, but she and her teary eyes were right. "I am," I squeezed her hand.

"Ya must miss the hell out of each other. I can't even imagine being away from Scotty as long as you two have been parted," she shook her head.

Fitz was engaged to Cecil's brother, Scotty, and I had to agree, I didn't even want to see what she would be like if he were gone for weeks at a time, or lived *across the pond*. They had a period of unwanted abstinence in Ireland and it made Fitz go a little, well the word bat-shit crazy comes to mind. The long distance thing; me in Hermosa Beach, California and him in Ireland, was not the relationship I had dreamed of as a young girl…or an older one, for that matter. But he was worth the loneliness that distance can bring as well as the excitement of finally getting to see someone you really love.

A moment passed before Fitz piped up, "I can't believe we won't be home for Halloween. It's such a big deal at the Pub!"

I knew the truth, Halloween was Fitz's *thing*.

"And I know the Ladies of the Moon had somethin' planned for our first Halloween as members," Fitz pouted.

I tried not to show relief that we wouldn't be in attendance for whatever the Ladies of the Moon had planned. Truth is they're a great group of women. At one point, I referred to them as a coven for lack of a more accurate term. But in reality, they were just a group of women from different social, ethnic and religious backgrounds who came together to celebrate something they all had in common; the divine feminine. These women loved each other, were a support system. The fact that my introduction to them left me standing in the plastic kiddy-pool of rebirth, covered in oil, wasn't one of my finer memories. But being honest, that moment, no matter how odd it seemed at the time, had helped put me on a path to self-enlightenment and personal growth. I wish I could say that my next two run-ins were less mind-bending. But my last, I was reluctantly inducted into the group as a *Daughter of the Moon*. And in keeping with a tradition of humiliation I had adopted at all of these rituals, now I was to be named. For the foreseeable future I was to be known as Clematis. I was named so by Fitz's bat-shit-crazy aunt, Marble, who at that moment became my spirit mother.

"Yeah, I know," I said to Fitz, feigning disappointment. "But Tovah said she may have something going on for the *Holiday*, as she called it," I shrugged. I wondered if maybe she would have a party at the gallery.

Tovah was an eccentric to say the least. From the way she dressed, talked and swallowed life whole, I couldn't help but love her. But, I did have to wonder if she was going to try and get me to skydive or swim with sharks.

"Are we bein' picked up at the airport?" Fitz asked.

"Tovah said she would have a car waiting to take us to the hotel," I answered.

"Is she meetin' us at the airport?" Fitz questioned.

"Actually, she said she'd meet us at the gallery tomorrow for lunch."

"She must be a very busy woman," Fitz shook her head.

I grinned, "Well, apparently, tonight is *date night* from what she told me."

"Really?" Fitz grinned.

"Yeah. She said she has at least one a week," I smiled.

Tovah was kind of my hero, not that Fitz had lost her ranking in the least. She just had to share it now. I guessed Tovah around sixty, a slight woman with a salt and pepper faux hawk, and a one-sided grin that left me wondering if she was amused by me or just humoring me. A great art lover, she had purchased the gallery in the eighties and built it up piece by piece. Since the doors first opened, the Schumer Gallery had had the pleasure of displaying the works of some of the greatest artists the world had ever known (both alive and posthumous).

Ironically, the first time I was in New York, I would have begged, borrowed and stolen to have seen the Schumer Gallery. Instead, I was *begged* by Fitz to have photos taken by a woman/man who had *borrowed* the photo equipment from a previous employer and had my time *stolen* as I sat in a jail cell after being arrested for being part of a black market fetish ring. I was also mugged for a tiny little rubber penis by a tiny little man. If I had to judge New York by that visit alone, I would never have come back to The Big Apple.

The voice overhead asked us to fasten our safety belts and prepare for landing. This wasn't my favorite part of flying, either.

In fact, the best part of flying was the booze, and I didn't have to leave the ground to get booze.

Down the ramp we went into the craziness of the La Guardia Airport. If LAX was a zoo, this place was a jungle. People rushed everywhere and it seemed there was no *flow* to the foot traffic.

Finding our luggage carousel we waited for our bags. I couldn't help but wonder if mine had ended up somewhere else. Not because I was being negative, but because it had happened before. I spied our bags tumbling down the conveyer belt onto the other conveyer belt that sent them to the carousel where they would ride in circles until picked up.

"There they are," I pointed. Fitz and I walked up to where they would be an easy grab. But before they made it to us, a strange dark haired woman with dark glasses and a scarf over her head grabbed one of Fitz's bags and started to walk away.

"That woman has your bag!" I told Fitz.

Off like a shot, Fitz flew through the crowd of people yelling, "Stop! Ya have my bag!"

I wanted to go after her and be of some assistance but I still had to grab my bag and Fitz's other two.

I could see Fitz, her red head bobbing in-and-out of people. The small woman tried to pick up the pace, but Fitz's bags were always packed to the max and weighed almost as much as the slight woman. The woman was struggling as Fitz continued to yell, closing the distance between them. Finally a security guard decided to intervene.

Stopping the woman, Fitz was three seconds and ten people behind.

"What? Why are you stopping me?" the woman asked. "I'm an old woman!"

"That's my bag," I heard Fitz say as I and a big cart of luggage finally arrived.

"No, this is my bag!" the woman insisted.

With her huge dark sunglasses, Fitz assumed the poor woman had sight issues. "Check the tag…that's my bag, sir," she told the guard.

The security officer took the bag and looked, but said, "There's no tag."

"See, it's my bag," the woman said. "I'll be off now," she turned to walk away.

At this point, Fitz's eyes slit. "Not so fast."

The three of us were escorted out of the way so that the security guard could try and figure out who owned the bag he was lugging.

"So what's in the bag?" he asked them both.

The small older woman spat, "This is ridiculous! I can't believe I'm being treated this way," she said dramatically.

"Ma'am, I understand your frustration, but you both say the bag is yours and only one of you is correct," the security guard said. "So please what's in the bag."

"My things," yelled the woman and began to crumple up her face like she was trying to fight back tears.

The guard looked torn, obviously not wanting to make a woman cry.

"Ma'am," he said to Fitz, who had honed in on the woman's game, "can you tell me what's in the bag?"

"My undergarments are in this bag," she told him.

"That's a generic answer if ever I heard one!" the woman lifted her chin indignantly.

"Um," the guard looked uncomfortable to even have to ask the next question. "Could you be a little more…specific…?"

One of Fitz's cheeks rose, "There are six bra and panty sets, red, green, white, black, nude strapless and black strapless. Three camisole night dresses, lace; red, green and burgundy. Four pairs of pantyhose in assorted colors still in packaging, made for someone 5'8" and a half, she stared down at the 4 foot 11 inch woman. Fitz's face took on her signature evil fairy grin, "a pair of SPANX, although I don't know what for." She motioned to her perfect figure, "Also made for a woman MY size, must I continue?"

"Sir," began the woman with a look of bewilderment, "I don't know how she knows what's in my bag…this must be…some kind of scam," she asserted.

Was this woman with a set of deflated fun-bags hovering just above her navel, really going to try and pretend that she and Fitz wore the same size bra, I wondered.

I saw the look on Fitz's face; her eyes slit and her tongue found its way into her cheek. I knew this look and cautiously took a step back.

"Fine," said Fitz, "we'll do it yer way, then," she told the woman. "Sir," she addressed the officer, "in that bag you will find a silver hard cased rectangular box. I give ya my permission to open it and take a look. If she can tell ya what's in that box, I'll give her my damn bag," she stared daggers into the woman.

The officer looked perplexed as he unzipped the bag.

The little old woman with the dark glasses stepped closer to see if she could catch a glimpse when he opened the mystery case.

"Ma'am, I'm going to need you to stand back," he told the old woman. Locating the box, he made sure the woman couldn't see and he stole a peek.

I was a little perplexed as well. It looked like it could have been used for makeup, maybe an expensive makeup brush holder. But this wasn't Fitz's makeup bag and she was anal about keeping everything in its place.

I saw the security officer's eyes round as he quickly shut the box.

"Fitz's grin was sardonic as she asked the woman, "What's in the box?"

I was shocked she didn't finish that question with *Bitch*.

The guard was having a hard time making eye contact with Fitz…any of us, really.

What the hell was in that box, I wondered as the woman stammered.

"Well, ugh, this is ridiculous, I shouldn't have to answer this!" the woman said indignantly. "Obviously…," she was showing signs of panic, "it's my…eyeglass case."

"No…no, it's not!" the officer shook his head. "Thank you, ma'am," he said to Fitz and handed her back the box which immediately began to buzz in her hand.

My eyes rounded, I knew of no makeup brushes that made that sound.

The old woman made a face like she was appalled, "You carry one of those…when you travel?"

"Hence the hard cover," Fitz's eyes bored into the woman.

The officer still looked away from Fitz's eyes as he apologized and escorted the woman to the security office.

As we watched them go, I struggled to find something to say, "So I guess it's good you had one of…those...with you, huh?" was what I came up with. "That poor officer looked like he was in shock."

"Please, they do cavity searches on people with balloons of heroin shoved up their bums. Unless today was his *first* as an airport security guard, I doubt I made the *top-ten-list* of weird things he's seen. "

"It's a nice case," I offered nodding.

"Ya like it? I would have chosen the gold case, but Scotty picked it out…a gift for when we're apart," she beamed as she tucked it back inside her bag.

I had run out of things to say that would make this less awkward. The only phrase going through my head was; *Say hello, to my little friend!* "We should find our car," is the only thing I said out loud.

Outside, we saw a very irritated looking man leaning against a limo holding up a red sign that read, **O'Connelly** in big black letters.

"Hi, I'm O'Connelly. I mean Janie," I smiled.

"Nice of you two to show up," he gave us a head nod. "I've been standin' out here for half an hour," his New York accent well pronounced. "What, did ya stop off at the bar for a drink?"

My jaw dropped slightly, "Actually, someone tried to steal one of our bags. We had to let a security officer go through the luggage to prove it was ours…hers," I added quickly, not wanting to be connected to what was in the box even in thought.

"Likely story," the driver huffed under his breath like he heard this excuse every day.

"Would you like to see what I have in my bag?" Fitz asked with a smile.

I bit my bottom lip and rounded my eyes.

"Why would I want to see what's in your bag, lady?" he gave her the palms-up.

"It just reminds me of ya, that's all," she winked. "And…that I need to purchase new batteries."

The drivers face dropped as he connected the dots, "Can we just go, now?"

"My sentiments exactly," Fitz smiled as the man grumbled about her excessive luggage.

In the limo, I turned to Fitz, "Jeez, we've only been in New York for half of an hour and already we've pissed off a driver and almost had your luggage stolen. Do you think New York just doesn't want us here?"

"Yer readin' too much into it. We're one of thousands who go through this crap on a daily basis. Ya actually think we were that old lady's first victims? And this guy," she pointed to back of the driver's head, "he's just an asshole. We have those in So Cal, too."

I nodded slowly. It wasn't like others hadn't told horror stories of their visit to The Big Apple. But as of right now, we were two for two.

As we headed down into the city, I remembered the rush, hustle and bustle I had experienced last time. Bright lights drew the eye in every direction. Our driver seemed less than thrilled with the traffic as well, as he yelled at pedestrians and vehicles, alike. I noticed after several miles that he was very fond of his middle finger and shared it as often as possible.

Pulling up in front of the Ritz-Carlton, our driver seemed in a hurry to unload the bags and get as far away from us as possible. A valet called for a luggage cart and helped the driver. When all of our bags were out of the limo, the driver stood in front of us and stared.

I wasn't sure what he was waiting for until he rubbed his thumb against his fingertips; the universal money sign.

"Ah," I said reaching into my purse. Once again the driver rolled his eyes at me. Pulling out a twenty and handing it to him, he made the "*Pfff*" sound.

"I'm sorry, what's wrong?" I asked him.

"You're riding in a limo…to the Ritz-Carlton," he raised his eyebrows at me. "I waited in the airport for half of an hour for you!"

As I started to dig for more money, so embarrassed I was turning a bright red, Fitz grabbed the twenty out of the driver's hand, "Yer right, we'll probably need this to tip the bellboy," she gave him her best *fuck you* smile.

"Ah, forget yous broads," he said, spitting a loogie right next to my foot.

Fitz made a hocking sound, "No!" I told her as the driver got back into the limo.

"That guy's got a lot of nerve!" Fitz said.

"I feel stupid, I really don't know what size tip is acceptable," I told her.

"Fer that asshole, none is fine."

"But I feel bad. I mean this is how he makes his living," I explained.

"Ya spend too much time feeling bad and makin' excuses fer people who treat ya like shit!" Fitz had lost all humor by now. "Would ya tip a waitress who was not only rude about the job she was being paid to do, but insulted ya on top of it?"

I gave her the *maybe* face with a shoulder shrug.

"See, right there, that's the problem. Tipping is done in the service industry, partly because yer bein' provided with a service, true. But it also depends on whether the person is being cordial about it, at the very fuckin' least. Their job guarantees a wage… their attitude decides the tip!" Fitz educated me. "I've bartended fer years, and this is a well known fact among all service providers. So if he wants to be an asshole, he already knows what he has comin'!"

ABOUT THE AUTHOR

Edith Scheffer is a SoCal native, now blissfully transplanted to the Pacific Northwest. A gypsy at heart with the soul of a witch, Edith has wandered but never been lost. She loves sleeping under the stars and moon, walking in her bare feet, dancing to an eclectic playlist of favorite songs, and proudly parenting her exceptionally fierce and fabulous daughter, Brenna. Edith can mix the perfect drink (bartender by trade), massage your aches away (licensed massage therapist), and entertain you with her many novels (yes, she writes, too!). Her works include The Janie Chronicles, *Winged*, and *Fallen Gracefully*. You can discover more at edithscheffer.net.

facebook.com/AuthorEdithScheffer

goodreads.com/edithscheffer

www.ingramcontent.com/pod-product-compliance
Lightning Source LLC
Chambersburg PA
CBHW061617190726
48288CB00007B/2364

* 9 7 8 1 9 5 4 1 7 4 0 5 4 *